C. F. Moberly Bell, Georges Montbard

From Pharaoh to Fellah

C. F. Moberly Bell, Georges Montbard

From Pharaoh to Fellah

ISBN/EAN: 9783337390518

Printed in Europe, USA, Canada, Australia, Japan

Cover: Foto ©Andreas Hilbeck / pixelio.de

More available books at **www.hansebooks.com**

From Pharaoh to Fellah.

From

Pharaoh to Fellah

BY

C. F. MOBERLY BELL,

AUTHOR OF "EGYPTIAN FINANCE," "KHEDIVES AND PASHAS," ETC.

WITH ILLUSTRATIONS BY GEORGES MONTBARD

CONTENTS.

CHAPTER VI.

CHAPTER VII.

CHAPTER VIII.

CHAPTER IX.

CHAPTER X.

CHAPTER XX.

CHAPTER XXI.

From Pharaoh to Fellah.

PROLOGUE.

IT was in the early part of the year 188-, and in the bright courtyard of the Grand Hotel de Noailles, that they met. The Scribbler, an unmistakable Briton, was moodily inquiring of the waiter whether eggs in Marseilles were invariably laid addled, and whether coal was the sole ingredient of black coffee, when his eye caught that of another stranger regarding him with some curiosity. The grumblings ceased, and with an exclamation of "Sketcher, by Jove!" the Scribbler sprang from his chair with enthusiasm. The terrified look of the waiter at this unusual form of insanity in an Englishman recalled the latter to a sense of his nationality, and falling back into his Anglo-Saxon shell, he said quietly, "How are you, Sketcher?"

The man addressed was evidently no Englishman. The light-blue eyes, under straw-coloured eyebrows, betrayed the Gothic basis as unmistakably as the light, lithe figure showed the admixture of the Latin—an unmistakable Frenchman with Burgundy in all his veins.

"And what on earth brings you here?" said the first.

"Sketching, of course, old fellow! What else have I done since the days at Clareton when you made me do your French exercises for you, and I in revenge got you a hundred lines by sketching the loves of the Integral and Differential Calculi in the fly-sheet of your 'Todhunter'? A sketcher with nothing to sketch, in search of the picturesque, and with at least as much right to be in my own country as you have. And you?"

"A scribbler in search of material—material that must be solid and dull, such as no man can read, so that I may obtain a reputation for untold wisdom and inscrutable depth, be voted a bore without a trace of frivolity, be elected a member of a statistical society, and eventually, in my toothless old age, be considered worthy of a seat in the Cabinet, or the editorship of a comic paper."

" And in search of it ? "

"I am going to Egypt. After mature consideration, I fancy that I shall find there precisely the style of subject I require. In the first place, the British public took some interest in the country last year, so naturally has none now; then it has been so much written about, that there can be nothing new to say; thirdly, we have vital interests in the country, so it is certain that a book on the subject will not be read; and, above all, the subject has been so frequently discussed in Parliament, that one can rely on utter ignorance of essential facts."

"What rubbish! You are going there, first, because you like it; second, because you know that it has become a British possession *à peu près*; and, thirdly—excuse the brutal frankness,—because it's the only subject on which you know anything. Egypt! the dream of my life! I would give my head to come too!"

"You would like to come! then why not join me?" said the Scribbler, with a second access of genuine enthusiasm. "You needn't," he added, relapsing into his old tone, "give your head, though you would probably sacrifice your lungs and your liver. You would get typhoid in Alexandria, of course, and probably cholera in Cairo; but, after all, the hospitals are the cleanest places to live in in Egypt, and you might get over it. What do you say?"

"Say!" said the Sketcher, laughing. "Why, that your invitation is so cordial, your picture so lively, that I've half a mind to take you at your word. To me, Egypt has always presented one inscrutable puzzle, one ever-increasing mystery, and perhaps, if we went there together, you would help me to solve it."

"And what is the mystery? The riddle of the Sphinx? the sources of the Nile? or the explanation of British policy in Egypt?"

"Neither; but one more difficult than either—the connection between Egypt of the Pharaohs and of the Fellah!"

"I hate all mysteries or riddles, and can't even understand the question of yours. The connection between Pharaoh and the Fellah has generally been one of stout hippopotamus hide, called a *kourbash*. I fear there's no difficulty in understanding that!"

"How dense you are, or pretend to be! Listen, and I will explain myself down to the level of your practical intelligence. The Egypt of the Pharaohs is the Egypt of an art hardly absolutely inferior to that of Greece itself, and, as its parent, relatively superior to it—the Egypt of a science which may be similarly compared to our own—the Egypt with a literature, the remnants of which, scant as they are, show traces of majesty worthy of Homer—the Egypt of an empire embracing half the known world. Such is Egypt of the Pharaohs. Now turn to Egypt of the Fellah—a people who for hundreds of years have given us nothing above the literature of a Kaffir, without a trace of artistic perception, incapable of all but the lowest manual labour, unfit to govern, not a nation only, but a village—a people fallen from the highest to the lowest. Does not this contrast present a riddle worthy of solution?"

"Certainly it would," said the Scribbler, "if any such contrast existed, but it does not. You make the common error of assuming that the Egypt of the Pharaohs and the Egypt of the Fellah are two distinct epochs, instead of two distinct classes, always existing side by side. Egypt of the Pharaoh and of the Fellah existed 7000 years ago, and the same Egypt exists to-day. In the Fellah there has been no change; in the Pharaoh there has been much. The same men to-day till the fields, tend the same cattle, work the same *shadoof*, make the same bricks, as in the hieroglyphs of thousands of years ago. One foreign ruler has followed another, styled either Pharaoh or Ptolemy, Caliph or Khedive, leaving behind them monuments either of their greatness or their littleness; but this is not a change in the people, who are to-day what you have described them, and what they have ever been within the record of seven thousand years."

"Then you give the Egyptian no part whatever?"

"If you mean by the Egyptian the Fellah of Egypt Proper of to-day—the Egyptian of Arabi—the Egyptian of Blunt, and of the ravers of "Egypt for the Egyptians"—I give them one unbroken past, a servitude of 7000 years, during which they have been hewers of wood and drawers of water to successive conquerors."

"Even then they must have taken something from their conquerors. You so-called English yourselves are but a mélange of different conquering races, and probably owe your best qualities to your conquerors."

"Precisely; but there is this peculiarity about the Egyptian: always conquered, the prey first of one conqueror and then of the other, he is himself the real conqueror in process of time. The conquering race passes over him, but leaves no trace. Just as Indian wheat or American cotton-seed, planted in Nile mud, becomes at the second crop Egyptian wheat and Egyptian cotton, taking its nature from the soil, so the human seed—mixed though it has been with Ethiopian, Assyrian, Persian, Greek, Roman, Arab, the race Egyptian has always re-asserted itself and remained one and the same, physically and morally. I believe, if you were to obliterate the race, and people the country with settlers from Nova Scotia, you would in a few generations have the lying, licentious, and easily governed Egyptian of to-day."

"Then you believe in no regeneration of Egypt?"

"How can there be regeneration if there has been no birth? Egypt as a nation has never existed; that is, of course, as an independent nation under its own rulers. Whether such an existence is possible to her in the future, who can say? None of her numerous conquerors has ever tried the experiment."

"Are you English trying it?"

"Ah! that is a question that requires a long answer; but, if you are serious, come with me and study for yourself both Pharaoh and Fellah."

"But are you serious? Will you not feel like Sinbad, with a man of paints and pencils on your shoulders—a pure idealist—absolutely ignorant of all relating to the country?"

"On the contrary, my dear fellow, you will be invaluable to me. Experience, after all, is frequently only another name for prejudice; you shall correct me with the impartiality due to utter ignorance, and instruct me in the beauties of oriental dirt, which I have never been able to appreciate. You shall sketch with the pencil, and I with the pen; you shall depict the Fellah, and I propound the Pharaoh; you sometimes travelling into my domain and I into yours, we shall together find the happy mean."

"And the result?"

"That we shall amuse and instruct ourselves, if no one else, and add one more book on Egypt."

CHAPTER I.

A FEW days later, and the Messageries steamer *Maris*, with
some hundreds of passengers, and its full comple-
ment of two stewards and a cabin-boy to attend to their
wants, was struggling out of Port la Joilette, in face of
a light head wind.

Verily, in sober truth, and not satirically,
the finest view in all *la belle France* is
seen as we leave its grand old Pho-
cæan port. "If Paris had its Canne-
bière, it would be Marseilles," say
its shoppy citizens; but Marseilles
could give Paris a hundred Canne-
bières, and still, from the height of its
2400 years, afford to look down upon
its gaudy parvenu rival. Beautiful it
looks now, nestling at the feet of its
golden Virgin of Notre Dame de la
Garde, glittering like a sun lighthouse,

guarded by its saints militant, Forts Saint Jean and Saint Nicholas. The Chateau d'If and the Isle Mairé stand stern and forbidding, but beyond we see the lovely coast of Provence, rich in all colour from sun and sea and sky.

The shouting, which seems necessary to safe navigation for the first few hours, was gradually toning down ; and the sailors, settling themselves into little groups against the bulwarks, and furtively smoking the vilest *caporal* from their short pipes, were discussing their experiences of the few days they had passed among the land-lubbers. The monotonous throb of the engines, the flapping of the cordage, the premonitory groans of a few passengers, who were inviting sea-sickness in their cabins, and the rattling of plates in the pantry, were the only sounds which reached the Sketcher and the Scribbler as they tramped the deck, and discussed the age, station, calling, and relationship of the few passengers who had not already gone below.

There was a portly Britisher, whose sense of dignity, and a desire to prove that he individually represented a nation that ruled the waves, was struggling hard with a conviction that the waves should be ruled straighter, and that at this particular juncture they were acquiring more control than was becoming over the region covered by his capacious white waistcoat. The mingled dignity and helplessness of his demeanour recalled irresistibly the Turtle of Wonderland ; and the two fresh-looking daughters who were with him fitted naturally to their sobriquets of Turtle-Doves. A lanky American, of some six feet three, was trying hard, with the aid of a telescope of about his own length and breadth, to assume a nautical air. But Nature reasserted itself ; for piteously appealing to a typical Englishman, who, arrayed in an ulster, was dealing death to him with every whiff of his cigar, he remarked, "We long-built men feel the motion a deal more than them as has their innards slung lower," and went below. A scion of England's later aristocracy was maintaining his reputation as a man about town by sucking the handle of his cane ; but these, a German savant, an English clergyman, and a lady of

uncompromising principles and bonnet, were the sole occupants of the deck.

Early next morning the sea had got tired of what the American called its

waltz, and had settled down to the demeanour of a stately chaperone. The sun shone as it only shines in the Mediterranean, without the vulgar ostentation of the tropics, and with none of that timid reserve to which we are accustomed in England. It shone as if it shone for its own pleasure, with a desire to make things pleasant for the insignificant world below; and the sea was grateful, for it answered with its merriest laugh, and gave itself up as a mirror to reflect His Majesty's glories. And Corsica, lying in the distance, looked grateful; the mountain tops were still covered with snow, but they blushed pink as the sun slanted across them, and made the dark rugged cliffs, scattered with sparse woodland, look their best.

It was one of the Turtle-Doves who began it, that merry cry of " Corsica!" and a group of muslin took it up, passed it on to a group of youngsters on the way to their regiments in Egypt, and so it went round the ship, sounding now like a *feu-de-joie*, now like a volley, and at last dying away in minute-guns. Corsica! Corsica !! Corsica ! ! ! and the laziest rose from his seat, to be able to say that he had seen it, while the more conscientious consulted their guide-books, and a Herr Doctor in spectacles took out a chart of prodigious dimensions, to satisfy himself that Corsica stood where it did.

The Turtle was a member of the British Legislature, who felt that his mission in life was the imparting of solid information, and who was not to be deterred from the fulfilment of it. Ostensibly addressing the Doves, but generously raising his voice for the benefit of the company, he raised his right flapper, and pointing in the direction of the island, said, " The birthplace of Bonyparty, a very remarkable man." Perhaps the Sketcher felt that it was a generous admission; at all events he said, " Yonder is Elba." The Turtle bowed, and again raising his flapper, said, "And there is where he died;" but, with sudden doubts as to his historical accuracy, he lifted the other fin, and pointed it in a direction which might be supposed to vaguely indicate the direction of St. Helena. He observed the Sketcher taking, at the moment, a hurried note, and, relapsing from his semaphore attitude, remarked to the Doves that the young man seemed intelligent and anxious to acquire information; "for a Frenchman, remarkably so," he added, as he glowed with a conscious feeling of toleration towards inferiors.

"Look at Monte Christo," cried the Sketcher, as a rocky outline appeared on the horizon. "History and romance facing one another, and who shall say which has the best of it? You now, Scribbler mine, who try to prove the world a thing of dry facts and figures, sewers and drains, practical man as you are, will you deny that even the creation of the wildest imagination has not been beaten by your own facts?"

"Facts, my enthusiastic friend! What are facts? Do you mean Thiers's facts, or Napoleon le Petit's facts? Do you expect me to take history as proof of facts, when you know the very man's existence is capable of logical disproof? There was probably a substratum of truth in Monte Christo. Reduce the two stories to their naked facts, and then we will judge."

The Turtle, who had never heard of Whately or Dumas, found himself out of his depth; but she, who had been already christened the Fond Dove, encouraged by the previous parental approval, smiled at the Sketcher, who lay at her feet from that hour. And the Fair Dove asked the Scribbler if he were going to Cairo; and when he replied that he was afraid so, she quoted to him pages of "Murray," and so the acquaintance began—an acquaintance pleasant indeed, but which had its drawbacks, for the ever-conscientious Turtle saw an occasion not to be missed. For years he had been struggling to catch the Speaker's eye, to unbosom himself on Egypt; and though, because he had once been a Cabinet Minister, he had twice hooked that slippery optic, it had, to his surprise, only resulted in a "count out." Now was his opportunity. Drawing his heels together, protruding his waistcoat and chin, and apostrophising the nearest mast as an imaginary Speaker, he began: "In the complicated series of blunders in which, so to speak, the mummy of the Egyptian question is swathed"—when the luncheon-bell ringing, carried away his audience, and left him speaking.

The next day brought the *Maris* off Naples, and the glassy stillness of the sea reflecting Vesuvius, Ischia, Nisida, and Procida as in a mirror, left the most inveterate of sea-sick sufferers no excuse to remain below. Even that never-absent female, who in any possible voyage is firmly convinced that she will be drowned in the Bay of Biscay, appeared on deck, arrayed in a bonnet which was apparently adapted to serve in case of need as a life-buoy. Is it necessary to describe the Neapolitan shore, from Castella-mare the stately to Posilipo the beautiful? Are we not rather intent on more Eastern scenes than these, sung of from Horace to Lamartine? Need we linger over the forgotten terrors of Scylla and Charybdis, the gardens of Messina, the majesty of Etna, and the cerulean Calabrian coast? The *Mœris* has passed them all, and is in the waste of sea that will not be broken till she sights the Alexandria light. The party have shaken down, as the stiffest of parties will do on a sea-voyage. The Turtle is less dogmatic; the Sketcher is pretending to give drawing lessons to the Fond Dove; while the Fair One is relaxing the cynicism of the Scribbler under a course of Browning. The Patrician has emerged from sea-

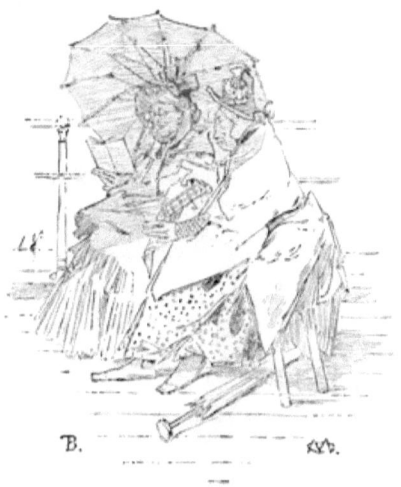

B.

sickness with more sense of toleration towards his fellow-sufferers; the American has vainly endeavoured to start a business connection in hides, which he explains is his specialty; and Ulster, ever genial and content, has managed to keep the whole party in good-humour with themselves and each other.

The last night had arrived; the *Mœris* was due early next morning at Alexandria, and our little party were pouring forth their stores of information or imagination regarding Egypt for mutual benefit. The young Patrician was naturally a violent Radical; and the Turtle, having made his money in soap, as decided a Conservative. "We should never have touched the country, sir, but for your fatal Conservative interference," said the first. "We should never have made ourselves contemptible there, if we had been in power," replied the other.

"Now that," said the Sketcher, "is the peculiarity of your English party politics. I invariably find that the party in power, and the party in opposition, are agreed on one point, and that is, that whatever has been done, has been done badly and under pressure from the party out of office. 'Why did you go to Egypt?' says one. 'Because you compelled us,' replies the other. The idea

B

that any one party, ministry, or man should have a policy of their own, is absent from English politics."

"Yes," said Ulster. "'Please, sir, 'twasn't me, 'twas t'other boy,' would summarise most of our debates on foreign politics. But perhaps it's as dignified as sending in an ultimatum one week and going off to Jaffa the next, to the tune of '*Partant pour la Syrie*,' as your fleet did, my good friend."

"Leaving to the British fleet the sole glory of bombarding a helpless town," said the Frenchman.

"The town was not helpless, and was not bombarded," replied the other. "The forts were silenced one day, and only one shot was fired the next day, while the 'helpless' soldiery were firing the town, massacring Christians, and ill-treating even native women. On the whole, throughout this Egyptian business we behaved with singular clemency and good faith."

The discussion became general and was getting warm. The Gallic blood of the Sketcher had been aroused against Ulster, and the Turtle and the Patrician were gradually working their way back into the Middle Ages, in an attempt to fix the origin of our intervention in Egypt.

The Scribbler, who had gravely followed the discussion with the silence becoming a person of authority, summed up the debate with cynical impartiality. "As for the origin of the whole matter, it would be about as useful to discuss the origin of the siege of Troy. Put it down as the offspring bred by human nature out of geographical position nursed by national imbecility. Let us go back a little. Palmerston, so far as I know, never read

A Fellah Woman.

history, but *knew* it, so avoided logical will-o'-the wisps with a true instinct. Perhaps you don't know that he refused the Protectorate of Egypt when Abbas offered to throw over the Sultan, but it's a fact."

"You mean from the Czar Nicholas?" said the Turtle.

"No, I don't; that was another offer refused; but I refer to a distinct, specific offer on the part of Abbas, then Viceroy of Egypt, to place himself under the protection of England instead of that of the Sultan. Palmerston refused; he said that we did not require Egypt; but when Abbas's successor encouraged the Suez Canal, Palmerston saw as clearly as Alexander that, if the project succeeded, Egypt would become of vital importance to the mistress of India. Did he believe all he said about the certain failure of Lesseps and his visionary schemes? I don't know; but in any case, the wish was father to the thought, and there is no better proof of his foresight than the cautious answer he gave as an explanation of his opposition to the scheme : 'Remote speculations with regard to easier access to our Indian possessions, only requiring to be indistinctly shadowed forth to be fully appreciated.' He recognised, and even predicted, that if a practical waterway were created between the two seas, England would be compelled, sooner or later, to annex Egypt,—that, in fact, we must either hold Egypt or lose India."

The Turtle opined that the Canal could never be depended upon, and that England would have to rely on quick transports by the Cape.

"Excuse me," said the Scribbler, "if I point out that that argument is the result of a singular confusion of ideas. The ordinary British mind can only take in one idea at a time, and that very slowly. It took it a long time to realise that the Suez Canal had altered the situation as regarded Egypt itself. Having at last grasped the importance of the Suez Canal, it dropped all idea of Egypt, just as a monkey drops one nut when you offer it another, though a smaller one. *1st idea:* Egypt is of no importance; *2nd idea:* Egypt is of importance because of Suez Canal; *3rd idea:* Therefore Suez Canal is of importance; *4th idea:* Therefore Egypt is of no importance. Now, because we realise that the Suez Canal is of importance, surely there is no need to forget the importance of Egypt's land route; and if we cannot rely on the Suez Canal (which is an open question), there is all the more reason to hold on to the alternative. If we found our advantage in transporting troops across Egypt during the Indian Mutiny, when there was no Canal, does that advantage disappear because there is another doubtful route running parallel to it? And when you talk of quick steamers round the Cape, you forget that there is nothing to prevent the same speed in the Mediterranean and the Red Sea. Quicken your transport either way, by all means; but you cannot get over the 4300 miles difference between the two routes, and, even at thirty miles an hour, that is six days. Six days in which you may lose or save your Empire ! Besides, if Egypt is useless to you,—if the Mediterranean is a *cul de sac*, leading to nowhither, through seas where you have to run the gauntlet of hostile fleets,—of what use are Gibraltar, Malta, and Cyprus? Be consistent ; and when you give up Egypt, give up those also. A year later you will have no trouble in getting rid of India too."

"Stop a bit," said the Patrician. "You said that we sent troops through Egypt during the Mutiny. Well, we didn't garrison Egypt then ; why should we not withdraw from the country now, and still be able to cross it if we wished to ? "

" Because, my dear boy, 1857 is not 1887. The Crimean war was just over then; France was our ally; Turkey our humble servant; Russia temporarily exhausted; Germany and Italy non-existent. Is that the position to-day? And, lastly, if you want another reason, because we were not in possession then, and we are in legal occupation now. To take is one thing, to give up is another."

" For a somewhat reserved son of honest Britain, I think," said the Sketcher, "that that is a very fair exposition of England's declared policy of retirement from Egypt."

"I am not called upon," replied the Scribbler, "to expound or to subscribe to the absurd engagements entered into by a Government which made two contradictory and equally impossible promises. I might, if I chose, refer you to Mackenzie Wallace's argument, and say that in such a case the less important promise must give way to the other; but not being politicians, let's do away with casuistry, and the cant—pardon me, Ulster—of 'singular clemency and good faith.' We showed just the same amount of the latter as you do when you pay an overdue bill under pressure. As to clemency, it's true that we only *fired* at the forts; but as our shells riddled that lighthouse, which by special order the gunners were instructed to avoid, perhaps it's of more importance to consider what we hit than what we fired at. We certainly didn't do much damage to the inhabited quarters of the town *directly*, but *in*directly, by failing to send troops, or even to land four hundred marines, we are morally responsible for all that happened and the burning of Alexandria must remain, what Wolseley called it, 'a lasting disgrace to the British navy.' As to our not firing the next day, let's be silent about it. There's not much merit in it when you happen to have fired away the last shot from your locker; and seeing that there were representatives of some half-dozen doubtfully friendly fleets within a few miles, it's not pleasant to think that if one or two had turned on us, we should have had to make a bolt for it."

" Is that true?" asked Ulster.

The Scribbler rose. "You had better ask the Admiralty, who, to save a few pounds in coal, sent the *Hecla* with the ammunition from Malta under canvas, so that she arrived twenty-four hours too late. Of course they'll deny it, as they denied sending the marines without arms, and the *Orontes* without troops on board, but it's true none the less."

"Scribbler," said the Sketcher solemnly, as they left the deck, "I have a favour to beg. To-morrow we land at Alexandria, and yonder light on Pharos is the morning star that heralds me to the glorious East. Let me entreat you to abstain from immoderate indulgence in Blue Books. Put your spirit in unison with the surroundings with which we shall be environed. Remember that we shall land amidst the ruins of Ptolemy; that we shall breathe the air of Cleopatra, and be pacing the groves of the Platonists. A few days more, and we shall have plunged into the dreamland of Haroun el Raschid; and yet a few weeks will see us in the temples of Osiris, amidst the shades of Ramses. Remember that the difference between life and death is only accordance or want of accordance with our environments; and let me live!"

The Scribbler was touched by the agonised tone of the appeal. "There doesn't happen," he said, "to be any light on Pharos, but only ruins, not of Ptolemy, but of Beauchamp Seymour. Your morning star is rising and setting every two minutes in a rather ugly lighthouse of the nineteenth century. You will find the air of Cleopatra very much like that of most other decomposed matter; and the groves of the Platonists are converted into peculiarly ugly buildings, mostly tenanted as *café-chantants* of a third-rate order. I might then ask you to put yourself in accordance with these environments, and become a practical travelling companion; but I will not ask impossibilities. I will do my best, and to-morrow shall see me a changed character."

CHAPTER II.

THE next morning at daybreak, the *Mæris* was steaming over the rocky bar into Alexandria harbour. To the Sketcher, with his strongly imaginative temperament, all things alike, old and new, were objects of delight. The low sandy shore to the west; the little villas of Ramleh to the east; the ungainly windmills and hideous palace of Mex; even the dilapidated stuccoed Ras el Tin itself seemed bathed in Oriental splendour. The pilot's "half-a-speed-astern" impressed him. "It had," he said, "precisely that mellifluous guttural sound which he had always associated with Arabic;" and it required some argument from Ulster to convince him that he was mistaken. As for the Scribbler, he had a preoccupied air, as of one who had been wearied with midnight study. It was abstractedly that he answered his companion's eager inquiries; uncontradicted, he allowed the Turtle to point to a factory chimney as Pompey's Pillar, and to expatiate upon the unmistakable grace of what he called "the Monolith;" and even when, later, one of the Doves remarked that the Monolith was smoking, his smile was unusually grave. He submitted with unwonted meekness to the obstreperous appeals of the numerous Alis and Mahomets, as they divided his portmanteau among them and struggled for his person. It was with a sigh of relief that he escaped from the Custom-House, seized the Sketcher by the arm, and, pointing to a Maltese engaged in a scuffle with a Greek, began as follows: "Do you see Abn Hassan at the city gate? and there is Haroun el Raschid quietly coming up in that disguise of a city merchant. There is Sinbad the porter, too, hurrying to Sinbad the sailor; these minarets make the city so beautiful; the heavy mound-like domes "——

The Sketcher was disturbed; in the dirty, semi-European faces around him he could recognise none of the wonders described by his ordinarily practical friend ; besides, the words sounded familiar to him. "There's something like that in an American book," he said.

"Good heavens ! you've read it, then ! Why, I sat up all last night learning pages on purpose to please you ; and there's lots more of it," he added pathetically ; "but what's the use ? "

"None whatever, my friend. I too have been striving to change my skin and become practical. That $97\frac{1}{2}$ pounds make a piaster, or $97\frac{1}{2}$ piasters a pound, I am convinced, but I cannot remember which. Let us give it up. Keep you to the practical side of this trip, and leave to me the artistic ! Is it a bargain ? "

"Agreed," said the other ; "I will write fact, and you shall paint pictures."

"Let us hope, at least," said the Fond One, "that the facts will be as true as Art."

"As true as Art ! As if Art, or painting, at least, were ever true. Your truest picture is a framed untruth ! "

"The Scribbler is only happy when indulging in paradoxes," explained his friend.

"Paradox ! do you call that a paradox which is self-evident. Take this sketch now," he continued, taking the block from the Sketcher's hands ; "what is that but a conventional representation of a street ? That house is a hundred yards away, this one is ten yards off, and you represent them on a plane. You call it drawn in perspec-

A Seller of Drinks.

tive ; but what is perspective but a term invented to get over the difficulty ? Your educated eye, as you call it, recognises its rules ; but the Chinese eye is just as educated, only with other rules ; so he ignores your perspective, draws in accordance with rules of his own, called *Ru-tew-shan*, and equally thinks he has got over the difficulty."

"But I see no difficulty to get over," said the Sketcher.

"Of course you don't. Your eyes have been so educated, that to you there is nothing absurd in a European picture drawn in accordance with the rules of perspective, just as to the Chinaman there is nothing absurd in his pictures drawn according to the rules of *Ru-tew-shan*. None the less the one and the other is equally untrue to nature, and equally false. If you want a proof, show a child of artistically uneducated parents that porter, and ask what he is. He will say, a man carrying a trunk tied on to his head, and a very shabby bag in his hand. From such a description you may recognise that it is a porter carrying my modest luggage. Now, show this sketch, which you all doubtless recognise, to the same child, and ask him what it is. He will say it is a white sheet of

paper with black marks on it. Turn it right way up or upside down, and he will say the same—a sheet of paper with black marks on it, that's what he would say; and he would be right, for that's precisely what it is;" and he returned it to the disgusted artist.

"You seem, sir," said the Turtle, "to have given this subject considerable and lengthy study."

"I have," said the Scribbler; "in fact," he added in an undertone, "ever since that fellow began pulling about my baggage; and now that he's done, we may as well go."

The rest of the party expressed an intention of going in carriages, but the Sketcher vowed that he could descend to nothing so occidental, and ordered camels. Nothing more resembling them than donkeys could, however, be found; and as the rest stoutly refused this mode of conveyance, a compromise was effected. The least disreputable-looking Mahomet was intrusted with the luggage, to take to the Hotel Abbat, and the whole party agreed to walk. The resolution was carried out not without persistent opposition from numerous donkey-boys, who loudly vociferated the excellent qualities of their beasts. Two of them, respectively named "Bradlaugh" and the "Bishop of London," were finally loaded with the luggage, and ambled ahead in genial fellowship, urged thereto with language of a character which even the Sketcher could not conscientiously mistake for Arabic.

A Native Shayal.

The way from the harbour leads through narrow streets, filled with the offscourings of all nations, and pervaded by an odour to which one becomes rapidly accustomed in Egypt; its basis is unmistakable dirt—rich Nile mud, but adulterated with saturation of garlic, peppermint, arachi, putrid fish, and worse. In different parts of the country, one or other of these extra ingredients predominates over the rest; but they are always all present in a more or less degree, and combine every odour which decomposed animal or vegetable matter is capable of producing. The Scribbler was useful as a guide, and comparatively cheerful; for he explained that he had already gone through all the diseases which were inevitable to first-comers, and so felt personally safe. On the left side of the narrow street up which they passed, he was able to point

The Harbour of Alexandria.

out the house from which had been supplied the "nabouts" with which, on the fatal 11th June 1882, the Christians had been assaulted; and close to it was the Zaptieh, or police-station, whither the unhappy victims fled, only to be shot down by the guardians of order. Turning here to the right, the old Heptastadium, now Frank Street, is entered, through which, amid flames and in danger of falling ruins, the marines entered the town a month later, after the forts had been silenced; and suddenly, at a point where, in Napoleon's time, ended the town, which then contained only six thousand inhabitants, opens out the great square, "Place des Consuls," now "Place de Mehemet Ali." In the centre of it stands the bronze statue of the great Roumeliote; and Scribbler told how, when he last entered it, the statue stood alone, red hot, the square an almost complete rectangle of fire strewed with corpses, and moving among them only two devoted priests, who had stood all the horrors of those nights. Let their names be recorded once more—Père Guillaume, a Franciscan, and Frère Mivielle, a Lazarist.

The ordinary traveller who comes to Egypt disdains Alexandria. He comes to see the land of the Nile, associated somewhat vaguely in his mind with vast antiquity, which he would perhaps describe as consisting of pyramids, Pharaohs, and mummies, or, at the very least, the legendary genii of the "Arabian Nights." Instead of this, he finds a modern town, possessing little pretensions to beauty, and small trace of antiquity: so he hurries on to Cairo, and can see nothing in the commercial capital of Egypt but the commonplace resort of Levantine usurers. And yet, if he would linger a little, he would gain all the clearer insight into the world which he is about to enter without comprehension. If we were as anxious to find indications of prescience in the works of man as in those of nature, we might prove that there was a secret and beneficent purpose in making Alexandria the first stepping-stone into the East. For not only the beauties, but the inconveniences of the Orient, are here broken to us gently. The streets are paved and watered; the shops rival those of any but those of the first European cities: and the very odours are mitigated to suit the untried

A Jewish Scribe.

occidental palate. On the other hand, the Eastern sky, though pleasant, is apt to be murky; the fierce sun is tempered by the cool breeze; and the interesting

Oriental who salutes you in the *Lingua Franca* is probably a Jewish saraffe, and possibly smells of spirits. And the position which Alexandria occupies towards the rest of Egypt, as the point of transition from West to East, is similar, though conversely, to that which she holds from an historical point of view. It is at Alexandria that the histories of the East merge with those of the West; that we find in the period of the Ptolemies a stepping-stone between the Egypt of the Pharaohs and the Egypt of the Arab. He who looks for many traces of antiquity will indeed fail to find them; but surely it is a dull mortal who requires the tangible object before him to excite his imagination, and who is unable to derive any pleasure from the dream of association alone. The town which was founded by Alexander, defended by Cæsar, and captured by Bonaparte surely merits some consideration.

Is it nothing to you that at almost the spot where you landed, landed some 2200 years ago the great Macedonian himself, at what was then the fishing-village of Rhacotis? Here, beneath the very streets through which you walk to reach the square, was the Heptastadium, the narrow causeway originally connecting "the rocky isle of Pharos" with the mainland, increased by accumu-lated soil, assigned as dwelling-place to the Franks in Arab times, and now, when the pushing Christians have extended the town to almost the limits of the old city, become the Arab quarter. Here, in the great square, we are in a modern quarter, formed by the soil which collected at the point where the Heptastadium joined the mainland. At the top of the square, and just as we enter Cherif Pasha Street, with the New Bourse on our right, we are really crossing the old city walls, and entering the town just where stood the public granaries, stretching down to the now unused harbour on our left. Walk up Cherif Pasha Street, named after Egypt's late easy-going Premier, and beneath these new-built houses and shops are the ruins of the old town; and when you get to the top of the street you will find yourself—where? If you consult the legend in black and white before you, you will see that you are facing the "British Main Guard;" but if you let your imagination lead you a little, you can think that you are facing the great Museum; for something more than legend makes us certain that it was here. Where that sentry is tramping, paced Euclid, and Clemens, and later Origen. In the groves which stretched behind, where now stand ugly buildings and the railway station, disputed Athanasius and Arius, Cyril and Hypatia—the disciples of Christ, of Aristotle, and of Serapis. Behind, again, lay the Library of 100,000 volumes, including the Septuagint—the Library destroyed not by Amru, but by the flames of the ships fired by the great Julius, which spread, and spared the Museum itself, but destroyed its never-to-be-restored treasures. It is to the labour of Alexandrians on this spot that we owe not only the text of Homer, but that translation of the Hebrew Scriptures into Greek which drew into the young Church of Christ all that was best and noblest from all rival creeds. "The Platonist saw in Christianity a fuller and clearer embodiment of the noble ideas of his philosophy than could be seen in Judaism; the Hebrew saw in it the extension of the fate of Abraham and the promises to the whole race of man; the Egyptian saw in it the great doctrines of the divine unity and man's future condition, which had only just disappeared from his religion in the shock of its contact with philosophy."[1]

Arab Beggars.

The very street we are standing in, now the fashionable drive to Ramleh and the Canal, thronged with luxurious carriages and needy beggars, is probably the very oldest in the world that still maintains its purpose. Laid out some 2000 years ago, it stretched from the Necropolis Gate to the west—where now you will find leviathan steamers loading cotton and grain at the quay—to the Canopic Gate, beyond the limits of the present town. That part which lies to our right as we face the Museum extends now but a little way, and then loses itself among foundries, Italian schools, and gardens, within which latter lies the old English Cemetery, containing the graves of some of those Englishmen who lost their lives in the Abercromby campaign of 1800. But to the left, going eastward, we can still follow the exact road as traced by the hands of Alexander. Here, next to the Museum, where you see lofty houses, was the Soma, with the bodies of the kings, and that of the great Alexander himself, in about the centre of his city; for Ptolemy Lagus stole the body of his great master from Perdiccas, who was carrying it from Babylon, and placed it here in its golden coffin. Ptolemy Cocæs stole the gold coffin, and replaced it by a glass one; but who shall find it now, whether of crystal or metal, beneath these deposits of ages?

> " Imperial Cæsar, dead and turned to clay,
> Might stop a hole to keep the wind away."

Still a little farther on, and always on the right hand, you see the hill now called Kom el Dikk (Hill of the Cock). Here stood the Paneum, an artificial

1 "Cities of Egypt." R. S. Poole.

height, as it seems to this day, "of a conical form, with a spiral ascent," says Strabo; but of this there is no trace now, nor from its reduced summit can you see any longer the whole city.   On the other side of the road, opposite to the

Rosetta Gate.

Paneum, but at some distance, and near to the sea, stood the Theatre; and passing still on, we reach the modern walls and Rosetta Gate, where stood the Gymnasium with its furlong porticoes; and beyond that, again, we reach the well-marked ridge of the French lines, carried by Abercromby in 1800, where stood the Canopic Gate and the walls of ancient Alexandria.   And of all this, nothing remains but the street itself, with here and there a granite pillar or a mutilated statue.

Retracing our steps to the point at which we have fixed the Soma, opposite to where now stands the Theatre Zizinia, we shall find a second road intersecting the first, and having the same claims to antiquity.   This road, now called after the Prophet Daniel, contains the tomb of a late Viceroy, Said Pasha, and southward leads to the Moharrem Bey Gate, passing between the sites of the Museum and the Soma.   Following it, however, northward, we find ourselves confronted at the end by the familiar "Lion and Unicorn" of the British Consulate.   The worthy representative of Britain exercises alike the justice of the Consular court and the hospitality of his own house on the threshold of the Cæsareum.   It overlooked the greater harbour, now singularly misnamed the New Port; beneath its waters you may trace the ruins, though little more than the foundations.   Here was besieged by the Alexandrians the great Julius, and here Cleopatra lost an empire with Mark Antony.   There, to the right, she could see the Lochias Palace with its royal port, the castellated island of Antirhoodos, the Timonium at her feet, which was to be the last refuge of her lover, and stretching away to the left the Poseidium and the Pharos of her ancestors. Here, too, in later days, under Theodosius, Cyril, real ruler of Egypt, held his priestly state, and issued his orders that revenged on the infidels the Christian massacres of past centuries.   Of its grandeur nothing remains; the two obelisks, which had survived the Roman and Arab conquests, were destined to fall into the hands of those later barbarians, the Anglo-Saxons of the nineteenth century. They stand on the Thames Embankment and in the Central Park of New York,

A Street in the Arabian Quarter of Alexandria.

as a testimony to the wealth, perseverance, engineering skill, and consummate vulgarity of the people who removed them.

> " And thou, Cleopatra's Needle, that hadst dared
> Great skirts of Time ere she and Antony had
> Dead hope!—hast thou too reached, surviving death,
> A city of sweet speech scorned, on whose chill stone
> Keats withered, Coleridge pined, and Chatterton,
> Breathless, with poison froze the god-fired breath?"
>
> —D. G. ROSSETTI.

Away to the south-west, crossing again the square, and passing through one of the gates of the town, we come upon a high eminence, crowned by the pillar which we may call Pompey's or Diocletian's with almost equal inaccuracy. That it had nothing to do with the great Pompey may be admitted; for not only did he never reach Alexandria, but he only came to Egypt itself to be defeated and killed near the modern Port Said: and certainly Alexandrians were the least likely of people to raise a column to a defeated hero. Nor has Diocletian much more right to have his name associated with it. It is possible, or indeed even probable, that, as it stands to-day, with its ungainly base and vulgar capital, it was erected in honour of the persecuting Emperor, who at last staid his hand. It may, too, have been still further disfigured by the statue, either

Distant View of Pompey's Pillar.

of himself, or, as others relate, of his horse, whose stumbling was interpreted as the omen which saved the city. But all this does not justify the title of Diocletian to a column which formed part of a building erected five hundred years before he was born. Similar nomenclature would justify the absurd title of Cleopatra's Needle, or, for that matter, Wilson's Needle, to the obelisk of Thothmes III. The column was a part of the Serapeum. On the highest point of Rhacotis, Ptolemy Philadelphus placed the statue of Serapis, and around it grew the Acropolis of the Greek town. The cult of the god (Osiris-Apis—Serapis) died hard in the city of Alexandria. Long after the religion of the Cross had driven the idolaters from the rest of the town, those who still resisted it found their refuge here. Here was their Library, with volumes greater in number at least than those

D

which had been already burnt.   Here mixed the philosophies of Egypt and of
Greece, hurling their Parthian shafts at their victorious foe.   And when "the
pious indignation of Theophilus" could no longer restrain itself at the furious
raging of the heathen, it was here that he pursued them; it was their temple which
they turned into a fortress, and where they found a horrible alternation to their
sufferings in torturing their Christian prisoners at the foot of the statue of their
god.   Nothing else remains of the arched portico, the hundred steps which
led to it, the stately halls, or the marvellous statues.   Through two thousand
years the column has looked down upon the struggles of rival creeds and rival
empires.   Greek and Roman, Turk and Arab, Infidel and Christian, Jew and
Moslem, have each struggled at its feet; and in the city of Alexander, where
Cæsar and Bonaparte triumphed, it remains the one memorial which survives
the British occupation.

A Copt of Alexandria.

CHAPTER III.

IT was at the particular request of the Sketcher that the party agreed to miss the evening's express, and devote the afternoon to an excursion to Ramleh. The Scribbler maintained that it was a waste of precious time; that the so-called Brighton of Alexandria was a Cockneyfied desert, with houses scattered like tombs in a cemetery, wherein the pious Alexandrians secluded themselves, to prepare for the next world by abusing their neighbours in this. On this one point, however, the Sketcher was immovable; and declining steadfastly to reveal the reason of his obduracy, he succeeded in exciting the curiosity of the Doves, and, as a matter of course, from this moment carried his point. Driving then from Pompey's Pillar to the Canal, they passed along the shady banks to the east, and were repaid by the beauties of a drive which is perhaps unsurpassable in Cairo itself. The Scribbler indeed refused to be charmed; the Canal to him was nothing but the grave of the 20,000 lives which had been sacrificed to digging it; in the beauties of light and shade he detected rheumatism; beneath the brightest foliage lurked malaria; and in a baker's shop, which the Sketcher styled picturesque, he found only a hot-bed of cholera.

Leaving the Canal with its gardens, the road turned sharp to the north, and passing between a couple of small lakes, reached the continuation of the old Canopic road, already described. Again turning eastward, it led across the Desert, past the hideous modern palace of Ramleh, built on the site and from the very stones of Cæsar's camp at Nicopolis—the scene of the victories of Octavianus over Mark Antony, and of Abercromby over the French. Another mile brought the party to the Beau Mer, an hotel apparently designed to attract from without and to repel from within. The Sketcher, in pursuit of his mysterious purpose, had desired to be introduced to the oldest inhabitant of Nicopolis; and the Scribbler thought that he knew one man, who, from the patient

endurance of his disposition, might still have been able to support existence in
the hotel. "He is," he explained, "a judge; but it is fair to state, in extenuation, that being an Anglo-Egyptian judge, he is naturally debased by no
technical knowledge, and is as necessarily unpractical and unworldly wise.
Were it otherwise, he would not have been appointed to the position, nor
would he have accepted it. On the other hand, he is socially charming; will
recite Tennyson and Swinburne by the hour, which will please you; and is

A Bakery at Karnoos.

utterly ignorant of the country,
which is an advantage for me."
The judge did not belie his reputation; he had been editor of
a newspaper, secretary to a Duke
—everything except a judge, and
was therefore all that could be
desired for the Egyptian bench.
In gentle, uncomplaining tones,
he stated the one hardship of his
lot—that for three days in the
week, during nine months of the
year, he had to sit for four hours
in a court where the noisy argu-
ments of counsel disturbed all
the charm of conversation with
his colleagues—"some of whom,
I must admit," he added, "take
their duties much too seriously,
and, in fact, are as solemn as if
they were beneficed clergymen of
the Church of England."

"Are they all English?" asked
the Sketcher.

"No," said the judge; "many
of them are of your country, and of other nationalities. It requires the united
intelligence of five nations to try every petty case. You see," he added
solemnly, "the balance of power in Europe might be disturbed if an Englishman or Frenchman alone were to decide a question of five pounds between
Ali Mahomet and Spiro Dimitri. So the other great Powers must be represented
too; and Greece, because Spiro is a Greek, and Egypt, because Ali is an

Egyptian; and if Greece, why not Holland and Denmark? And then consider the important interests of the United States!"

"And do you all have to listen to such a case?"

"Listen! well, we all *sit*, you see, and that is the main thing, next to our pay, which, I am glad to say, is regular. For myself, I generally do my private correspondence on the occasion."

"And the rest?"

"Well, you see there are some who have a difficulty in following the case, as they don't understand the language; but there are generally one or two who can understand if they listen, and they *do* sometimes."

"But," said the Turtle, "do you mean to say that this hollow mockery has to be gone through with every trifling offender—that the man who is guilty, say, of a common assault, is allowed thus to waste the time of this highly expensive bench?"

"Not at all, my dear sir, not at all. So expensive are we, that we are reserved as a luxury for purely civil and commercial cases. Neither we, nor, so far as I know, any other Power in Egypt, have criminal jurisdiction. An Englishman, indeed, committing a crime, is subject to the authority of his Consul. He may be transported for life or condemned to death; that is the peculiar privilege which he enjoys over every other person in Egypt—a privilege for which he pays five shillings annually. I believe," he added gently, "I am stating the fact; if not, my friend will correct me. A free-born Briton differs from all other foreigners in Egypt in two particulars—the one, that he contributes five shillings yearly to the revenue of his country; and the other, that he may be condemned to death by his country's representative."

"At all events," interposed the Sketcher, "you have had, in exchange for your five shillings, the protection of a British fleet and some 30,000 British soldiers. You cannot say that the charge is excessive?"

"No! perhaps not," said the other meditatively; "provided they remain in the country, I am not disposed to quarrel with the value which my Government attaches to its protection; in that case the five shillings is not excessive. But if to-morrow the troops are to be removed, we shall certainly be in a distinctly worse position than we were before they came; and I think I shall then be justified in reclaiming my accumulated five shillings with compound interest."

"But," asked the Turtle, "returning to this question of criminal jurisdiction, I presume that other subjects are equally liable to their Consulates; otherwise, what is the meaning of Consular protection?"

"Consular protection," explained the Scribbler, "is, in Egypt, synonymous with free-trade in crime. Except as regards Englishmen, there is no punishment for crime in Egypt. Natives, whether innocent or guilty, are punished or acquitted according to the price which it is convenient to pay for either condemnation or acquittal. As for other Europeans, they are amenable to their Consulates for misdemeanours; and for crimes, you may, if you like, prosecute them in Moscow, Athens, Copenhagen, or wherever else their supreme court lies."

" And these are the results of the capitulations?"

The Scribbler was preparing to reply, when the Sketcher interposed.

"Let me implore you to desist; the mere mention of the word involves a history of Egypt for the past seven hundred years. Let me change the subject, and ask you where is the temple of Arsinoe?"

The judge appealed to was mute.

"Do you mean, sir, that you have lived here all these years, and cannot direct us to the temple of Arsinoe, of Venus, of Berenice, of what you will?"

"I have heard of all the ladies in question," said the judge, "but have met no one of that description in Ramleh."

"And is this what you have brought us here for?" said the Scribbler; "is it for the sake of three miserable sandstone pillars that you have dragged us into the Desert? Come, you shall see them;" and he led the way to the sea.

The weary sand which gives its name to the little suburb was sprinkled with ice-plants, poppies, anemones, and early spring flowers, together, it must be admitted, with a goodly number of old sardine-boxes, bottles, and other less romantic objects. Here and there, tents of Bedouins mingled among the houses; but the Bedouin, in the neighbourhood of civilisation, loses his charm and preserves his dirt. Clambering up a gently sloping hill, the party found at their feet the blue Mediterranean in wide expanse to the east, and to the west the outlines of Alexandria, stretching round the bay, and terminating far into the sea with the graceful fort of Pharos. Behind them, the Canal, with its gardens, formed a belt of green; beyond, as far as the eye could reach the Lake Mareotis; and at their feet, half way down the cliff, the remains of a small temple.

The few battered sandstone pillars, possessing, indeed, in themselves no remains of beauty, were not without attraction, due to their position on the rugged promontory, beneath which were still to be seen the remains of what perhaps were catacombs, and a passage which may have led to some subterranean refuge.

"Have none of you a word of gratitude to me for bringing you here?" said the Sketcher, as he expatiated on the view.

"The sea," said the Scribbler, "we have seen somewhat more than enough of lately; the sand, except that this is dirtier, we shall see more than enough of by-and-bye; to that add two or three pieces of sandstone, and what have we to thank you for?"

"To thank me for? man who pretends to be interested in historical associations! You have to thank me for bringing you to a spot where the wisest men of perhaps the wisest age, and the most beautiful women of the most beautiful age, racked their brains for the solution of a mystery, and solved it by inventing a constellation. Listen: when Ptolemy Euergetes was away on his Assyrian war" (B.C. 238, interposed the practical Scribbler), "Queen Berenice came here to Zephyrium, and sacrificing a bull to the gods on this very spot, vowed that, if they brought her husband home, she would cut her beautiful tresses, hang them up in this temple, and dedicate them to the sea-born goddess who protected sailors. When Euergetes returned a conqueror, the vow was kept—the locks were yielded to the knife, and hung up here. Imagine them as they floated round this

Temple of Berenice.

pillar; and do you not see the pirate who, coming in round that point, is attracted by the glitter of what he mistakes to be gold. He has carried them off (for even pirates, Scribbler, had a love of the beautiful in those days), and the whole coast is in a transport of excitement at the audacious robbery. Here stood Ptolemy himself, the outraged Berenice, Callimachus summoned from his library at Alexandria, and Theocritus, genial poet-laureate. The king has said that it must be found, and search is made along all the coasts, from Cyrene to Pelusium, and throughout the seaboard of the Empire. But Conon, wise man, is courtier as well as astronomer, and he discovers it. He is busy at the time making a chart of the heavens, and where so likely to be the golden tresses of lovely Berenice? There, sure enough, is a glittering group of stars between the Bear, the Lion, the Virgin, and Bootes, and as it hangs over the temple, he proclaims his discovery of a new constellation, "The Hair of Berenice!"

Can the most exacting monarch inquire farther? Can Berenice herself complain that the glory of her womanhood has preceded her to Elysium?"

"Did you invent that on the spot?" said the Scribbler.

"No, I did not; but, to be honest, I read it in a book."

"Then you are a pirate yourself!"

"Possibly; but always one with an appreciation of the beautiful!"

The Turtle remarked that the story didn't seem at all probable. The Fond One looked appreciatively at the Sketcher, and hastily assured herself that her own hair had not gone the way of Berenice's. The judge sighed, and passed his hands through his own scant locks. "My Berenice was very beautiful," he said softly. "*Was* her name Berenice, though? No, it was Barbara I was thinking of; but *she* was very beautiful too."

The road back led through the old Nicopolis, where, 1900 years ago, Augustus defeated Antony; past a hideous palace, built by Ismail out of the ruins of Cæsar's camp; and the little white-domed mosque where Sir Ralph Abercromby was carried wounded during the battle of Alexandria, to be taken on board to die a few days later.

Peep-Show.

Reaching the high ridge known as the French lines, but marking also the walls of the town of Ptolemy, the party came on the recently excavated remains of a cemetery. Entering a doorway cut in the solid rock, they found themselves in a crypt containing tiers of cells, each with the remains of ten male skeletons; and beyond these more, some two hundred corpses in all. The rude cross, marked on the rock with the I.H.S., showed it to belong to the Christian era; not improbably it was the site of a monastery without the outer walls of the Cæsareum, and of about the sixth century.

"It is right," said the Scribbler, "that we should finish Alexandria with this latest discovery, and this latest of ruins, of the old city; for if, as seems probable, this is of the Justinian or Heraclian period, we have to-day seen almost the first and the last of the

Street Cooking.

city as one of the mistresses of the world. Perhaps some of these bones had life when Amru entered Alexandria, and when the Crescent of Islam triumphed over the Cross of Christ in the city of one of her four great Churches Fostat becomes the capital of the new Egypt of the Saracens, and for 1200 years Alexandria disappears from history.

We are so prone to measure everything by the standard of our own little lives, that we lose all count of time. We talk of Alexandria as an ancient city; connect it vaguely with Ptolemies, Cæsar, and sectarian struggles, and speak of an Alexandrian period as we speak of the Augustan or Victorian age. But the history of Alexandria is half the intellectual history of the world for nearly nine hundred years, and the two little ruins we have seen to-day are chronologically as far apart from one another as the Norman Conquest from our own day.

A Washerwoman.

E

CHAPTER IV.

THE next day, our travellers, who had apparently been definitely accepted as a recognised portion of the Turtle dovecot, had possessed themselves of a first-class carriage, and were crawling at the steady pace of an Egyptian loco-motive to Cairo. The Sketcher

Interior of a Third Class Carriage.

had again expressed a desire to attempt the journey on camels. The journey by Egyptian railway was, he argued, much less pic-turesque, and apparently not much more expeditious, than by caravan. The enduring Ship of the Desert, he maintained, would not lie down oftener than the engine broke down; the motion of either was equally likely to produce sea-sickness; and in both the time of arrival at one's journey's end seemed to depend upon the good-will of the drivers.

The Scribbler maintained that the comparison savoured of ex-aggeration. "The railway ad-ministration," he said, "like most others in Egypt, is managed by an International Board, and the working of the lines is therefore, to some extent, dependent upon the political relations of Europe, modified by the social relations existing between the directors' wives. The system is certainly not one which can be recommended, either for its simplicity, economy, or practical results. That considerable loss is occasioned to the Egyptian Government, and the maximum of annoyance caused to all who use the lines, cannot be denied; but the former should remember that it enjoys the protection of Her Majesty's Government, and must not grumble if it occasionally pays for it in the form of a useless official or two; while the latter should learn to subordinate their own personal comfort to the political exigencies of Europe."

"But I cannot see," said the Turtle, "how politics enter into the management of the railway."

"The difficulty is not unnatural," replied the Scribbler, "but I will make it clear. The railways having been made the guarantee for a portion of the debt, it was necessary to see that the revenues reached the bondholders. It is true there were four (now six) gentlemen paid £3000 a year each for the sole purpose of protecting the bondholders' interests; but this was not sufficient; the railway must be put directly under European control. Considering the length of line and amount of traffic, it would not have been difficult to find a man capable of managing it; but there arose a question of nationality. First, there must be an Egyptian, because it was an Egyptian railway; and as he was useless, there must be a Frenchman to look after him; and as, of course, the balance of power in Europe would otherwise be disturbed, a couple of Englishmen must be sent to look after the other two. A little later, the only capable man of the four having died, it was thought unnecessary to replace him."

"The arrangement seems preposterous enough," said the Turtle; "but still, after all, each one, I presume, took a department, and so dispensed with the charge of some subordinate officials, who would otherwise be necessary."

"But you cannot think," said the Scribbler, "that gentlemen occupying these exalted positions would condescend to attend to such details. On the contrary, there are chiefs of every department, who do the work and manage the line—a chief of the permanent way, a chief of the rolling stock, a chief of the traffic, an inspector of telegraphs, a controller of the Port—all these officials conduct the business of the administration as well as they can."

"And what are the duties of the Board of Management?"

"Well, you see, they have always a good deal of personal abuse of each other to get through. Irritating the chiefs of departments occupies a considerable portion of their time; and such as remains is spent in Europe, in hospital, or, on rare occasions, in prison."[1]

"And, under all these difficulties, does the railway pay?"

[1] The railway administration has quite recently been somewhat improved.

" Well, if you take the value of the line at £10,000,000, which I suppose is a very large estimate, the dividend would be roughly five per cent. ; but then you must not attach much importance to that. The railway in Egypt is a monopoly, able to charge whatever rates it likes over two-thirds or more of the country. Under these circumstances, it succeeds, at the cost of about forty per cent. of its receipts, in keeping the line in its present ragged condition. The Board is very proud of its success, and points to the forty per cent. as proof that their management is, if nasty, at least cheap; but if compelled by competition to carry cargo at rates charged in India or England, their working expenses would probably exceed their receipts, and the line prove as expensive as it is ill-managed. To give you an instance of mismanagement : Some years ago one of the chiefs of department found necessary a certain piece of work, which would cost £75. There was no question as to the necessity of the work, but it took fourteen months before the application had passed the necessary formalities before the Board. But then all was not over; the chief of department found that he would also require the use of a truck for the work. All the negotiations had to begin over again, and, for all I know, are going on still."

" But is it not a fact," asked the Turtle, " that the amount of working expenditure is limited by agreement to a figure which is insufficient ? "

" No ; that is a popular fallacy. The amount allowed may be insufficient, but they do not spend it : they reduce the receipts by gross mismanagement ; they allow the whole material to go from bad to worse ; and then they complain that the administration is starved."

" Well," said the Sketcher, " I for one am grateful to them for the leisurely pace, which offers a pleasant opportunity for surveying the scenery, and for the long pauses at the stations, which enable one to study the manners and customs of the natives ; " for the Sketcher saw beauty where the Turtle saw only squalor and misery, and where the Scribbler saw neither.

" Your beauty," he said, " is nothing but your love for novelty. Prettier effects of light and shade, more beautiful combinations of colour, you can find in nearly every village of England or the South of Europe ; you pass them there because you are accustomed to them, and fall into ecstasies over this because it is new. That woman carrying a *goulah*, that boy on a buffalo, attract your attention because of their novelty. An English farm-lad on a horse, a washer-woman at the village pump, is every bit as picturesque, and considerably cleaner. As to your squalor and misery, there is not a farmer in England, let alone Ireland, who would not change places with the poorest of the Fellaheen, so far as the results of farming are concerned. Had you passed through here twenty years ago, you would have seen squalor and misery; but then that was in the so-called golden days of Ismail."

The train leaving Alexandria passes over the swamp of Mareotis, stretching on both sides of the line, and cuts through the remains of Arabi's earthworks in 1882. A useless reconnaissance on the 5th August was here the occasion of our first loss during the campaign. Among the reeds to the right fell Howard Vyse and two privates, killed by falling spent shot. After this, for some six weeks, a cannonade with heavy guns from both sides was maintained daily, with the net loss of one buffalo and one horse. The latter gave the name to the clump of trees on the left. A picket of the 60th, on a dark night, found themselves, as they thought, at close quarters with the enemy. Valiantly they fired volley after volley, but their fire was not returned; and next morning they discovered the body of a stray horse lying in what has since been known as the "Dead-horse Picket." Kafr Dawar, the first station, must claim the honour of being the scene of perhaps the most ignoble surrender ever made by men bearing arms; for here 10,000 followers of Arabi surrendered to a sergeant of the Shropshire, armed with a stick. The surrender had, of course, been previously agreed upon; and there were perhaps 300 more of the regiment within call, but there was no need for them. The patriotic Egyptians came in, anxious only to get rid of their arms to any one who would take them. A line of trucks was drawn up by the station; and close to the trucks, with just sufficient room to allow one man to pass at a time, was a telegraph post. On one side of this stood Sergeant Tommy Atkins of the Shropshire; there

A Woman carrying a Goulah.

was no pomp and circumstance of war about him; he had taken off his coat, slipped his braces over his shoulders, and had his sleeves tucked up for business. On crowded the 10,000; and as they came to the post, one by one, they had to pass between it and the trucks; throw their Remingtons, bayonets, pistols, and trumpets into the latter, and pass on. Sergeant Tommy Atkins was one, and they were many; but he was not to be trifled with. Did any try and pass the wrong side of the post or smuggle through a revolver, he got a sharp rap on the knuckles, and a "Now, then, hand up," soon brought him to order. "It would have done Wilfrid Blunt, and other believers in Arabi

patriotism, good," said the Scribbler, "to have seen the cheerful way in which
these gallant and patriotic warriors accepted the situation. The 'valour of
the beaten host,' as Wilfrid calls it, was singularly like the playful excitement
of schoolboys who come bounding out of school. So anxious were they to
pass muster, that many of them handed their rifles to myself and others, to
get rid of them the quicker; and we got into amicable converse with them.
Singularly good-tempered were these victims of tyranny to their betrayers;
some of them shook me warmly by the hand, and said that, now all this

tomfoolery (*shoogly mushara*) was over, they were going
back to serious work; others were delighted at the noise
their guns made, 'Even more than yours,' they said, but
hoped sincerely they had caused no one any inconvenience. 'None at all,' I replied; 'we didn't lose a
man; but how many did you lose?' for great had been
the tales in camp of the slaughter we had effected. 'Oh,
no!' was the reply; 'you never came near us. You did
once,' he said, deprecatingly, 'kill a man's buffalo, but
then it had strayed in your way;' and he begged I would
not think of it. These were the patriots of Blunt," said
the Scribbler; "poor, innocent Fellaheen, ready enough
to be put into a uniform, to be given a gun, fair food,
and nothing to do, at so much a day. Why should they
not, poor wretches? There was nothing else going on;
the markets were closed. But fight or incur danger!
No, not for Arabi, nor their country, nor for anything
else. So when they saw troops they bolted."

Some of our Captives.

"And was 'all your campaign as glorious as this?"
asked the Sketcher sarcastically.

"Well, it was not very different; but you may spare
your sneers. The lines of Tel-el-Kebir were carried gallantly, and if there was
little resistance, you must remember that the troops were unaware whether there
would be any or no; and they stormed, without a moment's hesitation, entrenchments which it's easy to depreciate now, but which, if properly defended, would
have defied attack by twice the force. Still, I am willing to admit that the first
Egyptian campaign gave little opportunity for trying the mettle of our soldiers in
a hand-to-hand fight, but it established our reputation for other qualities not less
valuable, and chiefly for *audace*. Here, for instance," he continued, as the train
drew up at Tantah, "is the most fanatical town of Egypt, dedicated to the Sheikh

Said el Bedawee. Into it, a few days after Tel-el-Kebir, rode gallant Sir Archie Alison, with a single company of his Highlanders, and found, drawn up in the square there, some 4000 Egyptian troops, armed, and apparently ready to fight. What was he to do? The numbers were forty to one; any hesitation would have been fatal; and the plucky one-armed General showed none. 'Summon all to lay down their arms,' was the order given through an interpreter to the officer in command. Just a moment of anxiety, a glance at the perfectly composed face of the General, and the order was obeyed."

" And suppose it had not been?" asked the Sketcher.

" Precisely! there was the danger; but it *was* obeyed, and that is its justification."

" Justification for the summons to surrender, perhaps, as the best way out of the difficulty; but hardly any justification for getting into it."

" Well, that you may discuss with the General; but the presence of mind remains to the good in any case. Take the surrender of Cairo as another instance. After the wonderful ride from Tel-el-Kebir, the cavalry arrived deadbeat at the Abbasiyeh heights, within sight of Cairo. They were 900 men, and few of them capable of either moving a step in advance, or even of retreating if they had been attacked. There lay the city below them, with 8000 troops, and the citadel commanding their position. What were they to do? At any moment, if discovered, they might be attacked; and it was impossible that they could escape observation. There was only one way of gaining time—to show a bold front, summon the garrrison to surrender, and to await the result. To their surprise, the garrison of 8000 at once expressed their readiness to obey the summons. And now arose the question, how to take advantage of it without showing their weakness. With some difficulty, 150 men, able to get their horses on for another five or six miles, were got together. In command of them went Major Watson of the Engineers. Through the close streets of Cairo they threaded their way, till they drew up at the massive gates of the Citadel. Into it quietly walked Major Watson, leaving his tired men drawn up outside, faced by curious but respectful Egyptian troops numbering two to one. 'Where is the commandant?' asked the Major. 'Asleep!' was the reply. 'Then wake him up, and tell him to surrender.' The first order was obeyed, and the commandant came, sleepy but servile. 'Will you kindly turn your men out, and hand me the keys?' said the Englishman. 'Certainly,' said the Egyptian; and within the hour, but with profuse apologies for delay, the 8000 patriot soldiers of Arabi filed out to make way for the 150 tired men, who, unable to sit longer in their saddles, had thrown themselves on the ground for very weariness. The Major, who has a fine Irish brogue, adds reproachfully, as he tells the story, ' An' they ca'all that foightin ! '"

"And there is the Citadel in question," said the Sketcher, as some few minutes later the line made a sudden curve, bringing in view Cairo, nestling under the Mokhattam hills, with its green gardens, the pretty gaily-coloured houses of Shubra, and the slender minarets of the Citadel mosque on the heights above.

In a few minutes more the train drew up at the Cairo railway station.

Sayees.

View of Cairo.

CHAPTER V.

RIGHTLY called Angelo is the porter of Shepheard's to the weary traveller who arrives in Cairo. Like a good Shepheard does he gather the flocks of portmanteaus, and like a guiding Angel pilots his sheep through the crowd. Disdaining the colossal hearse of the hotel, our travellers have hailed lithesome *arabeeyahs*, and are being driven at a pace which would excite the horror and indignation of any well-regulated policeman. The citizens of Cairo despise the modern improvements of Alexandria. They recognise that the capital of Egypt exists solely by virtue of its reputation acquired in the dark ages, and they have determined that no vulgar innovation in the way of cleanliness or municipal regulation shall cast a slur upon their character. The streets, therefore, are neither paved nor levelled, and the carriage flies from one rocky eminence to another, so that one's first experience resembles a steeplechase on wheels. Railways, indeed, have to be submitted to, also bridges ; but no fastidious modern precautions are adopted for the one, and a hole or two is still left by way of protest in the other. So the engine puffs across the crowded streets without so much as a telegraph post to attract attention. If the carriage gets in the way, it must share the fate of Stephenson's coo ; and if, in dodging an engine, you should by chance land yourself in a hole of the bridge,—well, it is not big enough to let you through into the canal, and there is generally a policeman near enough to curse your driver. The bridge and the line safely cleared, you urge your Mazeppa-like career to the right, and clinging with both hands to your seat, you get into the comparatively speaking still waters of the road that skirts the hospitable house of Nubar. As you come near a succession of *café-chantants*, you suffer from what seems to be an after-swell, and are liable to be thrown over the back of the carriage, as you draw up suddenly at the steps of Shepheard's Hotel.

A Street in Cairo.

It may be admitted as an axiom that the man who has not stayed at Shepheard's has never really visited Cairo. Other hostelries, indeed, there are, possessing many and various well-advertised charms. This one is cheap, and that one is in the centre of the bazaars; another has the electric light, and a fourth has the best *table-d'hôte*. Shepheard's disdains offering such inducements. It is Shepheard's and nothing else; and it is enough. As the Nile to other rivers, so is Shepheard's to other hotels. It is not the biggest, nor the most handsome, nor the oldest; nor is it the dearest (not quite) in which mortal might stay and live. What is the charm, which no man can either deny or define?

You may dwell where you will, in private house, in pension, or in unorthodox hotel; but as surely as the needle to the pole will you gravitate to Shepheard's. One attraction, indeed, it has; but that is one which we only reap, like that of Paradise, at the close of our sojourn. Stately is the mien of the Shepheard king Luigi when he receives us the first time; but unutterable bliss accompanies the smile with which he bids us adieu. The man must be obdurate, indeed, who, having once basked in that farewell smile, does not seek its sunshine again. As for such a woman, be assured she does not exist. The attitude itself with which it is rendered is a bouquet; the final bow which accompanies it is its choicest rose, and the smile is its aroma. The feet, well drawn together, with stern determination to support the inevitable; the shoulders bent in agonised but silent despair; the hands clasped in mute entreaty; the head slightly to one side in pious resignation; the reproachful eyes which look tears; the melancholy smile which tells of joys buried in perennial gloom ; and then the final bow, which is the last dignified submission to fate. "It affects even me," said the unsentimental Scribbler, "and I have seen it for twenty winters."

"But he's quite young," said the Fair One, to whom the graceful proprietor had been pointed out.

"But the smile is part of the hotel properties," said the other ; "it has been handed down through a long succession of Shepheard kings, and the original is in the Hyksos chamber at Boolak."

The great man received them with becoming dignity, and arranged the party with all the promptitude of a skilful general. The Turtle was happy, for he learnt that the sitting-room allotted to him had just been vacated by a crown-prince. Damon and Pythias found quarters at a more remote part of the building, a good quarter of a mile from the landing, through infinite corridors, but commanding a view over the garden, and a tree which the Sketcher at once pronounced to be evidently the one under which Kleber was stabbed. "From this very window, perhaps," he said, "looked out the black woman who spotted the murderer, and pointed him out hidden away among those shrubs." The Scribbler remarked, drily, that this part of the building happened to be only a few years old ; still—there, or somewhere near it, was the tree, and here, or somewhere near it, there was such a window.

Great was the crowd at the *table-d'hôte* that evening in the big room with its long rectangle of tables. Imposing was the row of waiters, steadfastly waiting the word of command from Edgardo, general of brigade ; and a proud man looked Luigi, as at not rare intervals he came, like an able commander-in-chief, to survey the field of battle, and count the bottles which yield him his harvest of four hundred per cent. Lovingly he looked at the chickens—those chickens the lineal descendants of those concerning which wrote Adrian Augustus : "I wish them no other curse but that the Egyptians may be fed with their own chickens, which are hatched in a way I am ashamed to relate."

"And how was that?" asked the Patrician, who, together with the merchant in hides, had joined their late fellow-travellers at the table.

"I presume," said the Scribbler, "they were artificially hatched ; at least it's a flourishing trade now, and probably was then, in Alexandria."

"Wa'al," said Hides, "there is something to me attractive in eating what is to any extent the product of machinery. I reckon most things are better done by machinery than nature. These animals, now," he said thoughtfully, "could never have been brought to this state of sturdy endurance by the fondling attentions of a parent fowl; they will, for that quality, probably never be excelled until the laying itself is also the work of human ingenuity."

"They do reflect credit on the establishment," said the Scribbler; "they are a well-known speciality of the house, and their legs only reach this muscular state by dint of continual exercise up and down the Pyramids upon which they gaze."

"But I can find nothing but legs," said the Fond Dove.

"The wings are invariably made into *salmi* of duck, and the rest of the bird into game-pie; but, hush! the real excitement of the evening approaches."

It was Luigi, preceding, with ill-concealed pride, the waiters who were bearing that *chef-d'œuvre* of Shepheard's, "the ice-pudding," reserved for Thursdays and Sundays.

"You have dined well?" he inquired, as his guests went out; "you found the ice-pudding good?" And the whole *table-d'hôte*, with one accord, pronounced themselves feasted as if by the gods. Who would dare grumble at Shepheard's? What angry thought, what pang of indigestion, would not disappear before Luigi?

Smoking their cigarettes on the balcony that evening, there was much recounting of experiences, comparison of plans, and consultation for the future among the ex-*Mœris* party.

Hides and the Patrician had determined not to let the grass grow under their feet; they had caught the train for Cairo on the day of their arrival, and seen Pompey's Pillar on their way to the station. Hides checked the accuracy of his recollection by looking it up in his "Murray," and finding a mark against it, was convinced. The railway journey he described as trying. "They played bowls with me all along the line," he said. Arriving in Cairo, they had spent half an hour at the Boolak Museum, driven to the Pyramids, walked round the Sphinx, and got back in time to see the Citadel mosque. This last impressed the American more than anything in Cairo; for he measured it carefully, and found that it would make a magnificent tannery. Both were now prepared to take an affidavit that they had done Cairo. As for the Nile, the American was led to believe that it consisted mainly of buildings, mostly in a bad state of repair; and the Patrician had been disappointed in the reported shooting prospects.

The Turtle was anxious to see "the proper thing" in Cairo, and "to do" the Nile with as much regard to his pocket as his dignity would allow. He was opining towards Cook, but the Doves cooed rebelliously for a *dahabeeyah*, and indulged in some not profoundly original sneers at Cook's tourists.

The Scribbler, on the contrary, avowed himself an enthusiastic Cook, as the only feasible means of combining the exigencies of time, money, and the Nile. "Perhaps some of the people are not exactly those you would choose as companions, and perhaps, for that very reason, they are precisely the people whom it will do you good to travel with. You complain that Cook is too gregarious. I tell you it is exactly the reverse. Cook makes you go out of your own narrow set, and does for you what a public school does to the boy from home. Of course, you don't like it, nor does the boy at *first;* but you come away all the better—you have enlarged your ideas as to your fellow-man."

"Enlarged your ideas with a Cook's tourist!" said the Patrician.

"Certainly, my dear boy. It may be, in some cases, that you have enlarged your ideas as to their narrowness; but how can one arrive even at your own large and generous toleration of others, unless you have some experience of them? '*Odi profanum vulgus et arceo,*' say you; but how can you hate what you always avoid?"

"But they are so very unpicturesque," murmured the Sketcher.

A well-known Character in Cairo.

"Now, that," said the Scribbler, "is all cant. Look at ourselves, and tell me if we add anything to the beauty of the scenery? Where does Cook take them to? To Paris, where their worst bonnet-strings can compare not unfavourably with the flashy Saint-Chapelle. To the Rhine, where they look at least as graceful as the newly whitewashed castles on that tedious river. To Switzerland, where the scenery is already spoilt by the hideousness of the women. And here, where they are at least a comparatively bright spot of cleanliness. I tell you, sir," continued the Scribbler, getting argumentative, and consequently hyperbolical, "that against all the inconvenience which you, and a few like you, grumble at, is to be set the education of the most ignorant part of the British nation—the eradication of our greatest national vice, vulgarity. Mr. Cook is the educator of our middle class—the class through whose education alone we have any hope of remaining a nation. Do you think we should have had all this rubbish about non-intervention if John Cook had educated our grandfathers as he is educating us? No, sir! They were brought up in the belief that they lived in a nice little, tight little island; but their idea was to make that nice little island rule the world, of which they knew nothing. Their sons, who had imbibed the first part of the theory with their mother's milk, added a little knowledge of geography

from an atlas; thought England looked very small on a map; got frightened at
the Alexander idea of conquest, and jumped to the other extreme. This tight
little island was enough for them—let all the rest of the world go as it would.
Cook has made their children again travel, and they are slowly awakening to
a consciousness of the fact that there are other races as intelligent as they are;

that they have to fight to hold their own; and that the veins and
arteries of this tight little island are in every village and in every
country of the globe."

"The admission of which general principle," said the Sketcher,
"does not seem to bring us much nearer to Assouan, or the means
of getting there. It seems to me that, however we go, we are
bound to be despised. If we go by the post-boat, we are despised
by those who go by Cook. If we go by Cook, we are despised by
those who go by *dahabeeyah*; and if we go by *dahabeeyah*, we are
condemned by the Scribbler. Similarly, if we go to Luxor, we are
despised by those who get as far as Assouan; and these in their
turn are despised by the hardy travellers as far as Wady Halfa."

The notion of doing anything for which he could be possibly
despised was ungrateful to the Turtle; but comforted by the
reflection that the Archbishop of Canterbury and some royal
personages had travelled as Cook's tourists, he announced his
decision of starting by the steamer of that day week, and graciously

A Water Seller.

condescended to place himself and party in Cairo under the personal conduct
of the Scribbler for the intervening seven days. "You will understand," he
added gravely, "that we should like to see everything,"—which, thought the
Scribbler, as Cairo is supposed to contain 400 mosques, 1170 cafés, 140 schools,
300 cisterns, 70 public baths, 40 Christian churches, 13 synagogues, and 1265
okellas, is a pretty considerable order; but he saw the eyes of the Fair One
fixed on him, and consented with effusion.

The Nile near Beni Hassan.

CHAPTER VI.

Cairo from Mokhattam—Seventy centuries—Cairo of "Arabian Nights"—Cairo according to Ariosto—The Muski—Khan Khalili—Cairo of the Khedives— Sequence of history—A vast plan.

TO understand Cairo aright, the first view should be taken from the Mokhattam heights. The view which Murray ignores and Bädeker dismisses in a paragraph is generally neglected for the far inferior but more easily accessible one from the Citadel terrace. If he who has " not seen Cairo, has nothing seen," then assuredly the same condemnation attaches to him who neglects the Mokhattam, for there, below you, lies not only Cairo, but Egypt itself. The forty, or let us say seventy centuries, look across to us from the Pyramids ; the Sphinx, from even a remoter period, stands still waiting the answer to its never-solved riddle ; and down from long ages, with huge lacunæ indeed, we trace the history of the world, marked by the ruined footprints of time. There is Memphis, earliest of cities, built by the dissatisfied Prince of This ; there are the colossal tombs of the ancient empire, stretching from Sakkarah to Ghizeh. To the right lies Heliopolis, with its sun-temple of the Middle Monarchy ; and the Nile, hurrying by to Tanis of the Hyksos, to Sais and Bubastis of the new empire, to Naukratis of the Greeks, and to Alexandria

G

of the Ptolemies. There is Babylon of the Romans, away to the left, Fostat of
the Arabs ; El Askar of the Abbasides ; El Katayeh of the Tooloonides; and
Cairo itself of the Fatemites. At our feet lies the Citadel of the Great Salah ed
Deen—Saladin of our childhood, and founder of the Ayoubites. The minarets
of Kalaoun and Hassan, Kait Bey and El Ghoree, recall the Memlook dynasties ;
and there, by the Mosque el Mowayud, is the Bab el Zuweilah, where Turkish
Sultan Selim hanged Toman, last of his race, assumed the title of Caliph, and
secured Egypt to the hated rule of the Turk. Three hundred years pass, leaving
no trace on the map before us ; but the ever-standing Pyramids mark the site of
Bonaparte's victory over Murad ; the obelisk of Heliopolis, the triumph of his
successor over the Turk ; and the garden of Shepheard's recalls Kleber's assassination only three months later. There, along the river, marched the three
evacuating armies of England the victor, France the vanquished, and Turkey
who seized the spoil. In the Citadel at our feet, that grand old Roumeliote
brigand, Mohamed Ali, stood many a siege, pounding into submission the
miserable city below, until he had enclosed within those gates, massacring
within that courtyard, the last of the Memlooks, and waded "through slaughter
to a throne;" while beyond again lie the green gardens of the Ismailieh of
his grandson, and the barracks of the Khasr el Nil, where floats the Union
Jack.

So great is the interest of historical association, that we are tempted to
neglect the view itself. Yet the words of the old Arab legend, handed down
by tradition, and published in Cairo about the beginning of the sixteenth century,
come vividly to our memory : "He that has not seen Egypt has not seen the
greatest wonder in the world. All the land there is golden—I mean, it is so
fertile that it enriches its inhabitants. All the women of that country are
charming, either in their personal beauty or in their agreeable manners. If
you speak of the Nile, pray where is there a more magnificent river? What
water was ever purer or more delicious? The very mud that it carries along
in its inundations fattens the land a thousand times more than other countries
that are cultivated with the utmost care. Remember what a poet said to the
Egyptians when he was compelled to depart from the country, 'Your Nile
loads you with bounties every day; it is for you only that it flows from such
a distance. Alas ! in going away from you, my tears are doomed to run as
abundantly as its water. You are to continue in the enjoyment of its sweetness,
while I am condemned to absent myself.' If you look at the island or delta
that is formed by the two great branches of the Nile, what variety of verdure
have you there ! what embroidery of all sorts of flowers ! what a number

of cities, villages, streamlets, and a thousand other agreeable objects! If you cast your eyes in another direction towards Ethiopia, how many fresh causes of admiration are there! Then, again, is not Grand Cairo the largest, the most populous, and the richest city in the universe? What a number of magnificent edifices, public and private, does it contain! If you behold the Pyramids, you will be seized with astonishment. You will stand motionless at the sight of those masses of stone which tower to the skies; and you will be obliged to confess that the Pharaohs, who lavished so much treasure and employed so many men in building them, must have surpassed all the monarchs that have appeared since, not only in Egypt, but throughout all the world, in liberality and invention—monuments so ancient, that the most learned men cannot agree as to the time of their erection; and yet they have lasted to this day and will last throughout whole ages."

As one gazes on the crowded beehive below, and listens to the hum of life resounding through the clear atmosphere, one is almost tempted to believe Ariosto, who describes Cairo as "threaded by 18,000 streets, each house with three floors, one only containing 15,000 warriors, their families and their horses, under the same roof," until a calculation shows us that the estimate of the poet would account for the entire population of

the universe. But as the sun sets behind the Pyramids, and bathes the myriad minarets in a flood of ruddy golden light; as that wonderful afterglow, seen nowhere but in Egypt, rises over the horizon, and seems to shed its benediction on all the valley beneath, to soothe the swiftly flowing waters of the Nile, and to lull to sleep the city to the sound of the Muezzin's call, one seems to stand above it all in a dreamland, and to deem no legend too strange to be true.

Coming down from the realms of dreamland and imagination, from the Cairo of the Caliphs and of the Memlooks, we find ourselves at once in the everyday life of the capital of to-day, in the new street, which is but a continuation of the famous Muski. But what an everyday life it is! It is the everyday life of six centuries

Carpet Bazaar in the Khan Khalili.

ago still, varied only here and there by the unmistakable presence of a cheap and nasty civilisation. Here is the carpet bazaar of Halil, with carpets,

though some worn with age, still showing that velvet gloss and that indescrib-
able harmony of colours that we find equalled only in nature; and there,

not far from it, is the flashy store of the Levantine, with
hideous Brussels and Kidderminster patterns of brilliant red
roses tied into bouquets with mauve ribbons on a yellow
ground, over which are poring in ecstatic admiration some
young housewives of Cairo, in search for the very latest
novelties from Paris. Here are the red and yellow *babouche*
slippers from Tunis and Morocco; there, hard by, are the
high-heeled monstrosities of to-day—the old world mixing
with the new, the East with the West; and, singularly
enough, the denizens of each generally seeking for the wares
of the other. Not always, however; for here is a trade
with which we have dispensed in Europe, and which yet
flourishes in Egypt, and happily still among the natives.
Sometimes in the court of an *okella*, sometimes in an open
side-street, is the well of the quarter; a sturdy native raises,
in primitive fashion, alternate buckets of the muddy Nile

Shoe Seller.

water, and finds constant demand. Here is a Saga with his
goat-skin newly filled, which he
will distribute with careless generosity about the feet of the
passers-by in the dusty streets,
or perhaps carry to some private
customer, who will let it filter
itself imperfectly through a stone
zeir; others are waiting for their
supply in jars, graceful as is the
rudest pottery of the Nile Valley;
while hard by a venerable vendor
of what he avers to be "Water
sweet as honey! water from the
spring! Drink, O faithful! the
wind is hot and the way long!
Water sweet as honey!" is bending his back, and pouring from
the quaint jar over his shoulder

Water Carriers.

C. MONTBARD.

Water Sellers.

a sparkling stream into the little brass cup, religiously inscribed with verses from the Koran. Perhaps the water does not answer to his description; but then the meanest Egyptian is a poet, and must be allowed poetic license. It is better than the fire-water of the Greek baccal yonder, he will tell you, and is cheap at least; for if he will take a piaster from you, he will, on the strength of it, give it gratis to the first poor beggar who asks for it. "Bismillah! in the name of God!"

With the taste of honey, or mud, in your mouth, turn to the right here, where the crowd seems thickest; follow the close-packed, narrowing street; salute copper-coloured Abdallah, the carpet-man, and pass on to your right again, into the Khan Khalili, named after Caliph El Ashruf Khalil, son of Kalaoun, and built in his day 600 years ago. Here was then the business quarter of the town, as now it is of such as deal in carpets, jewels, silks, brass-work, and biblots of all kinds; but, in the old days, the life of a merchant was by no means so quiet as now. Memlooks would ride through the streets, pillaging the shops and houses, carrying off women and children; free fights took place in the roads; missiles of all kinds were discharged from the houses on to the enemy below; and the terrified merchants of the Khan Khalili would gather into its narrow alleys, shut to the heavy gates, and remain for days at a time trembling in a state of siege. No signs of such terror do we see now. Like spiders in their webs sit the Persians, Spanish Jews, and Turks, warily watching for the European fly who may be tempted to enter. Some are stately and Oriental; receive you with a solemn bow, explain that all their goods are yours; scrutinise keenly your expression as they open before you their wares; and when they catch the glance that tells of approval, vow that the article which has attracted it is the one jewel of their collection. Others, again, affect an eager anxiety to finish

B

A Merchant.

the work they have in hand; hardly can they spare the time to look at you; never were there such industrious workmen, even though you may have seen them only a moment before enjoying their *kef* and gossip. Such are the workers in brass. Do you want such a thing? That is the price, and there is no more to be said—they have no time to waste; only, when you turn to go, and a hurried look shows that you mean it, does the chisel and hammer fall, and the hard-pressed workman become the anxious bargainer. A third class there is, who affect the superior ways which they fondly imagine to be in accordance with English ideas. "Have cup coffee? Have cup tea? How's y'self?

How's y' family? Sit down. Want anything? All cheap; low'st price." Of such
are Faraway Moses, so named by some facetious American—title duly registered
in a guide-book, and accepted by the worthy old Hebrew in a large board over

his stall; Coen, dealer in curios, and
dabbler in stocks, rich in embroideries,
and of more than average Khan Khalili
honesty; and "Low'st Price," so named
on the *lucus a non lucendo* principle.
Many are the hours and many the guineas
that you may wile away, not altogether
unprofitably.   Nowhere better, perhaps,
can you find Cairo epitomised in miniature
—its crowded streets, its veiled beauties,
its Eastern treasures, its projecting roofs,
its fine dilapidated Saracenic architecture,
and—its beggars.

Leaving the Khan Khalili, we cross
the road into the silver bazaar; but it requires much enthusiasm for light filagree
work, or determination to unearth the

Silver Bazaar.

occasional specimens of good old Hedjaz silver manufacture, to tempt us to
linger in the fetid atmosphere of the Sug el Fuddah, and a turn to our left
brings us again into the Grand Muski. Here, until recently, was the most
prosperous quarter of Cairo, the site of banks and the
largest Levantine commercial houses; while the little *"rond
point"* in the middle of it, with its four trees, was the
fashionable lounge of Young Egypt mounted on donkeys.
Now, it is the meeting-place for auctioneers, offering well-
worn remains of cheap European furniture; the shops on
either side of the street are more frequently European than
native, and slimy Levantine touts assail you to buy their
spurious wares. Still, if we take the Irishman's view, and
regard the street disassociated from its houses, we may
realise that we are in the East. Camels pass, laden with
wares from Mocca and Barbary, gingerly placing their feet
in the mud to the warning "Hât" of the driver; donkeys

A Jeweller.

laden with balloon-like women, who sit cross-legged on the very summit of
the saddle, crowded with sail formed by their black *fadlas*, and held on by

The Khan Khalili.

sympathetic donkey-boys. The rattle of the water-sellers' cups, the jingle of the donkeys' bells, mingle with the cry of the seller of pistacchios, of *rahatlakum*, of Helowa, of all the luxuries for Egyptian sweet-teeth. And here comes the *cafeijee*, with coffee suitable for grave seigneurs—coffee which, for a copper, we drink, not in vulgar draughts, but sip as nectar, more precious than golden chartreuse or precious curaçoa; and the seller of cheap iced sherbets or liquorice-water, that the faithful may imbibe without intoxication, if with colic. Turning through a wide door to the right as we leave the Muski, we find ourselves in a quaint old *okella* where congregate the cooks to buy rich stores of fruit and vegetables—the Covent Garden of Cairo—in one corner of which we find Parvis Magnus, maker of much furniture in beautiful antique, both Pharaonic and Saracenic Egyptian style, as tempts the æsthetic spendthrift to speedy ruin. And so we pass on, past the place where stood the statue of Ibrahim, victor of Konieh, but where it stands no more, since the iconoclastic Arabi relegated it, as an impious representation of nature, to the Boolak Museum—on to the Esbekieh, formerly a lake round which stood the gay kiosks of the Memlooks, and now an artificial garden, with sham lakes, sham rock-work, sham grass, fit emblem of the sham civilisation of its creator, Ismail.

Cafeijee.

For the Cairo of to-day—the Cairo in which the average traveller spends nine-tenths of his time—is the creation of the last twenty years. Old Mohamed Ali was fain to be content with his Citadel for the first few years of his reign, for therein alone lay safety. Later, when his power was more secure, he built his palace at Shubra, to the north on the banks of the river, not without taste of a barbaric oriental sort. Abbas, who deserved a better character than most historians have given him, half Bedouin as he was, loved the desert, and made his palaces in the Abbassieh and at Mex. Easy-going, voluptuous Said loved Alexandria, the sea, and the Canal. Ismail, the vaunted, over-praised civiliser of Egypt, had no higher ideal than that of making Cairo a miniature Paris, a city of boulevards and ballets, casinos and *café-chantants*.

And so it is that the capital of Egypt has come to be the one city in the world near which you may trace the life of 7000 years.

The Scribbler, who was a nervous man, felt somewhat appalled at the idea of carrying the unsympathetic Turtle through a course of history at the rate of a day per ten centuries; but he had been rash enough to consent, and being withal conscientious, he determined to do it as thoroughly as possible.

"It was the misfortune of my life," he confided to the Sketcher, "to acquire at an early age a considerable amount of desultory historical information, without any chronological sequence. By the time I was eighteen, I was deeply learned in various periods of history; my reading had ranged from Herodotus to Macaulay, or I should speak more correctly if I said from Macaulay to Herodotus, for I had the vaguest notion of what I will call the sequence of history. The longer I have lived the more convinced I am that half of even the educated world suffers from the same defect. They are deep in periods, and yet are ignorant of the most rudimentary knowledge of the connection between them. I met once a man who had given much study to the religions of the world; he was well versed in the niceties of the early Christian sects; could discourse for hours on the Ego and the Logos; was equally informed as to the life of Mahomet

A Pistacchio Seller.

and the rival pretensions of Ali and Othman; but it happened one day at a dinner-table that a question arose as to the right of Mahomet to the title of "Prophet of God," and the learned one denied his right to the title because he had not predicted the Messiah. Of course, in the next moment he saw his mistake, but the confusion was there for a second. Well, I feel that the soft and succulent brain of our friend the Turtle has been committed to my keeping for a week; that it is my duty in that time to make such impression as I can upon that yielding pulp; and as in the period I can hardly pretend to give a history of 7000 years, I will try at least to make the chronological framework or skeleton."

A Seller of Liquorice Water.

"Have you the remotest idea that he will ever be able to fill it in?"

"Very little, I confess; but besides the chance of interesting the Doves, there is, I confess, the hope that I may interest you, or at all events myself."

"And how do you propose to begin?"

"With the Sphinx, of course, starting our little trip somewhere before the date of the creation, according to Archbishop Ussher; leading him, metaphorically at all events, over the Pyramids to Boolak; hurrying him through the ancient empire and the Hyksos, and allowing him to linger over the mummies. The Ptolemaic period I tried to instil into him at Alexandria;

and, with a vault of some few thousands of years, we will carry him to Bablun, and then through mosques, beginning with the Gamr Amr, and finishing with the El Goriah. We will (metaphorically always) hang him at the Bab el Zuweilah with the last Borgite ; massacre him at the Citadel with the Memlooks ; let him realise Mohamed Ali at Shubra ; and finally leave him panting and struggling on his back at one of Tewfik's receptions at Abdeen. Dost thou like the picture ? "

" At first sight it seems, like ' Murray,' more instructive than amusing ; but, I confess, it has its advantages—mainly that we shall be for 7000 years in the company of the lovely Enid and Iris, as I discover they are called."

The Scribbler looked grave. " Remember, my Gothic and inflammatory friend, that you have to do with the stern British *père de famille, capable de tout,* as Talleyrand said. The British paterfamilias is as stern a despot in his family circle as the Turkish Pasha ; and if too attentive to the Doves, your headless trunk may be flung into the river with as little ceremony as that of Goroun, or, at the best, you will be asked to state your intentions."

" Which," replied the other, " I should at once state as evanescent and unmercenary."

CHAPTER VII.

I N accordance with the plan, our travellers started early the next morning for
the Pyramids, and duly experienced all the totally contradictory associations of all travellers, from Herodotus to the latest of American Howadjis.
These impressions may be studied with advantage from numerous guide-books,
and are probably not much more accurate, and certainly less interesting, than
the description given by that "simple man, void of learning," worthy Edward
Webbe, who, in the time of good Queen Bess, was carried as a slave to the
"Gran Caer," where he saw "Seauen Mountaines builded on the out side like
vnto ye point of a diamond, which Mountaines were builded in King Pharoes
time for to keepe Corne in, and they are Mountaines of great strength. It is
also saide that they were builded about that time when Ioseph did lade home
his Brethren's Asses with Corne, in the time of the great dearth mentioned in
the Scripture ; at which time all their Corne lay in those mountaines ;" or that
other by Richard Knolles, author of "The Generall Historie of the Turkes,"
who wrote some twenty years later, presumably from hearsay :—"About fiue
miles distant from old Caire, on Affricke side, stand the Pyramides, monuments of the barbarous Ægyptian kings vanitie ; whose proud names and titles
Time hath worne out of those huge and wonderful buildings, of purpose made
for the vaine eterning of their fame and endlesse wealth, so that of them it may
now well be said,

> Miramur periysse homines ? monumenta fatiscunt
> Interitus saxis nominibusque venit.
>
> What wonder we that men doe die ? the stately tombes do weare ;
> The verie stones consume to nought, with titles they bid beare.

Within them are the sepulchers of the old Ægyptian kings, divided into
chappels, garnished with stone of great price curiously wrought. Yet are those

places loathsome of smel, and for darknesse thereof, dreadfull to behold : for as men go downe to come into them by a narrow way, almost swarved up with rubbish, their lights are often times put out with the dampe of the earth and swarmes of remise flying about their eares. Some having got to the tops of them, report, that the watch tower of Alexandria, and the mouth of the river Nilus where it falleth into the sea, is from thence well to be scene : and that for the great height of them, a man cannot shoot an arrow so high as the midst of the lower tower wheron the spire standeth. Of these outragious buildings, are written many strange and almost incredible things, as that an hundred thousand men should be occupied continually by the space of twentie yeres, in building one of them : during which time, the charges for roots, garlike, and onions only, amounted to 1600 talents of silver."

The young people determined to scale these "outrageous buildings," but returned without having seen any of the wonders averred. Going inside, they were more fortunate, and pronounced the description of the old author painfully exact. The Turtle was not to be induced to try either experiment ; he sat stolidly on a stone, disregarding the flattering assurances of the well-known Pyramid "Doctor," who offered to carry him "up one side, down t'other, twenty minutes, no bone broke, and you very happy, only two shillin.' Perhaps he was much impressed—more probably he was bored—but he felt it was his duty to see the Pyramids ; and he saw them, if not with reverence, at least with compassion for the misdevoted energy which, properly applied, as his had been, to soap, might have proved largely remunerative. Still, he paid his dime, bought a coin or two, and was repaid by being pronounced "a very straight man forward"—a well-meaning compliment which his waistcoat belied.

From the foot of the Great Cheops the "Doctor" led the way to the Sphinx, which he described as "very old, and very soon naked quite"—an expression which might have caused the Turtle to pause, had not the Scribbler explained that it had reference only to the recent excavations, and that it was a monster safe, *virginibus puerisque.*

But a few steps farther brought them in presence of that monument, which neither the least emotional nor the least flippant can face without reverence.

> " Age cannot wither her, nor custom stale
> Her infinite variety."

Even in Egypt itself, the hardiest conception stands aghast at a figure which has confronted time for 7000 years ; for Mariette, at all events, places its date before Menu, who lived 5000 years before Christ. The guide-books, which mark it, like second-class brandy, with a double star, and speak of it as "next to the Pyramids the most famous monument in this vast burial-ground," insult its majesty, for it stands *the* monument of the world, one and unapproachable. We may leave it to such critics to describe its length and breadth, and to suggest to the traveller to "stand upon the upper part of the ear," to measure the nose and the mouth! The Arabs appreciate it better, who call it "Abou Hol," Father of Terror. Even patronising Harriet Martineau is impressed at last, though at first she took it, with her superior ignorance, "for a capriciously formed rock, forgetting that I should not meet with limestone at Ghizeh," she adds by way of showing us that her knowledge of geology might have saved her from overlooking it. Even she, at last, had to own a feeling of awe. Wonderful tribute to the Sphinx power that it drew admiration from Harriet! And ingenious Verulam, who, let it be said in extenuation, had never seen it, found a parable therein. The whole, he says, is Science, regarded by the ignorant (Harriet) as a monster. As the figure is heterogeneous, so the subjects of Science "are very various;" the female face "denotes volubility of speech." (O Harriet!) Her wings show that "knowledge, like light, is rapidly diffused;" and so forth. Enough of such criticism; rather let us watch her in reverence, striving, if perchance may come to us the solution of that mystery which she has asked in vain, with her yearning, prayerful gaze, at every morning's rising sun since time was. No Œdipus has solved that riddle—the mystery of immortal life—the mystery "of going on and still to be."

> " The Sphinx is drowsy ;
> Her wings are furled,
> Her ear is heavy ;
> She broods on the world.
> Who'll tell me my secret
> The ages have kept ?
> I awaited the Seer
> While they slumbered and slept." [1]

And she has watched them, not slumbering and sleeping alone—

> " Nations have fallen round her, but she stands ;
> Dynasties came and went, but she went not.
> She saw the Pharaohs and the Shepherd Kings,
> Chariots and horsemen in their dread array,
> Cambyses, Alexander, Anthony,
> The hosts of standards and the eagle wings,
> Whom, to her ruinous sorrow, Egypt drew,
> She saw and she forgot." [2]

---

[1] Emerson.   [2] Stoddard.

The Sphinx Uncovered.

But since Harriet and our sympathetic friends, the compilers of guide-books, have been there, much has been done. Hitherto the head only stood above the desert, encroaching around it. Seventy years ago, English enterprise, for once not purely mercenary, enabled Caviglia to uncover the flight of steps leading to it ; but the sand ruthlessly buried it again, until Maspero began the work of excavation, continued by Grébaut, his successor at Boolak. At present they have bared the whole front of the body, the small sanctuary between its paws, and the wide flight of steps. The work still goes on, and may eventually confirm the surmise that it stood in the midst of a huge artificial amphitheatre hewn out of solid rock. The paws are red brick, tawdry looking, and of far later date than the head. We might even regret the excavation of them, were it not that without it we could never get the most perfect view, which is obtainable about half way down the steps, and that but for it we should not have been able to read on the stela of Tutmes IV. how the great king lay down to rest one midday in the shadow of the Sphinx (it was then more than 3000 years old), and the sleeping king dreamed in a dream how the venerable image above him conjured him to clear away the sand in which it was already nearly buried. Then the prince awoke, and in the silence of the desert "made silence in his heart," and vowed to perform the bidding of the god.

It is cruel to spoil such an idyll, the sleeping king and his dream ; but there comes, in this iconoclastic age of ours, one Flinders Petrie, most flintstone-hearted of antiquaries, who hints, nay, almost avers, that the pious Tutmes actually pilfered, like a nineteenth-century antiquary, a red granite block from the neighbouring temple of Khafra. Dreadful it is to think of, and of the righteous indignation of Erasmus Wilson when he meets the royal pilferer in Elysium !

If you will, you may, after seeing the Sphinx, go to the temple of Chefren, and the tomb, which Colonel Vyse, with true Anglo-Saxon taste, has rendered ridiculous by associating with the name of a worthy British Consul-General, and which (such is the value of tradition) the Pyramid Arabs point out as the grave of Colonel Campbell. But the Doves were impressed, and unwilling to with-draw from the sight of that face, and the imagination of that sleeping king, pirate though he may have been. Nor did it enter into the plans of the Scribbler, who was unwilling to overladen the non-receptive brain of his pupil. So as the sun was setting behind that stupendous image they drove away, wondering, with Dean Stanley, "what it must have been when on its head there was the royal helmet of Egypt ; on its chin the royal beard ; when the stone pavement by which men approached the Pyramids ran up between its paws ; when immediately under its heart an altar stood from which the smoke went up into the gigantic nostrils of that nose now vanished from the face never to be conceived again."

The long drive through the avenues of acaccia had lasted for a few minutes before the Scribbler, anxious to ascertain the effect his first lesson had produced, ventured to ask the Turtle his impressions.

As became an ex-minister, the reply was Socratic.

"How old did you say that—er—that object was?"

"Roughly, 7000 years."

The Turtle paused and made a mental calculation.

"It cannot," he said, "be more than 5890 years old, for the world was created on Sunday, 25th March, 4004 B.C."

"*Mais nous avons changé tous cela,*" sang the Sketcher airily.

The Turtle looked shocked, and glanced uneasily at his daughters.

"I think, sir," said the Scribbler, anxious to allay a storm, "the date you mention is wanting in confirmation. It is, if I may say so, not official," he added, seeking words which might appeal to his feelings.

"I think," said the man of Blue Books, somewhat mollified, "I think you will find that date attested in Scripture, and you will not, I hope" (glancing at the Doves), "attempt to—er—to traverse that authority."

"I will not," replied the other; "but you will, I am sure, excuse my pointing out that the date rests on no divine authority. Without even questioning the *verbal* inspiration of Scripture—a point which, I believe, many undoubtedly orthodox men have given up—nay, without even calling in question the still more doubtful point as to the verbal inspiration of the Authorised Version, we are still not compelled to accept the chronology, which rests on the assertion—let us say the investigations—accurate so far as they then could be, of Archbishop Ussher."

Now, the Turtle had never heard of Archbishop Ussher; but it so happened that he had once had a question with his rector in reference to tithes, and in a friendly way had referred the question to an archbishop, in full confidence that his claims of social superiority would be recognised. The archbishop, however, had given the case against him; and, though accepting the decision, and abstaining even from his first idea of voting for the abolition of the Establishment, the Turtle had held a poor opinion of archbishops ever since. He had already begun to realise, from casual conversation, that Egyptian chronology would not fit in with his preconceived ideas; but he had held tightly to the latter, under the conviction that the received chronology was one of the Thirty-

Nine Articles of the Church of England. It was, therefore, a secret relief to him to hear that it rested upon no more secure foundation than the opinion of one of that order of the hierarchy, of whose want of judgment he had in his own case had such a conspicuous example.

"I am quite willing to admit," he said, "that the archbishop you speak of may have made a mistake of a few years in his calculation;" and the Scribbler felt that his point was gained.

"Accept, then," he continued, "that we have been contemplating a monument created 7000 years ago; and, without further inquiry as to what period it required to bring art to that pitch of perfection, let us assume that the Sphinx is the beginning of creation, as it is the beginning of human creation, so far as we have any existing complete vestige of it, and to-morrow we will skip a few thousand years or so, and continue the subject at Boolak, in presence of the wooden man and the founders of the comparatively modern Pyramids."

Tomb of Mariette—Entrance to the Boolak Museum.

CHAPTER VIII.

THE Boolak Museum is reached by a long drive through quarters where the lowest European class has added some of its ugliness to, and borrowed some of the extra filth from, the native. It is not here, assuredly, that you would expect to find treasures which no capital in Europe can parallel, and the loss of which no Rothschild could replace. And yet, perhaps, the resting-place for these records of past Egypt has not been ill chosen ; for it lies on the banks of the ever-mysterious river, keeping touch, as it were, with the life-stream of the people whose history it records. The Pyramids look down on it from the opposite bank ; and the nineteenth century, with its military casernes, its busy cargo-boats, and its sugar-stores, crowd it in on every side. It would be easy to find a more costly habitation. The palaces of Ghizeh or Ghezireh might afford more ample room for the relics of 5000 years, now crowded into a few square yards ; but as no building that modern art could devise or imitate would ever look aught but shamefaced in comparison with the glorious contents themselves—as no style could ever be harmonious with the remains of periods reaching from the prehistoric Second Dynasty to the Ptolemies—it

is perhaps better that there should be no attempt to render the casket worthy of the jewels, and that we should plunge, as it were, straight from the hideousness of the lower life of to-day into the quiet garden washed by the Nile, where the tomb of Mariette guards the portal to the mysteries of a giant past.

> " Her beauty hangs upon the cheek of night,
> Like a rich jewel in an Ethiop's ear."

The Scribbler, in pursuance of his plan, would permit no loitering, but led the way straight to the statue of Khafra. The builder of the Second Pyramid of Ghizeh, whose char-

acter would seem to have been handled with unnecessary severity by Herodotus, has a face of benign shrewdness, and, unless phrenology is at fault, possessed a considerable sense of humour. That it is a likeness, and not a mere conventional representation, is evident. Seated in solemn state among his descendants, he looks every inch of his colossal frame a king. Near him stands the perhaps yet more lifelike figure of the wooden man.

Statue of Khafra.

"Do you suppose," said the Turtle, reading from his "Murray," "that there is any truth in this story, that the villagers recognise a likeness between this image of some thousand years old and their own municipal magistrate of to-day?"

"Of course it's true," interrupted the enthusiastic Sketcher. "Here you have the statue of a man hidden at Sakkarah some 6000 years ago. His sons have buried him, succeeded to his camels and his honours, and lived on the same spot. There was a man, whom your soldiers came across in the last war, who had lived his life of some sixty years within thirty miles of the Nile, and had yet never seen it. So lived this man and his descendants—

K

never moving, always living within the same square mile, marrying and intermarry-ing, until, when this statue is discovered, it is found that the lineal descendant, through some 200 generations, has preserved an exact resemblance to his ancestor. Would it not be strange if it were otherwise? That goose, which you see in that 3000 years old picture, is the goose which we saw outside; that trefoil is the *berseem* growing to-day. The biped man has been as much localised as the biped anser or the clover."

"I don't know," said the Scribbler, "that we need attach much importance to the alleged likeness to the individual man. The Egyptian is not observant in physiognomy. This man has two legs, two arms, and one head; so has their Sheik El Beled; that would probably create in their minds sufficient resemblance for them to cry, 'Wallahi zei el sheikh betana.' Whether it were so or not is immaterial; but the *type* of man represented here is the exact reproduction of the type of the Fellah of to-day; and it proves, not exactly the Sketcher's family-feature theory, but the fact, established beyond a doubt in hundreds of ways, that the successive conquerors of Egypt have always ended by being physically conquered by the children of the soil. Was it an innate knowledge that they would in this way ultimately subdue their conquerors which reconciled them to perpetual conquest?"

"But have they always been so easily governed?" said the Sketcher. "The history of Egypt seems to me nothing but a series of conquest and revolt."

"Precisely; but hardly ever, if ever, of resistance to invasion in the first instance, nor of revolt afterwards, except in favour of a new conqueror. The Egyptian of all ages has grown up in the belief that it is his destiny to be the slave of some one; that some one, whoever he may be, he respects and hates, but has no idea of resisting. Not unnaturally, however, he is like an Irishman, 'agin the Government;' and when another some one comes to attack the reigning some one, his sympathies are with the former, and he revolts in favour of a new master. So each conquest is tolerably easily accomplished, and equally easily overthrown. The Egyptian, always submitting, and always secretly hostile, is ready to welcome a third conqueror, or perhaps the old one."

The most well-intentioned chronological plans were doomed to failure, owing to the restless spirit of the Sketcher and the Fair One, following whom, the party found themselves suddenly confronting the mummy cases.

"Here, for instance," continued the Scribbler, "you have an instance. This is Sekenen Ra Taaken, conqueror of the Hyksos, leader of the so-called war of Egyptian independence, which lasted 150 years some 3600 years ago. But note that Sekenen himself is but one of the Theban despots fighting against the

Hyksos despots. The Egyptians who fought with him against the Hyksos had probably aided the Hyksos against his ancestors. However, he fights for what he assumes to be his rights; gains them for his descendants, but loses his life. Look at him closely, and read his history, told as graphically as if by Macaulay, and perhaps more truthfully. That wound there, inflicted by a mace or hatchet, which has cleft the left cheek, broken the lower jaw, and laid bare the side teeth, was probably the first, and must have felled him to the ground. See there, how his foes fell on him! That downward hatchet blow split off an

Mummy of Sekenen Ra Taaken.

enormous splinter of the skull, leaving a long rift through which some portion of the brain has escaped; you can see it in that large white blotch on the cheek. That other blow, just above the right eye, must have been a lance wound, passing through his temple, and probably finished him. Look at the agony in the face, and the tongue bitten through in anguish. He gave his life dearly, did Sekenen Ra; and after the fight the body has been embalmed and had decent though hurried sepulture. A tall, slender, but muscular man, small, long, barrel-shaped head, covered with long black curly hair; the eye large and deep set; the nose straight and broad at the bridge; a massive lower face with projecting jaw and cheek bones, probably a Barabra; and note one singular detail still visible after thirty-six centuries—he must have been shaved on the very day of battle.

"Here, close by, is his descendant, Aahmes of the eighteenth dynasty, who

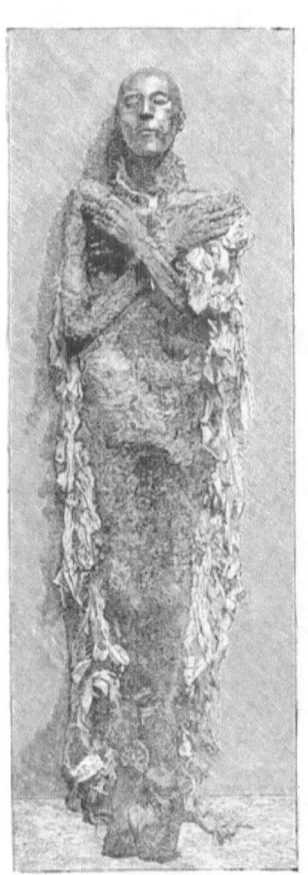

Mummy of Seti Menephtah.

reaped the fruits of victory. He is bandaged; but see next to him his son, Amenhoteb, covered still with garlands, which, when the sarcophagus was first opened, had not lost their colour; and hidden among the flowers a wasp, who had slipped in as the coffin was being closed, and remains there preserved after 3000 years, probably the only wasp ever dignified with the rites of mummihood. In his day must the family of Joseph have increased and multiplied; for I forgot to say that the Hyksos adversary of Sekenen Ra was probably Joseph's friend. And here is Seti Menephtah, son of the first, and father of the second, Ramses. A beautiful old man is Seti, with refined intellectual face, and a sweet smile that fascinates after thirty-two centuries. A hale old man, too, for his teeth are white and well preserved, and only his fingers show the signs of that even then aristocratic disease, gout.

"Ramses II., the great Sesostris of tradition—the Pharaoh who knew not Joseph—is a singularly hard and powerful likeness of his father. Like him vigorous and robust, for he reigned sixty-seven years, and must have been over a hundred when he died; the chest broad, the shoulders square, and the arms crossed; the head long, but small compared to the body, with thick, smooth, straight locks of hair about two inches long, probably white at time of death, but rendered yellow from the process of embalming. The forehead is low and narrow, the eyes close together, with thick short eyebrows; a long, thin, and Bourbon hooked nose slightly crushed at the tip; the cheek-bones prominent; the jawbone massive and strong; the chin prominent, with small but thick-lipped mouth; the teeth worn and brittle, the round ears pierced for earrings. The moustache and beard are thin; perhaps he shaved during life, and this is the growth of the last illness. On the whole, the expression is not intellectual, perhaps even animal, but withal shows resolve, majesty, and pride. And here you have two of a very different type—can you not recognise the priest in both these faces?—the priest Nibsoni of the twentieth, and the priest-king Pinotem of the twenty-first. They want only the *berretta* to be Don Basilios."

"And here, again, Ramses III., last of the warrior-kings of Egypt—a face not equal to that of old Seti, but yet better than that of Ramses II., of which it is

a small imitation, though more delicate and intelligent in expression — 'of pompous piety and inordinate vanity,' however, if we may trust Mr. Maspero."

"*De mortuis*," said the Sketcher gently, at the end of this somewhat long oration; "don't let's abuse the man over his coffin. Even in a cemetery of unknown dead, one cannot help feeling a little generous and grateful to the hundreds who have

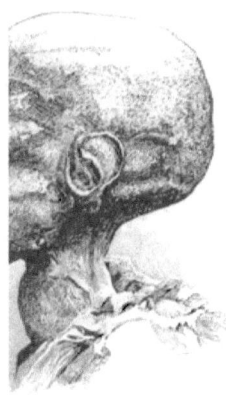

Mummy of Pinotem.

probably each done some one little act of kindness, which has begot others, and these in turn more, multiplying like the grain of mustard seed, and so producing, generation after generation, a kindlier feeling to each other—a feeling which we are now learning to

Mummy of Ramses II.

extend to the brutes, and in time shall bestow on the flowers. And these men left us something besides their own mummies and the records of their wars. If they were conquerors of savages, they conquered Art too, and Nature itself. Their blood may not run in our veins, but their brains have helped to

form ours. We are never tired of owning our debt to Athens and Rome, but
we forget that Athens herself was what she was only thanks to Egypt, and that
the intellectual ancestors of Phidias and Homer are around us."

"What, then, is the date of the mummies?" asked the Turtle.

"Of these, from 3000 to 3500 years; but a bald statement like that hardly
conveys anything. Remember that we are only
1000 years removed from Alfred; little more than
2000 years from the destruction of Carthage; and
that Ramses III., the most modern of all these,
was probably ruling in Egypt when the well-gyved
Greeks were starting on the mythical Trojan war."

"Then does real History begin here?" asked
Enid.

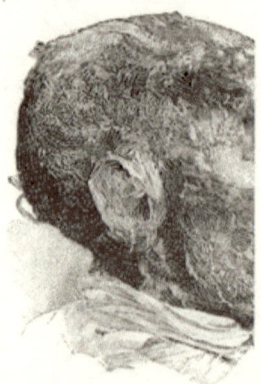

Mummy of Ramses III.

"Begin here! Say rather that it ends here;
for from henceforth the Egyptian
empire declines. The 3000 years
seem immense to us; we find it
difficult to carry back the imagination so far, and to picture these
poor mummies as making history.
But remember that, if they could

Statue of Rahoteb.

rise and walk into the next room, they would see relics as far
removed from their age as they are from ours. Roughly, 3000
years separates you from Ramses, but 3000 more separated
Ramses from these two statues of Rahoteb and Nefert, looking
as if carved and plastered yesterday. And Rahoteb himself
may have pointed out to Nefert the Sphinx as an antique, the
mystery of whose creation was already buried in a thousand
years. As I said in Alexandria, we talk glibly of Egyptian
antiquities—walk through this museum, and carry away the
notion that we have seen something of an interesting period
of the world's history; but how few realise that within these
four walls they are in presence of records extending over
some 5000 years; that if you collected together specimens
of all Art and records of History between the dates of say
the siege of Troy and the battle of Alma, you would only
then in point of time be rivalling Boolak! These half-dozen mummies we have
spoken about, which we regard to some extent rightly as an epoch, cover the
same period of time as from Magna Charta to the French Revolution."

"But," said Enid, "this is bewildering! Let me repeat my question. Are these statues, at all events, the beginning of History?"

"Of History, perhaps, or of such History as has left any trace (the mysterious Sphinx always excepted), but certainly not of Art; for you have here the same difficulty which meets you in your researches into Nature. You know that the tree comes from the seed; you may be able, perhaps, to give a scientific explanation of the process of transformation; but go as low as you will, you are baffled at last when you seek to explain the origin of life itself. So it is with Egyptian Art. Here is your mummy, your hieroglyph, your statue, and, finally, your Sphinx; you trace back through the 7000 years, but the mystery is always increasing; for the more you recede, the more perfect you find the work. You are working, in fact, up a stream of decadence in Art, and when you reach the most remote date, you reach also the most consummate Art. Now, perfect work implies previous study and time for development. Art did not spring into the world ready-made, like Athene from the brain of Zeus. We know roughly the ages it took for the rude Cyclopean masonry to develop into Greek Art. In Egyptian Art we may or may not have reached the summit. There may yet be lying hid treasures more ancient and more perfect than the Sphinx; but what is certain is, that there must have been a long period through which Egyptian Art struggled to the perfection at which we already find it 7000 years ago."

Statue of Princess.

They had seated themselves on the little stone balcony that overlooks the river. The Nile rolled past them with its swift torrent, breaking with dangerous force against the very walls of the little Museum; below lay the little port of Boolak, with its busy lateen-sailed craft; to the left, the great Kasr el Nil bridge; beyond, the island of Rhoda, with its Nilometer; and on the other side of the river, the ever-present Pyramids in the setting sun.

"Who was it," asked Enid, "who called them petrified prayers? The expression is perfect."

"Some one with more talent for alliteration than observation, I suspect," replied the Scribbler. "Call it poetical if you will, but not perfect, because inappropriate. The Pyramids are not prayer, but the negation of it; 'petrified presumption' would be as alliterative, and more appropriate."

"Surely," said Iris, "you are not going to rail against the Pyramids, after the enthusiasm you have shown to-day?"

"I confess the Pyramids inspire me less than any monument in Egypt."

said the Scribbler. "Pure antiquity, as such, has no charms for me; and vulgar piles of stones, erected at the cost of intense physical suffering to thousands, and which have served no other purpose than that of exciting the ingenious curiosity of a few mad theorists, are vulgar still, though old."

"Is the idea so vulgar after all," said Enid? "It seems to me that the man who took such pains over his tomb had some instinct of immortality in him; that he recognised death not so much the end as the beginning of life; that he built a more durable palace for his last home than he had thought it worth while to build as his earthly one."

"But even admitting that," said the Scribbler, "and Chateaubriand himself could not have put it more poetically, is not his idea of immortality a vulgar one? Fancy an immortality which wants a stone house to live in!"

"It's something," said the girl, "to have had an idea of immortality at all 6000 years ago."

"Besides," interrupted the Sketcher, "why should you persist in looking at it simply as a tomb? I am not going to ask you to accept it as a yard-measure or an inverted bushel; but unless you deny the value of all monuments, and of all desire to leave a memento to history, surely one valuable quality in a monument is that it should last; and if one has devoted one's life to such a monument, surely it is not mere vulgarity to wish to be associated with it, and to be buried in it."

"A power of endurance," said the Scribbler, "may be one valuable quality in a monument, but surely you will not argue that it is the only, or even the most important one. What is the value of them, however ancient, if, as old Fuller has it, 'They dote with age, forgetting the names of their own founders'? Did they exhibit a single hieroglyph of value, or had they saved a papyrus, I would forgive them. As it is, they make a good background for a picture, but that is all you can say for them; they have added little or nothing to our knowledge of man."

"And what have we gained from the hieroglyphs or the papyri?" asked Iris.

"History, Poetry, and Romance. You will admit, at least, that the two last are worth something, even though you despise the first."

"Do you mean Poetry that you can read and understand?"

"That," said the Scribbler, "must depend on what you call Poetry, and what you call understanding it; but I saw the Sketcher last night struggling to get a hieroglyph into verse, and the result is probably as intelligible as Browning."

"I am afraid," said the Sketcher, laughing, "my efforts over a hieroglyph would result in poetry compared to which Sordello itself would be intelligible.

The Harbour of Beshik.

I.

The papyrus was a sheet of foolscap, and I made a rhyme out of some verses of a translation of a hymn to Amen Ra. I will read it if you like, but please remember I am only responsible for the doggerel; the sentiments belong to the Nineteenth Dynasty, and the words are almost identical with those of Goodwin's literal translation :—

> " Hail to Amen Ra the Bull !
> The chief of all great gods in An ;
> The good god beloved, whose rule
> Gives life both to cattle and man.
> Hail, Lord of the thrones of the Earth !
> Amen Ra, the Sun-god of Thebes,
> Who, with feet in the land of his birth,
> Rules heathen in Araby's East ;
> The ancient of Heaven, the oldest of Earth,
> Sustainer of all things that owe thee their birth.
>
> " One in thy works, and one in high Heaven,
> Beautiful Bull of the Cycle Divine ;
> Chief of all gods, and maker of all men,
> Creator of beasts, and feeder of kine.
> Lord of existences, herbs, and of trees ;
> Sun-king, Truth-speaker, and chief of the Earth ;
> Maker of all things, the light and the breeze,
> The gods give thee honour, and own to thy worth.
> Begotten of Ptah, youth fair and beloved,
> That sailest in Heaven, peaceful, unmoved.
>
> " Thou deliverest the meek from the mighty ;
> Thou judgest the poor and oppressed ;
> Lord of wisdom, whose precepts shine brightly,
> At whose pleasure the Nile gives its best.
> Lord of Mercy, of Love, Light, and Life,
> Great giver of rays to each star ;
> Men live, and gods joy in thy sight,
> When they see thee approach from afar."

" Do you mean," said Iris, " that all that was written 3000 years ago ? "

" All that, and some seventeen verses more ; but you must make allowance for it as an adaptation."

" And what about Romance ? " asked Enid.

" Well, I can give you a romance of a slightly earlier period, if you will ; but I warn you it has one great defect."

" Which is ? "

" That will become apparent, if you allow me to read it. Listen ! this is the tale of the Doomed Prince, word for word, from the Harris Papyrus :—

" There was once a king who had no sons ; he prayed for an heir, and the gods listened to his request. When his son was born, the Fates came to greet him at his birth ; they said that he would die either by a crocodile, a serpent, or a dog. When the people who were about the child heard it, they went and told these things to his Majesty. His Majesty was exceedingly grieved at the evil tidings. His Majesty gave orders to shut the child up in a house in the country, provided with attendants, and all kinds of good things from the king's palace, and that the child should not go out abroad. When the child grew big, he ascended to the roof of the house, and he saw a dog, which was following a person who was going along the road. He said to the attendant who was beside him, 'What is that which is in the road?' He said to him, 'That is a dog.' The child said to him, 'Let one be brought to me like it.' The attendant went and repeated these things to his Majesty. His Majesty said, 'Let there be got for him a boar-hunting dog to run before him.' Then they got for him a dog. Now it came to pass, some time after this, the child became a man. He sent to his father, saying, 'Why is it that I still remain shut up? I am destined! Let God do whatsoever pleases him!' He went, and a servant, and all kinds of weapons. The man conducted him to the East. He said to him, 'Go now withersoever thou wilt;' and he went, and the dog with him. He went up to the country, according to his will; he lived upon the best of all the beasts of the field. He arrived at the country of the Prince of Mesopotamia. Now there was no child of the Prince of Mesopotamia excepting one daughter. He had built a house for her, of which the window was distant many cubits from the ground. He had sent for all the sons of all the princes of the land of Syria, and said to them, 'Whoever shall scale the window of my daughter, she shall be his wife.' It came to pass, many days after this, while they were engaged in their daily occupations, the youth rode up to them. They received the youth into their house, washed him ; they gave fodder for his horse ; they did all sorts of things for the youth. They lodged him, they shod his feet, they brought him to their lodging. They said to him, 'Whence comest thou, thou good youth?' He said to them, 'I am the son of one of the horsemen of the land of Egypt. My mother died, and my father took another wife, a stepmother. Thereupon she hated me, and I fled from before her.' He was silent. They kissed him. He said to the youths, 'What shall I do?' They advised him to scale the window of the tower. Now it came to pass, many days after this, he said to them, 'Do ye go out; I will invoke a deity; I will go to climb among you.' They went to climb according to their custom every day. The youth stood afar off, looking on. The maid-servant of the daughter of the Prince of Mesopotamia was upon the tower. Now it came to pass, some time after this, the youth went to climb with the children of the princes ; he climbed, and he reached the window of the daughter of the Prince of Mesopotamia. She kissed and embraced him. Some one went to congratulate her father, and said to him, 'A man has scaled the window of thy daughter.' The Prince inquired about him, saying, 'The son of which of the princes is it?' They said to him, 'It is the son of a horseman who has run away from the land of Egypt on account of a stepmother.' The Prince of Mesopotamia was exceedingly angry. He said, 'How can I give my daughter to a runaway from Egypt? Let him go back again.' They went and said, 'Go back to the place from whence thou camest.' But the girl clung to him. She swore by God, saying, 'By the name of the sun, Horus, if I am prevented from keeping him with me, I will neither eat nor drink.' She was on the point of dying. A messenger went to announce all she had said to her father. The Prince sent men to slay the youth. He was in his house. The girl said, 'By the sun, if he is slain, I will die too ; I will not pass an hour of life without him.' One went to her father ; the fear of the youth came upon the Prince. He embraced him and kissed him. He said to him, 'Behold, thou art unto me as a son!' He replied to him, 'I am the son of a horseman of the land of Egypt; my mother died ; my father took to himself another wife ; she hated me ; I ran away from before her.' He gave him his daughter to wife. Now it came to pass, some time after this, that the youth said, unto his wife, 'I am predestined to one of three deaths, either by a crocodile, a serpent, or a dog.' She said to him, 'Let the dog be killed.' He replied, 'I will not cause my dog to be killed. How should he do it?' The woman urged her husband greatly. He would not allow the dog to go out alone. He went in the land of Egypt to catch birds. Be-hold, a crocodile at the door of his own house in the

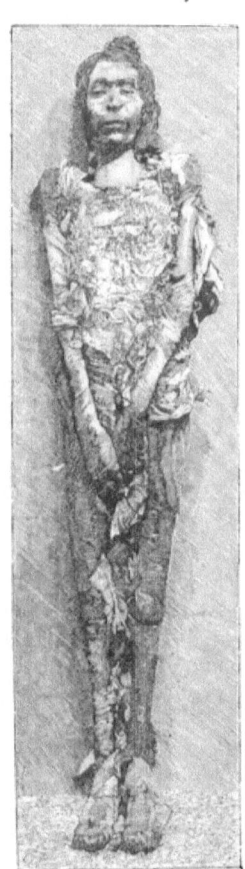

Mummy of an Egyptian Prince.

village. Behold, there was a giant by him. The giant did not suffer him to go out; he shut up the crocodile. The giant went out to walk. Now, when the dawn appeared, the youth went out every day for the space of two months. Now it came to pass, some time after this, that the youth was sitting and making a feast in his house. Now it happened that, when night approached, the youth lay down upon the mat, and sleep overcame his limbs. His wife was bathing. There came a serpent from a hole to bite the youth. Behold, his wife was sitting beside him. She was not reposing. Then she gave honey to the serpent; he drank of it to intoxication; he lay down overcome. The woman killed it, and threw it into her bath. She said to him, 'Behold, thy God hath given one of thy dooms into thy hand.' He proceeded to make offerings to God, to worship Him, and exalt His presence every day. Now it came to pass, some time after this, the youth went out to walk at a distance from his dwelling. Behold, his dog followed him. His dog seized the head of some animal. He began to run after him; he got near to the river. The dog was standing near the crocodile; he led him to where the giant was. The crocodile said to the youth, 'I am thy doom; I am come after thee.'"

"And now," said the Sketcher, "we come to the defect."

"Pray never mind," said the girls; "do go on to the end."

"Alas! the defect is, that there is no end."

"*La suite au prochain numero,* I suppose, in some other papyrus."

"I am inclined," said the Scribbler wearily, "to consider the defect the chief charm of the story. I feared that it might be endless in another sense. Suppose we start back, and you can draw on your brilliant imagination for the rest."

"The end," said the Sketcher, disdaining the insinuation, "is as clear as if it existed. The loving wife has saved him from the serpent; the faithful dog saves him from the crocodile; but nothing can save him from fate, and in some way he is unwittingly killed by his dog."

"And do you suppose it is only a story or an allegory?" asked Enid.

"For Heaven's sake," said the Scribbler, "spare us any Max Müllerisation of hieroglyphs, or we shall learn that the Shepherd kings were myths, and that Aahmes was but the sun chasing away Rasekenen, the dawn."

The Turtle was awoke with difficulty; he had at the beginning felt some doubts as to the possible propriety of a story which, so far as he knew, had not acquired the guarantee of respectability by circulation at Mudie's; but the blessed word Mesopotamia had reassured him, and he fell asleep, dreaming uneasily that a crocodile was trying to scale the balcony from the river below. But he thanked the Sketcher heartily, and still more cordially seconded the proposal of the Scribbler to return to the hotel.

[*The illustrations of mummies are reproduced from photographs, for which we are indebted to* H. E. EMILE BRUGSCH BEY.]

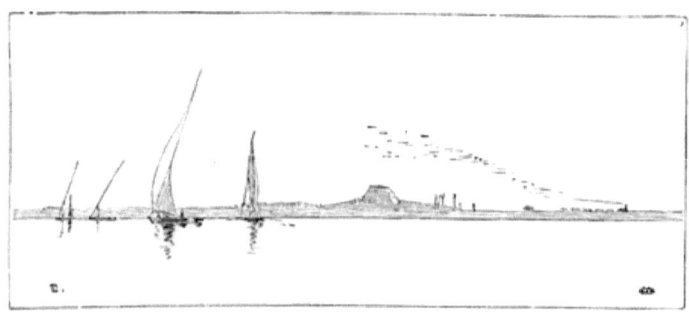

CHAPTER IX.

THE attempt of the Scribbler to study the Boolak Museum in chronological order having failed, is there any need to supply the deficiency ?

The serious student of Egyptian history will find abundant material for study in the scholarly works of Birch, Brugsch, Mariette, and Maspero. The casual traveller will find much useful information in the guide-books of Murray and Bädeker; but it may yet be useful to attempt a very brief *résumé* of the salient points of Egyptian history, and to show in the course of our journey the chrono-logical sequence of the relics of antiquity, and the relations which their records bear to the history of the past.

It is a striking fact that the earliest authentic story of living man represents him as dissatisfied with the circumstances in which he found himself, and impelled with that restless desire for change which is popularly supposed to be the marked characteristic of a later era.

Who was Mena, "first earthly king of Egypt"? We do not know, but he B.C. 5004. was probably a member of the royal family that ruled at This, near Abydos, where was supposed to be the tomb of Osiris. We can imagine him an

Advanced Radical of the period, dissatisfied with the old town, where life was
dull and made up of traditions; brimful with new ideas as to where and how a
city ought to be built; admonished, it may be, by his elders, who felt that the
world was going ahead at a dangerous pace, and who looked back with fond
regret to good old times, before the Sphinx allured northward the giddy youth
of the day. Mena, however, was not to be dissuaded, and built his new city of
Memphis near the mighty mystery, at the point where the Nile spread into many
mouths, and continued its northward course, as mysterious to him as was its
inaccessible source. The exact spot chosen by Mena cannot now be ascertained;
but later, at all events, it covered all the ground between the Bahr Jussef and
the river, from Ghizeh in the north to Schinbab in the south. The famous
temple of Phtah or Vulcan is now covered by the village of Mitrahenny; and
the Pyramids of Ghizeh, Sakkarah, Abousia, and Dashoor, were its cemeteries.

Thenceforward Thinis was but the religious centre of Egypt, around which
gathered the legend of Isis and Osiris. Near it Abydos was reputed the
burial-place of the latter, and here the pious sought to be buried. "To go
to Abydos!" was an expression equivalent to death. But as Thinis could not
hold the bones of all who sought the honour, it became a custom to bury the
mummy in the nearest cemetery, and to send to Abydos a votive stele. Perhaps
from this first arose, among the Egyptians, the idea of separate existences of
body and soul. Hitherto, they seem to have believed that the body itself would
revive; but with the practice of sending to Abydos their votive stele, while the
visible remains were enclosed in the sarcophagus near at home, arose the belief
that an unseen portion of them had gone before the judge.

B.C. 5004-3951.   At Memphis ruled the first four dynasties for some thousand years of apparently profound peace. Prosperity in the Valley of the Nile was on the increase;
the buildings improved; the middle, if not the lower class, had considerable
leisure, and were able to indulge in hunting and fishing, while attention was
evidently paid to the cultivation of flowers. Something, too, even at this early
period, they seem to have known of medicine, anatomy, and astronomy. The
year of 365 days was introduced, consisting of twelve months of thirty days
each, and five supplementary days. To this period we owe the Pyramids—
that at Sakkarah, known as the Step Pyramid, is probably the oldest, and may
possibly be of the first dynasty; the pyramid of Maydoom belongs to the third
dynasty; the pyramids of Ghizeh to the fourth. The diorite statue of Khafra,
the wooden statue of the Sheikh el Beled, the torso of his wife, and the life-like
statues of Rahoteb and Nefert bear witness to an artistic development which
no later period rivalled.

The next 900 years of Egyptian history comprise six dynasties. The B.C. 3951-3064. fifth dynasty reigned obscurely, and allowed the aristocracy to encroach little by little on the central power; the reins of authority were slackened; and in the sixth dynasty we find two Pharaohs reigning, probably contemporaneously— the one, Teta, at Memphis; the other, Atis, at Elephantine, near Assouan. Later, Pepi I. seems to have restored Egyptian unity, and to have repelled an invasion of Negroes from the south. To this period belong the interesting tomb of Tih at Sakkarah, the statues of Tih, Nefer Kha-ra, and Ra Nefer, as well as

Statue of Tih.

the oldest known mummy, that of Sokar Em Saf. The sculpture, though still fine, shows some falling off from that of the earlier period. Of the other four dynasties of this epoch, the seventh, eighth, ninth, and tenth, we know little or nothing: the two first reigned at Memphis; the two following at Heracleopolis, where gradually the sacerdotal caste seems to have more and more usurped authority. The tribes of Asia had begun to pour in from the east, and perhaps among them was Abraham; but all is conjecture.

The Middle Empire commences with the eleventh B.C. 3064-2851. dynasty, which established itself at Thebes, destined to become the capital of a great empire, and seems first to have commenced what may be termed an active foreign policy. Hitherto Egypt had held itself aloof from the outer world, but increasing civilisation created new wants, and commercial relations were first opened with Arabia; an Egyptian colony was settled on the shores of the Red Sea, which was connected with Coptos, north of Thebes, by a canal to the river. With the twelfth dynasty we find Upper and Lower Egypt united into one kingdom; and though its first Pharaohs had to repel an invasion of the Negroes, the 200 years covered by this and the preceding dynasty were years of peace, material prosperity, and agricultural activity. In the hieroglyphs we read how the most important chiefs of the Government occupied themselves in superintending the cultivation of their lands; we see the operations of shearing, of milking, of butter-making, and vine-culture; we learn how there were corporations of the different artisans; we watch the making of rich articles of furniture with gold and ivory from Ethiopia, the rich embroidery of cloth, and the use of cosmetics to colour the eyebrows. Music and dancing

M

to the flute and harp was common throughout Egypt. Games of chess and draughts for the amusement of the elders; dolls, paper balls, and wooden animals as toys for children. Sportsmen hunted the wild bull, the leopard, and the lion, as well as the fox, the hare, and the antelope, the last with a lasso. Rich houses adorned the banks of the Nile, from the balconies of which the predecessors of Izaak Walton indulged in the melancholy vice of angling. And with all these riches and luxury rose into importance the scribes, who later, in union with the sacerdotal class, were destined to become the first and ever-existing spoilers of the Egyptians. Memorials of the twelfth dynasty are found as far south as Semneh, beyond the cataract. To this period we may attribute the restoration of the old temple of Heliopolis, the colonnade of Karnak, the tombs of Beni Hassan, the Fayoum Pyramids, and the great irrigation works of that province.

B.C. 2851-1703.   And now for nearly 1200 years the curtain descends, and the history of Egypt becomes a mysterious and almost impenetrable blank. Of the thirteenth and fourteenth dynasties there are but a few scant traces near Assouan. At this period the whole of Western Asia was in a state of fermentation. Similar to the barbarian invasion which later in Europe overwhelmed the Roman Empire, hordes of Nomads issued from the overcrowded regions of the Euphrates. The fertile valley of the Nile was an irresistible temptation, and they demanded pasturage for their flocks. The haughty Pharaoh of civilised Egypt was not likely to accede to a request which would place his rich lands at the mercy of barbarian shepherds; but years of peace and Capuan luxury had enfeebled the state, and the Egyptians were unable to resist the martial horsemen of the Hittites and others of the Hyksos. Completely routed in the first fight, probably near the present Suez, they were compelled to retreat into Upper Egypt, and here they were possibly allowed to hold at Thebes some sort of dependent sovereignty. The Hyksos, or Shepherd kings, ruled from Zoan, the Greek Tanis, as the fifteenth, sixteenth, and seventeenth dynasties, and built the stronghold of Avaris to repel farther invasions similar to their own. Nor do they seem to have exercised their authority cruelly; the social and administrative organisation of the Egyptians was not only left untouched, but even adopted by the conquerors.

This darkest period of Egyptian history must always possess peculiar interest, because generally supposed to be that in which Joseph, and later his brethren, came to Egypt to settle in the land of Goshen. Modern research at Tanis may yet throw light on this period, but at present all is the barest conjecture.

The people of Egypt seem to have supported the conquest with the same indifference as they exhibited later under similar circumstances; to them one Pharaoh was very much the same as another. The scribes became functionaries of the new lords, and were probably content at a change which gave them inexperienced masters in place of more experienced ones. The sacerdotal element alone maintained a sullen opposition, ready to take advantage of any favourable moment, when they were certain to find the people as ready to rebel against their new rulers as they had been to serve them. A demand made by the Hyksos Pharaoh, Apepi, for the cession of a well held by Sekenen Ra, who ruled

Sphinx of Hyksos Period.

probably as representative of the old line at Thebes, formed the pretext, and civil war, or, as it has been called, a War of Independence, lasted for eighty years. At a final battle the Egyptians were at last triumphant; their leader, Sekenen Ra, was indeed killed, and his B.C. 1703. mummy lies, as we have seen, at Boolak; but his son, Aahmes or Amosis, drove the Hyksos into Syria, and starting the eighteenth dynasty, established his authority over the whole of Egypt.

Under the eighteenth dynasty Thebes became definitely the capital of the Egyptian empire, Memphis remaining the commercial capital; and the history of the subsequent period can be better studied in Thebes itself.

CHAPTER X.

The Dovecot flies south—A luxurious offer—Rail to Asyoot—The Pasha and the Nabob—Coinage and character—Secretary and interpreter—Crichton and Sara —Capitulations—Pyramids—Zeitoun—St. George and Horus.

THE Turtle and his party, exhausted with the study of 3300 years and expeditions to Boolak and Sakkarah, had made a plaintive appeal to the Scribbler to be allowed to postpone the rest of his historical course until his return from the Nile, and the Scribbler having given a grateful assent, the entire Dovecot started by an early Cook's steamer for Luxor, accompanied at the last moment by the Patrician and by the American, who had consented to waive his objection to ruins, in the hope that he might be enabled to paste an advertisement of a new tanning process he had patented upon the tower of Syene or the temple of Karnak. The Scribbler and the Sketcher remained behind, the latter not without some sentimental regret, and the former not without hope that he might be permitted in peace to avoid the river altogether. Meanwhile they sauntered through the never-ending bazaars, or mounted on those gondolas of Cairo, the Egyptian donkeys, and, attended by Ali, sablest of gondoliers, explored the recesses of the Mokhattam oases, braved the desert of Sakkarah, or shot the wily snipe in the delta.

An Egyptian Donkey Boy.

"Sketcher," said the Scribbler, one evening as he joined his friend on the balcony, "we are saved ; the difficulty is solved. Dismiss all those hungry dragomans thirsting for your yellow ore ; abandon your hopeless efforts to make three months at £60 a month less than £100 ; forget your fears of gregarious crowds and of wild women. Your dream is coming true ; we shall see the Nile ; we shall have the speed of a steamer, and none of the discomfort ; the luxury of a *dahabeeyah*, with none of the delay, and a third of the expense. Congratulate yourself on your friend, and your friend upon his omnipotence. Be ready to leave on Monday ; in a month we shall be back again ; and during that month you shall have seen Wady Halfa and the second cataract."

" In a month ! by post-boat then ? "

"Post-boat ! Man, I tell you that you shall repose on the downiest of divans, the pampered companion of Pashas and Beys, lord with myself and one or two others of the largest *dahabeeyah* on the river, and subject to neither wind nor tide, for the fastest steamer on the river shall tow us. Listen ! a certain Pasha of my acquaintance is bent on a journey of inquiry to Wady Halfa. The Government sends him ; stern duty compels him to go. A Government *dahabeeyah* and a Government steamer are at his disposal. Pining for company in his exile, he asks me to accompany him. 'I cannot ; I have a friend.' ' What sort of a friend ? ' quoth he. Then, Sketcher, I painted your character with the pencil of love, flattery, and self-interest. To cut a long story short, we are both asked, not exactly as guests, for we cannot any longer, even in Egypt, travel at the expense of the Fellah, but the *dahabeeyah* and steamer have to go ; our weight will not necessitate extra fuel, and we pay our mess bill. So, unless you object, we are off on Monday."

"Object ! " said the Sketcher joyfully. " But the Pasha ! does he—does he travel with a very large harem ? "

" Don't be afraid," said the other, laughing ; "wild women are excluded. The party, in addition to ourselves, consists of the Pasha (an Englishman and ex-Life-guardsman) ; his brother (a Nabob, I believe, from India) ; an English secretary, who is an Admirable Crichton, possessed of superhuman knowledge ; an interpreter, who is at the same time a Bey ; with about two servants for each member of the party. Have you any other objection ? "

To have reached Wady Halfa, the Sketcher would have sacrificed his dearest friend to Moloch ; and to such a project no objection could be forthcoming.

Three days later, and the worst carriage on the worst railway line in the world was hurrying the party of four southwards to Asyoot. The first sight of the Pasha had calmed the still lingering fears of the Sketcher, who had been unable to shake off the conviction that he would meet an unspeakable Turk. Unmistakably English was the face, figure, and greeting of Apollo Belvedere Pasha, who at five-and-twenty had held and resigned Her Majesty's commission, had wrestled with the intricacies of Turkish finance, written a Greek grammar, and was now engaged in the labyrinth of Egyptian budgets. The Nabob, his brother, was apparently the senior; he had the wearied *nil admirari* look peculiar to Anglo-Indians, who seem ever weighted with the responsibility of governing 250,000,000 souls, and unable to descend to the consideration of smaller numbers. The Sketcher was apt to form rapid judgments, and to evolve startling theories therefrom. Like the traveller who declared all women in Belgium to be ugly and red-haired, adding, " At least the only one I ever saw was," he was apt to argue from the particular to the general.

"That peculiar expression and frame of mind," he said, "is due solely to the unit of coinage. You will find that every nationality corresponds to its monetary unit. In Egypt it is a piastre; and you will admit that they are eminently a twopenny-halfpenny lot. In France it is the franc; and I confess we are trivial. In Germany, it is the mark; not very much better. In England it is the sovereign; good, solid, but heavy. In India it is the lakh; I don't know what a lakh is," he added frankly "but I believe it's a very large coin, in which the salaries of Anglo-Indian officials are paid, and it accounts for that supercilious air of superiority."

But the Sketcher's judgment of character was not much more accurate than his knowledge of the Indian currency, and when he got to know the Nabob better, and had had the mysteries of the rupee explained to him, he squared his altered opinion with his theory, and found that the Anglo-Indian was, like his coin, inclined to undue self-depreciation.

In the next carriage was the Admirable Crichton, English, or, more strictly, Welsh secretary, who wrote shorthand, and spoke numerous languages with a Cymric accent; and Sara Bey, prince of interpreters, the dreaded inspector of finances for Upper Egypt.

As the train left the station of Boolak Dacrour, the Pasha pointed plaintively to a wooden shanty on the very edge of the station, surmounted ostentatiously by the blue and white flag of Greece.

"There," he said, "you have an example of the Capitulations. That man, a Greek, has squatted on that land for some years, built that shanty, and opened a grocer's shop, paying possibly some rent to the Government year by year. The station increases, and we want the land, which is Government land; but not all the king's horses and men can make him move. For six years have we been trying to evict him, but he defies us. If we build him up, he carries off our palisade. If we try to eject him, he uses a revolver. There he reigns, paying no taxes, subject to no law, no tribunal in the country, safe in the shadow of the Capitulations."

"You don't mean to say," said the Nabob, "that even his own Consul can't turn him out, or that he receives Consular protection?"

"Whether he can or not, I don't know," said the Pasha; "but I do know that he won't, or at all events that he doesn't."

"But," interrupted the Scribbler, "don't run away with the idea that so many have, and be led away by the words 'Consular *protection*,' a word which takes

In illianah.

many astray. That Greek is not relying on Consular *authority*; he is relying on the *absence* of Consular authority. Probably his Consul is more in need of protection than he is, for his Consul has no control over him; and Dimitri will have as little compunction in putting a ball into his Consular Janissary as into the Government policeman. It is the fashion, of course, to blame the Consuls, and particularly the Greek Consul; but he is powerless. If he gives his subjects too much trouble, they have plenty of means of getting rid of him, even if they hesitate (which they wouldn't do) to use the knife. Dimitri the grocer has prob-

ably as much influence in Athens as the Consul, and the Government there have
not much more influence over their subjects abroad than their subjects have
over them."

   " But this is not the case with all ? " asked the Sketcher.

   " No, not quite with all ; certainly not with the English, who can be tried by
their Consul ; but with others it is the case, though in a less aggravated form.
An Italian, perhaps, would not use his knife so readily, and is more under
moral control of his Consulate ; but there can be no real control where, except
for the pettiest offence, the venue of trial is Ancona, or Moscow, or Aix.   And
as for the French colony, we may thank our stars that their particular form of
hostility to the Government does not take the form of homicide, for there is no
Consul-General more completely under the control of his colony."

   The Upper Egypt line follows the left bank of the river through fields and
gardens as it leaves Cairo ; to the right lie thick palm-groves, with desert
beyond, and here and there are seen the Pyramids of Ghizeh and Sakkarah, the
Step Pyramid standing in strong relief against the horizon.   On the other side,
beyond the river, lies Cairo, the graceful Citadel in the distance, the effective
background of the ruddy yellow Mokhattam, and nearer the hideous palaces
of Ismail.   The cultivation gets more scanty, and seems confined to small
fields of tobacco.   On the right, as we sight the Pyramids of Lisht, and later
the libelled lying Pyramid of Maydoom, oldest and perhaps grandest of all, as
it stands like a sentinel in the desert.   And as we go farther south, we pass
through Zeitoun, land of olives from oldest time ; and near it see the little
Coptic convent of Marazee ; and through Benisouef, still the flax-growing
portion of Egypt, and formerly famous for its linen fabrics, where we catch

sight of the Pyramid of Illahoun; and Bayad, from whence starts the track leading to the Monasteries of St. Anthony and St. Paul, in the desert.   There, to our left, is the site of Heracleopolis, where dwelt the destroyers of the great Labyrinth; and Bibbeh, centre of the sugar-industry, with a Coptic Convent and an apocryphal Moslem Saint, one Bibbawee, who is no other than our good friend, George, Saint, butcher, bishop, and dragon-slayer, whose picture has been made to do service as the representative of a Moslem, thus to secure the Christian Church from sacrilege.   Verily, we admit there is nothing new under the sun, when Mons. Clermont Ganneau identifies St. George of England with Horus.   Feshne, Maghaga, and Aboo Girgeh are passed as we travel through sugar-lands; and Gebelel Tayr appears in the distance, the mountain that shares with another at Asyoot the legendary tale of the ever-watching bird.   Minich, with its factory, and Manfalot, which the lover of tradition loves to call the "abode of Lot," are passed, and then appears in the distance the pretty town of Asyoot.

CHAPTER XI.

Asyoot— No kourbash, no taxes—Mosquito nets of Herodotus—Fanciful origin of the Lycopolis—Asyoot en fête—Sub-Mudir—Egyptian in authority—Turk versus Egyptian—Can the Egyptian rule?—Bazaars—Apathy of sellers—Asyoot trade past and present—Asyoot worthies—American Mission—Reform of Coptic Church from within and from without—Sincerity of converts—Education of pupils and education of people—Both ab initio—Asyoot Cemetery—View from Libyan range —Pasha and Mudir—Information at Asyoot viâ Cairo.

THE train draws up at the station of Asyoot. Great is the bustle, for the Pasha is a man of note, and has come to inquire into matters connected with taxation. Sleek and fat Copts try in vain to assume an air of dejected misery, but the oil of good living running down their countenances betrays them. Sara himself, a Copt, has evidently a very poor opinion of them, and they as naturally have the very highest opinion of him. "They all rich as pigs," he remarks, with some confusion of metaphor; and his lips water as he thinks how remuneratively they might be bled if he were only allowed to employ the methods of the "good old days" of Ismail. "No kourbash, no taxes," is evidently still Sara's theory at heart, though he has to profess differently when he comes down to Cairo with well-filled money bags, the proceeds of the month's taxes. The anxiety of the fellah to pay this charge is then, according to Sara, something remarkable. "No difficulty whatever," he avers. "Kourbash! of course not, is it not abolished?" He is hurt at being asked the question, and appeals plaintively to the Mudir, asking whether he ever heard of the practice. And the Mudir, with a suspicious protuberance in his cheek, but with an air of innocence that would convince the most hardened inspector, asserts that that sort of thing is all over. Still, the experience never seems to shake Sara's theory, and in confidence over his cup of coffee he will reiterate, "You believe me, sir, no kourbash, no taxes."

But the Pasha, majestically walking through the crowd, profusely salaamed and profoundly indifferent, has nothing to do with all this; he comes to see results only, and is, moreover, weary with his journey. Addressing the Mudir in fluent Turkish, he announces his august pleasure that he be not bored until to-morrow, and that for the present he will take his ease at his inn. A row of shantys at the end of the station is designated as the hotel, and thither the pilgrims betake themselves. A frugal repast closes the labours of the day, which give place to those of the night.

For Asyoot is *par excellence* the town of mosquitoes, and assuredly it was here that Herodotus observed the fishermen originating the mosquito net. "Every man," he says, "has a net, with which in the day he takes fish, and at night uses it in the following manner; in whatever bed he sleeps, he throws the net around it, and then getting in, sleeps under." And, perhaps, the fishing nets of those days were strong enough and close woven enough to exclude the monsters of the night, but not so the modern muslin nets of to-day. In other places mosquitoes buzz, but here they roar; and the Nabob descends to breakfast with a theory, that they are really the wolves which gave to the place its Greek name of Lycopolis. The Scribbler has another more obvious and incorrect derivation; and the Sketcher is only able to indicate vaguely that he had seen "birds the size of vultures flying away with bits of him in their mouths."

The breakfast accomplished, it becomes evident that Asyoot is *en fête*. The depressed railway officials have an anxious time in keeping the platform clear of the crowds who have assembled to see the great men, who are interrupted in their coffee by the arrival of no less a personage than the Sub-Mudir himself. He is dressed as becomes the ambassador of a great man to a great man on a solemn occasion. A Stambouli surtout, which had belonged to a remote and slender ancestor, was vainly struggling to maintain its hold round his well-favoured body; two buttons had abandoned the attempt, and one was still hanging by a thread at the post of duty. The ancestor for whom the garment had been built, or at all events some of its subsequent possessors, had evidently not been men like Miss Austen's favourite heroes, "careful in their eating;" for the remains of Lucullus-like feasts adorned the front. *Per contra* the check trousers were clean; they had, in fact, been recently washed, and somewhat hurriedly wrung out. The boots, however, made amends, for they were of shiny patent leather, evidently bought for the occasion; and the tarboosh, though posed over the eyes in an attitude of perpetual obeisance, was otherwise irreproachable. Yacoub Bey was altogether unmistakably pleased with himself, and felt that his toilet had risen to the occasion. As he blighted the hopes of the last button by a rapid salaam before Apollo, the side of his face nearest to that great man assumed an expression of abject humility; but the side turned towards the populace bore a look of unconcealed pride.

"His Excellency the Mudir was waiting for his Excellency the Pasha; would his Excellency deign to follow his servant to his Excellency?" Such was the message delivered. Apollo lazily stretched out his hand for his hat, and with an "Are you coming, you fellows?" passed through the door over the almost prostrate form of the humble ambassador. Yacoub saw him through with deference; but no sooner was the great man's back towards him, than he felt it necessary to reassert the dignity of his position, which he did by knocking together the heads of the nearest onlookers, invoking, at the same time, a curse on their female ancestors of the past three generations. Then he deftly recovered ground by a shambling trot, and appeared again the fawning slave of the great man from Cairo.

"That," said the Scribbler, "is the type of an Egyptian in authority. Your Turk may be a brute, but he is not generally a contemptible one. He is probably a thief, but it is on a liberal scale. The Egyptian, as a governed animal, possesses many excellent qualities; as a governing one, he is as a rule the incarnation of brutality, ignorance, servility, and corruption."

"That proposition," replied the Sketcher, "is peculiarly your own—one of good, general, uncompromising assertion; but before you thus condemn the whole race, is it not fair to remember that the Egyptian has been for thousands of years a subject race, while the Turk has been for as many hundreds a governing one; and that the vices you mention are only the natural consequences of the position they have occupied, not a vice of character."

"But do you not see, my friend, that you are only proving inductively my deductive assertion? I am dealing with the Egyptian as he is, not as he ought to be, as he might be, or as he would have been under different conditions. In my opinion, in spite of all differences of race, the prehistoric Turk and the prehistoric Egyptian would have been very much of a muchness. There is little difference now between the Egyptian fellah and the Turkish raiah; but it's not much good discussing such a question. Assume them originally the same. The Turk has been a governing race; the art of governing, like all others, has to be learnt; and with experience he has learnt it. He *does* govern—well or ill, is not the question—but he governs."

"Doesn't that rather depend upon your definition of government?" said the Nabob.

"I think not; for government in its first and most naked sense is the maintenance of authority, the power to preserve order."

"*L'ordre regne à Varsovie,*" murmured the Sketcher.

"Well, I will accept even that challenge. I do not assert that the keeping of order is the highest duty of government, but that it is the one absolutely necessary one. I do not maintain that any given body of men are justified in taking any measures to restore order. It may even be their duty to refuse to do so, but then they are refusing to govern. The keeping of order is a necessary condition to the existence of a government; the people who cannot do it, cannot govern; the people who can do it, whatever the means, are able to govern well or ill. The Turk, then, knows how to govern; the Egyptian does not. He has no experience of it; he has been prevented from gaining that experience. He may have all the embryo virtues you please, but there is no good leaving him to govern, for he cannot."

"But," said the Nabob, "may not the Turk's power of governing be worse than the Egyptian's ignorance?"

"Are you propounding a general problem, to be solved in the course of æons, or are you asking a question in the practical politics of to-day? Let me for once argue by analogy. You want a man to play a tune on a fiddle. Here is a man who has played it for years, and has always played it badly, without an idea of music in his composition, but able to read it. Here is another, whose soul is full of music, if you will, but who never saw a page of music or a violin—which will you choose? If you want to train up a musician for the future, by all means take this latter; but if you want the fiddle played on the spot, you must take the former, and be content with bad playing."

"I think I'd do without my tune," said the Nabob.

"Ah! or play it yourself—just so; but that's not the point; for I suppose we admit that we are talking of Egypt in parables. Govern the country yourself, if you will; but failing that, you must, for the time at least, let some other alien govern it badly for you."

"All which," said the Sketcher, "is based on your assertion that the Egyptian can't rule."

"Which assertion you proved yourself by induction to almost a certainty. But do you want a proof? Let us go into this factory, or that shop, and if the proprietor is a native, ask him who keeps his cash, a Syrian; who writes his books, a Copt; who attends to his machine, an Englishman; who directs all the work, an Armenian. When you can show me half-a-dozen natives managing their simplest affairs without the intervention of the aliens, then I will be prepared to argue with you as to whether they can govern the country."

"I rather thought that you had been doing that all along," said the Sketcher drily. "However, judging from the sample, I think I'll forfeit the discussion, give up the point, and enjoy this."

And the Sketcher was not wrong in preferring what he saw to the Scribbler's prose; for, in the conversation, they had gradually worked their way unwittingly into the centre of the town, and were standing at the entrance of the principal bazaar. The long narrow lane with its roof here arched, and here covered with low hanging beams, lighted up with flashes of sunlight, which seemed to burst through the rafters rather under the direction of some cunning artist, than at that of chance, and to flood with its glory the most picturesque corners; the stately inhabitants, who barely turned to observe the group, much less to tempt them with their modest wares; the graceful forms of the black and red pottery; the colours of the scarfs which hung like banners from the walls; the low murmur of the few bargainers mixed with the jingle of the donkey's bells, all contributed to awe the *blasé* frequenters of the Khan Halili. Do you wish to buy in Cairo? brokers and dragomans pursue you up the Mooskee; flashy rubbish is displayed before you as you pass the shops; and when at last you find the object of your search, you must consent to long and weary bargaining. But the stately merchants of Asyoot descend to no such solicitation or chaffering. Are you a buyer? they are there, and will so far unbend as to show you what you ask to see; but it is a favour they are doing you, or at most a pious duty, which they are too hospitable to neglect. And if you think their price excessive, there is no vulgar astonishment; no noisy pretence that you have been offered the goods at less than any one else; no insolent suggestion that you do not appreciate the value of their wares. The piece is rolled up again or put aside, and the stately vendor continues to smoke his pipe in supreme indifference. It may be admitted, perhaps, that there is little to sell, and that keen competition to get rid of cheap articles which may be seen in every shop along the bazaar would be out of place. Pottery, in fact, appears to be the staple trade; you may have it in red or in black, and in pretty well every variety of shape that the potter can mould the thick Nile mud. Vases which will hold flowers, but not water; ink-pots which will not hold ink ; and scrubbers for the soles of the feet : beyond this all variety ceases. Graceful and useless is the manufacture of Asyoot, but harmless, and different to the hideous trade for which it was not long ago famous ; for here formerly were mutilated the unfortunate slaves destined as guardians for hareems. Of historical interest the old Lycopolis possesses little. Here was the magic fountain *"cujus potu signa virginitatis eripiuntur."* Plotinus, founder of the Neo Platonic school, who was born early in the third century, is per-haps its most famous son, but he belongs rather to Alexandria and Rome than to the city of the Wolves. Coluthus the poet, a feeble imitator of Homer, flourished here in the fifth century; and here dwelt Holy John 50 years, "without opening his door, without seeing the face of any woman, and without tasting any food that had been prepared by fire, or any human art ;" on two days of the week only did he grant audience to his suppliants, and to one of them, the messenger from the great Theodosius, he promised for his Emperor a bloody and infallible victory over Eugenius. Modern Asyoot, too, has its holy men with ways of devotion different indeed, but perhaps more profitable, than the fifty years' seclusion.

The Scribbler had been furnished with a letter of introduction to the American Mission, and had received from the chief thereof a cordial greeting. Very pleasant it was to meet the homely Scotch accent and an English home-stead. Twelve hours only had separated them from Cairo, but the travellers already felt that they had left the civilised world and were glad of a sight of it again. And the Chief was a man whom one might be glad to meet even else-where than at Asyoot. A Scotchman, and as he said simply, a collier boy, who had spent only three months in America, but who had been attracted by the practical and unselfish devotion of the American Mission, had given his life to it, and spent some thirty years in Egypt, of which twenty in Asyoot. Full of information he was, and spoke lovingly of his work, with zeal tempered by common sense. The Mission, he explained, started with an endeavour to reform the Coptic Church from within. They were anxious to give it the chance of self-reformation, but the attempt failed, owing to the opposition of the priests who themselves profited from the abuses. Then, recognising their mistake, they began again, and practically started a separate Reformed Church.

" And with what success ? " asked the Nabob.

" He that knoweth the minds of men can alone determine the amount of success, and He who searcheth the hearts may be able to make allowances

which are difficult to us. We have to do with a people who have a past of
their own, traditions of their own, and, to some extent, a morality of their own,
which, if falling short of the True Ideal, may be as near it as our own
nineteenth-century morality. We Anglo-Saxons attach, for instance, a value to
Truth, which has grown up in us, and is not as pronounced in other, even
European, races. With us it is not only a point of religion, but perhaps more
often a point of honour. Do not think that I value it the less on that account;
I only say that even the strictest of us have a double incentive. Is the Copt as
truthful? Certainly not. For generations it has been his interest, and perhaps
his only safeguard from tyranny, to deceive. These inherited predilections are
not eradicated in a day, nor by the preaching of a doctrine, however pure. We
have to hold high our standard, but we cannot refuse all who fail to reach it.
On the other hand, persecution, which has made them untruthful, has
encouraged in them the virtues of adversity: they are loving, and tolerant, and
generous. These, too, are Christian qualities, which we, as a race, perhaps
neglect, and which we can cultivate in them. The men who are of our con-
gregation may be untruthful, and scheming in their business relations; but
they are sincere. We have some 1700 families, say eight to ten thousand souls.
By joining us they have gained neither worldly rank, social position, nor riches.
On the contrary, they are rather despised, and have to answer money calls
which they meet and might avoid. Why then do they join us? I have no
explanation of it unless it is that they see dimly the truth, and strive as through
a glass darkly to realise it."

"Is it not," said the Scribbler, "rather that they recognise a social superiority
—a higher moral superiority if you will—in Europeans like yourself and companions, that they attribute this to your religious dogmas, and think to attain
it by going through the routine of your Church?"

"And even if it were so," said the other, "would this not be a recognition
of some value, that the purer religion gave a higher tone of morality? But it
is not a mere going through the routine of our Church; the interest they display
in abstruse questions sometimes surprises me. They will ask questions that
show they have thought not superficially; and when I preach a sermon, I must
expect to be catechised upon it."

"You preach in Arabic of course? Have you no difficulty in explaining
yourself?"

"No; I would choose Arabic rather than English to preach in, even if it
were not necessary. The language is richer, more full of synonyms and
poetic metaphors. But I am detaining you with an essay on myself," he added,

with a smile, "and you have come to see Asyoot. Will you let me be your guide?"

The four passed through the schools, where clean, bright-faced little children were receiving instruction from kindly-looking Americans, too much interested in their work of love to do more than acknowledge the presence of strangers. "You begin at the very beginning, I see," said the Scribbler, noticing a boy rising four who was absorbed in a game of letters.

"Yes," replied the Chief; "as your Government should do in Egypt. Eighteen days after the bombardment of Alexandria I was in London, and was asked by Lord Aberdeen to meet Mr. Gladstone. I told him very much what I have told you as to our failure, so long as we attempted to reform by propping up a decayed and corrupt institution ; and I added, that England's work in Egypt would be the same, that you could do nothing until you did as we had to do, begin at the foundations."

"Do you mean that we should transplant our English institutions into Egypt?"

"Excuse me, you are changing my metaphor. You do not transplant foundations, you build them. The foundations are much the same whether you build in one style or another. Make your foundations solid, and then build in accordance with the requirements and possibilities of the country if you will, but solidly always, and in accordance with principles invariable in all solid buildings."

"Scribbler," said the Sketcher, who was following behind with the Nabob, " I detect you talking politics out of keeping with the environments again."

The party were entering the Cemetery, which seemed to occupy more ground than the town itself. Scrupulously clean, with bright white-washed domes, shaded by *Acacia Nilotica*, it is not ill chosen as the promenade of the town. Here loitered, not sadly yet not boisterously, alike Copt, Jew, and Moslem. There were groups of women seated round a grave, not visibly, at all events, depressed by the "*Memento mori.*" Here, on a fallen column, rested a venerable ulema ; and there was a group of children munching dates by a fountain.

Passing across the Cemetery, one finds oneself at the very foot of the Libyan chain, which Pliny wrongly called the boundary of the Thebaid. Here, according to Abu Feyda, is the mountain to which the birds perform an annual pilgrimage, one remaining ever as a sentry until relieved by another. The ascent is steep, but worth the exertion, for it is from them alone you get a fair idea of Asyoot, and what may be called the first view of Egypt. The panorama from the citadel in Cairo, unequalled as it is, either in Egypt or elsewhere, is hardly one of the country itself. There the imagination is too strongly impressed by the historical aspects of the scene to grasp the scene itself. Here, as you ascend, the view, enlarging at every step, reveals, like a kaleidoscope, new beauties at every turn. At last, creeping through a narrow tunnelled rock, called the "Needle's Eye," you clamber the last few yards across tombs excavated from the mountain side, the bones of antiquity are beneath your feet, and you stand on a Pisgah height, with the Land of Promise beneath, the plain which Amru described as "at once a green undulating meadow and a garden ornamented with the most varied flowers." There, hurrying from far south to north, you see the great river, in innumerable serpent-like curves,

Cemetery of Asyoot.

scattering broad-cast to east and west its golden benefits. Asyoot lies like a star at the foot, studded with domes and minarets, embowered in green gardens; still nearer is the Cemetery; and closing round the living and the dead, in one warm embrace, is the brilliant green of the young cornfields. Here and there the mud villages lie "like the marks of a soiled foot on a rich carpet," which the blue flax, the yellow cotton blossom, and the crimson poppy enrich with colours that even Shiraz cannot copy. Rich, too, is the gold of the border ; for the hungry desert stretches beyond, and bluest of Egypt's skies is that which looks down on the Stabl Antar.

Even the Sketcher was awed. "This," he said, "is beyond your pencil or mine. I understand now why the Sermon was preached on a Mount."

The Pasha, the Moses of the party, had meanwhile been compelled by the stern call of duty to abstain from the view of the Promised Land, into which, however, he was to be permitted to enter. Escorted by the slimy Yacoub, he had proceeded through the town to the Mudirich, followed by a motley crowd, who evidently experienced some difficulty in deciding as to the rival merits of the clothing of the pair. There is an air of official dignity attaching to the black Stambouli, which, be it never so ancient, it retains to the last in Arab eyes. Apollo in light tweed, swinging along at a good stride, bore, however, the marks of dignity too. His six feet three impressed the beholders, but then he was certainly less well fed than the Sub-Mudir, and breadth counts for more than height in Oriental eyes. Still, the former was a novelty, and so enjoyed as much respect as was compatible with the fact that they had not felt his kourbash; and the votes were already turning in his favour, when he was seen to enter the Mudirich, to fling himself unbidden on the divan, and casually order the Mudir to be seated. This decided the matter; he was evidently one in authority, an Ingleez of the highest rank, possibly the English Sultan himself, or his son at least—the fame thereof went up the river, and the rest of the party shone in that reflected glory for many days. The Pasha was a conscientious man, and part of the mission for which he had left Cairo was to ascertain on the spot the ruling prices for produce. He asked the Mudir, and that official at once realised the importance of the information required; to be more exact, he would, he said, get very careful information, and let him know in the morning. Then he sent off a telegram to Cairo. "The English Pasha wants to know the prices of produce in Asyoot; what shall I tell him?" The reply came back; the information in accordance with it was handed to Apollo, who remarked subsequently, that there was "nothing like making sure of your facts at the place itself."

Let it be said at once, though, that all the information collected was not of this origin. English Pashas are taken in at times, and detestable is the character of him who is never deceived; but sound common sense is well supported by personal observation, and perhaps Egypt would be more intelligently administered if more of its officials would take the pains to see something of the interior of the country, as well as of the Club Khedivial.

CHAPTER XII.

THE next morning's sun had hardly gilded the Libyan hills before the
Cleopatra, most æsthetically furnished of *dahabeeyahs*, had taken on board
its living freight. Rightly was she named, for the *vainqueur des vainqueurs du
monde* herself had never travelled in more luxurious comfort. The whole of
Apollo's house, itself one of the sights of Cairo, had been ransacked to bedeck
the roomy craft. There were carpets from Khiva, silks from Damascus, and
embroideries from Broussa; luxurious chairs and pretty little inlaid tables
strewed the centre of the deck, surrounded with luxurious eider-down couches,
and covered with a gaily coloured awning. The Egyptian flag fluttered in the
breeze; the steam-tug twenty yards ahead gave a shrill whistle, and, amid the
prostrate salaams of the Mudir and entire population of Asyoot on the banks,
the *Cleopatra* followed in her wake with the stately motion of a swan. The first
day on board a *dahabeeyah* is generally devoted to making a pint-bottle contain a
quart; to unpacking one's travelling treasures; to exploring the nooks and
crannies into which they may be hid with some possibility of rediscovery, and to

stowing away your wardrobe in a cabin seven feet by four, which must also contain yourself, and possibly another. But no such necessity existed on board the *Cleopatra*, and no degrading household cares were allowed to trouble the fortunate travellers. The luggage had been got on board nobody quite knew how, and had been stowed nobody knew where; but everything that could possibly be wanted was at hand. The East, from India to Albania, had been apparently put under levy to supply obsequious servants, who obeyed a wish before it was expressed, who produced one's heart's desire before the tongue could give it utterance, whether it were a delicately-scented pocket-handkerchief, a volume of Plato, or an appropriate quotation. The cook was a *cordon bleu;* fresh flowers and ice appeared to be manufactured on board; and stern janissaries with swords stood at arms, ready to protect the Pasha with their lives, or to hand any of the company a firearm ready loaded, cocked, and pointed in any promising direction.

The first sight of the Nile from Asyoot is disappointing; you seem to be leaving a rich plain to enter a narrow gorge. On the east, sloping reaches of mountain come close to the river, leaving at times a bare bridle-path; while to the west the Libyan range draws nearer and nearer. Village follows village with painful monotony, bearing names which sometimes recall, but more frequently disguise, more famous predecessors. Aboutiz, the old Abutes, marked by a few curious rocks standing straight from the water's edge; Gow-el-Kebir, the famous Antæopolis, where tradition tells us Antæus was killed by Hercules, and where was fought the battle between Typhon and Isis after the death of Osiris. Diodorus, however, assures us that it was fought on the Arabian shore, and some other is certain that it was in the Delta. Seeing the doctors differ, perhaps we had better agree with Wilkinson, who says naïvely, "But as it was an allegory, it couldn't have happened at all." Signs of Ptolemies and the Cæsars are here, however; but the *Cleopatra* wisely shuns them, and passes to Tahta, on the opposite bank; perhaps the site of old Hesopis, but better known for the cruel practical joke perpetrated on Pope Pius VIII., who, induced by a forged petition of the Egyptian clergy, and an equally forged letter of Mohamed Ali, named a Catholic Copt Archbishop of Memphis, with the title of Prince of Tahta. Directly opposite to the principality of this spurious Patriarch stands a singular rock, a Gibraltar in miniature; the sailors as they pass throw in, attached to sticks, a few coins, by way of conciliating either the Sheik, who, however, died a few years ago, or the miraculous serpent who preceded him in the alleged possession of miraculous powers. Whichever it be, there is no doubt that the sailors are anxious to appease him; and so intense is the anxiety lest the offerings should not reach the shore, that one is tempted to suppose that there must be much tradition proving the fatal effects of neglecting to perform the rite. The Arab captain, however, is like Herodotus, and declines to speak of the mystery; while Sara, who mingles with the scepticism of Abraham's wife much calculating superstition, sums it up thus: " All foolery, of course, but can't do no harm; and who knows? perhaps he do good." So he encourages the practice, though with vicarious piasters. But along the whole banks one notes a singular absence of life; the river is getting low, and a few buffaloes and goats scramble down the banks for water, but little of humanity, until, with much whistling, the steamer draws the *Cleopatra* to the bank at Sohag. Then indeed there is excitement; for the Mudir and his deputy come on board, and the whole populace of the capital of Girgeh crowd to catch a sight of the party. Solemnly the Mudir crosses the plank and greets the Pasha. He is a

Turk, and to his satisfaction, expressed with dignity, finds that Apollo can speak to him without the intermediary of a dragoman. Thereat Sara is hurt, and disposed to be contemptuous of information given in a language which he does not understand; so he stands behind the pair, indulges in numerous deprecating nods and winks to the Scribbler, and keeps up a *sotto voce* comment: "All he say lies; great scoundrel; you tell Pasha not believe word." But true Copt, there is reverence on his face as he passes the coffee to the dignitary whom he dare only secretly despise.

As it is already late, it is decided to halt the night at Sohag; the governor providing innumerable Gaffirs along the banks, who light their fires, and keep up a volleyed cry of " Wahad," while the party dine on deck and discuss the first day on the Nile.

" It's my impression," said the Nabob, "that all rivers are swindles. The Rhine is; so is the Danube; and it looks as if Father Nile was very little better. Water and dreary banks of mud as a basis; add to that sham castles to make the Rhine; a few trees, and you have the Danube; or worn-out waterwheels, and you have the Nile."

" Though I confess it's ungrateful, I'm inclined to agree with you," said the Pasha, "and feel relieved; for my orders are to be as quickly as possible in Cairo, and I shall hurry you through. I told you at the commencement I couldn't promise you much in the way of sight-seeing, and I'm afraid it will be less than ever now. However, I'll run you up to Wady Halfa, and leave you, if you like, to get down by Cook's."

The Sketcher alone looked somewhat disappointed; but he looked round the luxurious *Cleopatra*, and felt that he could never surrender Capua.

" You will let us stop at Karnac, at all events?" he asked.

" Yes; my idea is to take a day at Karnac, and at each of the Cataracts, perhaps a few hours at Edfou, but otherwise to push on, only stopping for information at a few of the chief Mudiriehs."

" Do you suppose you get any information worth having at places like this?" asked the Scribbler sceptically.

" Well, it's very doubtful. Ask Crichton here; he will tell you that he has picked up an immense mass of information; but I'm not certain that one wouldn't have found it in Murray; and whether one would or not, Sara Bey is prepared to swear that it's all false; but it's always worth while seeing men and places that you have anything to do with."

" It's the only way to learn geography," said the Nabob sententiously.

" Not only that; one forms some sort of idea of the men one has to deal with, and it keeps them up to the mark if they feel they are liable to be dropped upon."

" And is that all the control you have," asked the Nabob, "over your people in the interior?"

" No; we have armies of control of sorts—Sara Bey there, and others; but then the difficulty is to control the controllers."

" Will you let me," said the Scribbler, "give you some startling figures as to the cost of government in Egypt? I suppose you can't tell me the number of Egyptian Government employés of to-day, but in 1882 a Blue Book gave them as 54,041, costing £1,953,599 per annum. Well, these figures were misleading, for they included the army and police; but deducting those, we get about 30,000 employés, costing about £1,550,000. Now the population of Egypt is 6,800,000.

Assuming that one-fourth are able-bodied men, nearly two per cent. of the whole able-bodied male population are Government servants. The whole civil service of the United Kingdom, with its population of 35,000,000, requires only 29,000 civil servants, at an aggregate salary of £4,000,000."

"I admit the figures are startling," said the Pasha, "but the comparison is not quite fair. In the 29,000 for the United Kingdom, railway employés are certainly not included; and I should like to see how the English four millions are made up before I admit of any comparison at all."

"Well, I confess I can't meet you; and I asked rather for the sake of obtaining than giving information. My authority for the English civil service, 29,000 persons, with an aggregate salary of £4,000,000, is Mulhall; the authority for the 30,000, costing £1,550,000, I have given you; and making all allowances for railway employés, &c., the difference seems enormous."

"The comparison is valueless," repeated the Pasha, "without details."

"And that, as I have said, I can't give you, and ask only for information. The invaluable Whitaker gives 'Salaries and expenses of civil departments, total £2,477,258,' and in that he includes Treasury, £59,506. In the Blue Book I have quoted, the salaries alone of the Ministry of Finance are put at over £75,000, in addition to which there is financial services in the provinces £131,990, and your Budget for 1884 shows a total expenditure of £87,697 and £263,000 for collection of taxes."

"In India," said the Nabob, "the salaries and expenses of our civil departments come to something between eleven and twelve millions—say about eight times as much as yours in Egypt—and we have at least forty times the population."

"At that rate," said Crichton, who had been making careful calculations with a pencil, "the salary charge in India is 1s. 1d. per head; in England, 2s. 4d.; and in Egypt, 4s. 6d. The difference is too great to admit of the comparison being accurate."

"Look here!" said the Pasha, laughing. "If you fellows want statistical information, I wish you'd come to me at the Ministry, and Crichton and the rest of them shall read you to death with Budgets; but I'm not going to stand cross-examination here; and the first man who mentions figures or is guilty of the smallest interference with the multiplication table shall be pitched overboard."

"Seconded and carried unanimously," said the Sketcher; "but unless you can give the Scribbler continual mental pabulum in the way of facts, he will die of ennui."

" According to Ampère, *il faut s'être ennuyé dans un pays pour le bien connaître*," said the Pasha ; " if that's true, we shall be doing him a service."

" And if that's true," said the Nabob, yawning, " I know this beastly country very thoroughly already, and may as well go to bed."

The next morning at sunrise the *Cleopatra* was already on her way, and passing Akmeen, site of Chemmis or Panopolis, the city of the great god Pan. Hither to this day come worthy wives who love their lords, and offer vows to the great god Priapus ; in spite of which, says the gentle Sir Gardner, "the population of the country is still on the decline." Chemmis, according to Strabo, was also famous for woollen manufactures, and for an enlightened toleration of Greeks, which their descendants have probably learnt to regret. A few miles off it is conjectured lay the old city of Thomu, but, *pace* Murray, neither "mounds nor crude bricks " are now to be found, except in the pages of Wilkinson; and beyond, again, are Menshech (Ptolemais Hermii) and Girgeh, once capital of the province, but now washed away by the ever-changing river, near which are the ruins of Abydos, and north of them a large circling wall of crude brick, the cradle of the Egyptian monarchy—the capital which proved too small for the vaulting ambition of young Menes, founder of Memphis. At Abydos stood the tomb of Osiris, the Holy Sepulchre of the people of Egypt. Thither sped pious pilgrims from the most distant parts of the land, and there, according to Plutarch, the wealthy were brought to be interred, in order that they might repose close to the tomb of their god. At Abydos, too, are the two temples of Ramses II. The one, indeed, is variously known as the temple of Sethi, the temple of Osiris, or the Memnonium, but was more probably built by Ramses himself in honour of Sethi his father (Osirida of the hieroglyphs). As for the name Memnonium, used by Strabo, it originated from the practice of the Romans, who, innocent of Egyptology, and knowing only the mythical Memnon of Homer, the beautiful son of Tithonus and Eos, king of the blameless Ethiopians, attached the name of their one Egyptian hero to any temple, tomb, or statue which took their particular fancy. In this temple were found the cartouches of the seventy-six kings, headed by the name of Mena, venerable founder of the Egyptian monarchy. The other temple, of which only the walls remain, was undoubtedly begun and completed by Ramses II. Leaving This of 7000 years ago, and starting again from Bellianeh, we pass the red convent of Amba Mussars, Farshoot, with its sugar-factory of to-day, and How (Diospolis Parva), and the tomb of one Dionysius, son of Ptolemy, and scribe of King Ptolemy, and the Kasr-el-Syad, or Sportsman's Mansion, the ancient Cheno-

boschion. All that remains is an inscription apparently of the time of Antoninus
Pius, telling us how some one did something or other "at his own expense."
May the reward have lasted as long as the record !

The *Cleopatra* was now going due east. The setting sun was turning into
a rosy red the distant mountains and desert on either side, and, following them
with its last rays, turned the Nile into a rippling Danæ stream of gold. The
moon was high overhead, struggling against the greater glory, and waiting till
its sinking rival would allow it to show its own pale beauty in the clear blue
sky. The narrow strips by the river's bank, green with uncut corn, the graceful dom-palm mingling with its more stately sisters, the increasing number
of long lateen-sailed boats, the circling flocks of pigeons, and the faint hum

of distant voices, showed that a large town was near ; and ahead, half hidden
by a bend in the river, lay the minarets and white domes of Keneh.

The hideous whistle of the steamer suddenly broke a charm which had been
felt by the whole party ; and the Reis came hurrying forward asking for orders,
whether he was to lie under the east bank at Denderah or cross over to Keneh.
The Pasha explained that the former meant pleasure and the latter duty ; could
he hesitate ? The Sketcher urged that the former meant dancing-girls ; the
latter the face of Cleopatra and the temple of Athor. The Scribbler declared
that he saw little choice between the two ; but the Nabob, who by force of
apathy always got his own way, solved the difficulty. The *Cleopatra* was to lie
at Keneh ; the receptions of the Mudir could be undertaken by his brother in
solitary state, while the rest of the party would patronise the Ghawazee ; the
next morning, while the Pasha was pursuing his arduous inquiries, the other

three could cross to Denderah in the steamer alone. Great, apparently, had
been the excitement at Keneh while this decision was being arrived at. The
anxious Mudir had noted that the steamer had stopped in mid-river, and began
to fear the worst. Had his enemies managed to traduce him at some place
en route? Was there on board another Mudir to replace him? Had the Pasha
come to carry him off? No idea is too ridiculous for an Egyptian mind, and
this seemed so probable ; but he was relieved when the steamer began puffing
towards Keneh ; effusive joy took the place of fear, and, without waiting for
the plank, he climbed on board in a most un-Mudirian manner, and clasped
with affection the knees of Sara Bey. Nor was Sara himself unmoved ;
perhaps he liked the tribute to his power ; perhaps he is at Keneh even a
greater man than in other parts of the river. Certain it is that he displayed
a distinctly increased sense of dignity from this point ; his demeanour was that
of a monarch returning to his faithful subjects ; he knew them all, he said ;
"d—d rascals," he muttered *sotto voce*, and they cringed before him. There
was a dare-dog air about his tarbouche, and an unusual swing in his gait as
he walked the deck ; and he was almost condescending to the Pasha himself
as he introduced the Mudir, as if abrogating his own dignity, but only for
a time. It seemed as if he felt a little like the old Eton Doctor, with his
"Pardon me, your Majesty, but I must take the precedence here ;" and the Pasha,
like *Georgius Rex*, entered into the joke, and maintained the spirit of discipline.

The usual questions had to be put and asked ; the Mudir expressed
the most intense personal interest in every person of any influence in Cairo,
and placed himself and his administration metaphorically at the Pasha's feet.
Meanwhile it was late for business, and he had arranged an entertainment for
the party, similar to that, he explained, which was prepared for the Prince of
Wales and other royal personages. Sara gave a contemptuous sneer, but such
an invitation could not be refused. Sara and the great ones led the way, and the
rest followed humbly, surrounded by an admiring crowd. The way led through
the unlovely streets of the town, the site of Cœnopolis, the new city, past shop
rows of earthen *ghoolas*, the chief staple manufacture of Keneh, to a large
booth. Two sides, facing each other, were already filled with potent, grave,
and reverend seigniors, who rose at the approach of the party, and whose age
must have averaged sixty. Along the third side sat some half-dozen women
of surpassing ugliness ; one might have been only twenty, the remainder were
certainly of an age at which English spinsters remain for a decade ; in front
of them a row of tambourine and rebek players. The fourth side, facing them,
was reserved for the Mudir and his guests. As they seated themselves, the

whole audience again rose, looked preternaturally solemn, and then re-seated themselves.

A horrid thumping of the instruments, a low wail gradually rising into a shrill shriek, and a single Ghawazee came forward; the least offensive of the six, perhaps, and yet very hideous. It requires a Frenchman of strong imaginative powers to see "*le portrait vivant de ces figures d'Isis ou de Cléopatre*" in the unwashed, coarse, sensual face that, covered with paint, and half hidden by unkempt hair, loaded with tinsel, leers at you with a wolfish grin. Very slowly, and with sliding, panther-like steps, she made the round of the floor, changing into a heavy circular movement as she gradually approached nearer the centre, where she assumed a position from which every element of grace was excluded. Then, accompanied by tomtoms, rebeks, and a guttural falsetto shriek, she began that series of physical contortions in which some have seen grace and others sensuality. One by one the others rose and joined her, the music played more fiercely, the venerable elders joined with their appreciative long-drawn "*Aah,*" and in the centre were six repulsive women, who appeared without effort to distort their limbs, and to destroy every vestige of the human form divine.

"Licentious they may mean it to be," said the Pasha, as they escaped again on deck, "but to most men it would be a striking incentive to virtue. The drunken Helot could not have answered his purpose as well as these modern Paphians."

"The view down that reach of the river repaid everything though," said the Sketcher. "Come, admit that even you retract your expressions of contempt for the Nile."

"Well, I'm willing to admit extenuating circumstances at least ; but one-half hour's sunset is not compensation enough for a two hours' discussion on Egyptian finance and two hours of dancing-girls, and I reserve final judgment until Karnac and Thebes."

"Meanwhile," said the Scribbler, "will any one tell me the authority for placing either the tomb or temple of Osiris at Abydos?"

"*Abydus Memnonis regia et Osiridis templum inclytum,*" said Crichton promptly.

"Precisely ; but that's Pliny, and you've already pulverised him, Strabo, and the Romans generally by your contempt for the expression Memnonium ; and in any case, that only refers to the temple. What about the tomb? Plutarch names Abydos, Memphis, Busiris, Philœ, and Taposiris as all laying claim to his burying-place, but gives the preference to the first two. In both of which, how-

The Dance of the Wasp.

ever, he couldn't have been buried; besides, we've decided that he's an allegory, and you can't bury an allegory even on the banks of the Nile, though you might build a temple to one."

"But the idea that it's a temple to Osiris is given up," said the Sketcher; "that was Pliny's first misnomer, but it's admitted now to be the temple of Sethi."

"Precisely; but now you come to the bottom of the fiction. First comes Pliny, who imagines a temple to Osiris; next follows Plutarch, who finding a lot of graves, thinks it only natural that the temple should have been built near the tomb, and so imagines the tomb of Osiris; then come later Egyptologists, proving that it's a temple to Sethi; and yet they can't relinquish the tomb-theory, and so we are told that this was the Holy Sepulchre of the Egyptians—a myth created on an exploded myth."

"But surely you might leave us a few myths, at least in Egypt," said the Sketcher. "If we sacrifice William Tell and Joan of Arc, is not that a sufficient burnt-offering to the Moloch of modern research?—leave us Isis and Osiris and the gods of Olympus."

"There is no fear of our losing myths," said the Scribbler; "the tendency is to create quite as much as to abolish them. All I say is, let us keep them in their place. Leave the myth of Osiris, pretty as it is, but don't mix it up with historical fact. I don't mean to say that Egyptologists maintain Osiris to have been buried at Abydos, but they can't resist the temptation of making out that it was regarded as his tomb, and so create the new myth of the 'Holy Sepulchre of the Egyptians,' for which there is not as yet a shadow of foundation."

"Does it much matter after all?" said the Pasha languidly.

"Perhaps not in this case; but look at the confusion that was made by the unfortunate romancing of the earliest French Egyptologists over the zodiac found at Denderah. Desaix discovers it; he at least—good soldier, but no scientist—was not to blame. Bought for a fabulous price by Louis XVIII., the Voltaireans saw in its alleged antiquity a triumph over the authority of Scripture. If the zodiac dated some 15,000 years back, then the monuments of Denderah must also be ancient. Thereupon Jollois and Devilliers find '*qu'ils sont les plus parfaits sous le rapport de l'exécution et qu'ils ont été construits à l'époque la plus florissante de l'Egypte ;*' while the orthodox opposition, who are anxious to prove it modern, declare that they are detestable."

"And who was right?"

"As to the date, the latter, for it proved to be of the time of the Cæsars; as to the value of the monuments, you can judge for yourself to-morrow."

"And to-morrow evening Karnac by moonlight!" sighed the Sketcher, as they turned in.

CHAPTER XIII.

DENDERAH is Tentyra Tei an Athor, the abode of Athor or Aphrodite, according to etymology; but according to Pliny and Strabo, the abode of a people whose crocodilephobia gave pain to the pious crocodilephilians of Ombos. The feuds between these cities partook, according to Juvenal, of all the cruelties of most religious wars, terminating with a cannibal feast to the advantage of the conquerors.

The temple was begun by Ptolemy Auletes. Our Lord was probably living when this temple was completed, so that it has been finished barely 1900 years, and in Egypt hardly merits rank as an antiquity. Nor can it pretend to compare architecturally with the buildings which it imitates; its value rather lies in the fact that it is an imitation, however defective, yet in a comparatively perfect state of preservation, of a style which we can otherwise only study in a state of complete ruin. Its columns are barbaric, but the portico, taken as a whole, is grand, and enables us to realise what we have lost. It is what a

Q

photograph is to a painting; what a painting is to its original. As we pass
from court to court, we gather a general idea of the Egyptian temple and the
uses to which it was put. Its purpose must not be confounded with that of our
modern churches; it was not a place where the faithful or devout met to unite
in prayer; neither did it resemble our old colleges, nor the later Roman
temples. We find neither dwellings for priests, nor halls for initiation, for
divination, or for oracular utterance. So far as we can judge, the worship of the
gods in Egypt in their temples was reserved to the cultivated few, and none
but the king and the priests were permitted to enter. The temple was the
dwelling-place of the god, the sacred resting-place of his images, a place for the
consecration of king and of priests to his service.

From the hieroglyphs which cover the walls we learn much of the religious
rites of later days, imitated doubtless, like the temples themselves, from those of
an earlier age. There is the large portal, through which, clothed in his long
robe, with sandalled feet and leaning on his staff, the king alone could pass;
but before even he could do so, and so penetrate into the temple itself, it was
necessary that the gods should recognise him as king of Upper and Lower
Egypt. Thoth and Horus must anoint him with the emblems of power;
Ouate and Suan must crown him with the double crown; Mout of Thebes and
Toum of Heliopolis must conduct him into the sacred presence of the goddess
Hathor herself. Here within, sombre and silent, are the priests assembled,
passing in solemn procession, ascending the terraces and descending them
again, in order to encompass the encircling wall, according to prescribed rites,
with the four boats holding, carefully concealed, the sacred emblem. Here is
the court containing the offerings and the limbs of the victims of the sacrifice.
The king consecrates the offerings, and, followed by thirteen priests, carrying
on high poles the emblems of the divinities, ascends the northern staircase,
stops on the terrace of the twelve columns, and descends by the southern staircase. Below the temple, again, are the secret hiding-place of the treasures of
the gods, statues in gold, silver, and *lapis lazuli*, only brought out on the rare
occasions of the most solemn ceremonies.

The principal divinity of the temple is Hathor—Aphrodite or Venus;
goddess of beauty; pupil of the sun's eye; goddess of the lovely face; the
beautiful goddess; the goddess of love. Such are her titles, but she is more
than all these. She is the divine mother, giving life, fecundity, and abundance to
mortals, animal and vegetable. She is the emblem of youthfulness, of expansion, of resurrection, of truth. She is the type of that universal harmony
necessary to the well-being and life of the world.

And in the temple of Hathor is the picture of one who, if not a follower of the goddess in the highest attributes of her character, must ever be thought of in connection with the queen of beauty. Thence, from the walls, smile on us Cleopatra, *vainqueur des vainqueurs du monde*, mistress of all contemporary masters of the world. "In a word, all Cleopatra, fierce, voluptuous, passionate, tender, wicked."[1]

When the Nabob, the Sketcher, and the Scribbler got on board, they found the Pasha, who had tired of Denderah, extended at full length on the deck, swathed in a dressing-gown of delicate hues suitable to his complexion, apparently idle; but by his side were Crichton and Sara, the former engaged in receiving, and the latter in giving, an Arabic lesson, which the Pasha was attentively following. We have said that he was a linguist, and he claimed the merit of having discovered a royal and pasha-like road to knowledge. "It has

always," he said, "been my conviction that the only way to study any subject is to teach it; this is theoretically equally true in languages, but practically I am met with the initial difficulty that you cannot dispense with a preliminary knowledge of a few words; and, moreover, I find that when I try to teach Crichton, he gets so far ahead of my feeble intelligence, that it resolves itself into the ordinary form of a lesson to me, which I deem fatal. But I have solved the difficulty; I make Sara teach Crichton; I try and imagine I am teaching him myself, and at all events, by listening to both teacher and teachee, I get the advantage of both." So saying, he majestically dismissed both his secretaries, and signified his intention of proceeding.

[1] Hawthorn.

As the *Cleopatra* was setting off, she was hailed by a small boat, on which could be seen a European standing obsequiously hat in hand. From the evident determination of the stranger to board, the Pasha conjectured that it was a messenger with a recently arrived telegram, and gave orders to the steamer to slow down, in order that he might be at once brought forward. An anxious twenty minutes having been thus wasted, the gentleman in question at last appeared, and breathlessly commenced a rapid sentence, which apparently comprised his known stock of English. " Very good beer—pale ale—stout—powder —cartridges—shot duck—ginger ale—tea—sugar—what you want—buy—sell— 'bedient servant, sar." The Pasha with difficulty restrained his indignation, and ordered the importunate bum-boatman to be flung into the river—an order to which he had apparently become indifferent owing to frequent repetition without serious result. As he went over the side, we heard a melancholy whisper, gradually getting fainter, " Pale ale—stout—powder—shot duck," &c., &c.

"Another consequence of those infernal Capitulations," said the Pasha. " That fellow now is dealing in Heaven knows what rubbish, paying no taxes, subject to no law—and probably making a fortune."

"Why on earth should he pay taxes?" said the Scribbler in a spirit of contradiction. " What is he to pay them for?"

"Pay them for !" said the Pasha, still irate, "pay them for ! Why, to maintain the Government, of course. What are all taxes for? You don't wish to defend exemption from taxation, do you?"

" Not entirely; but still there are always two sides to a question. Let me take the other for a moment; not in reference to this individual Greek, but foreigners generally in Egypt. First of all, are not the Europeans taxed already in import duties?"

" Of course they are, but so are natives; only the latter have to pay other taxation in addition, from all which Europeans are exempt."

"Not from all, because at least they pay land-tax ; and as regards import duties, the Europeans probably pay seven-eighths of the total, as the main consumers of those imports."

"I don't quite see that argument," said the other. " If they choose to import, they must pay. The native doesn't choose it ; he doesn't pay ; but you can't argue that that entitles the man who chooses to use imported goods to escape other taxation."

" Certainly not, as a principle ; but when you say that natives are taxed when Europeans are not, you must also remember that, if there were no Europeans, there would hardly be any imports ; that if so, there would be less revenue from the customs; that you would then have to cover that deficit by farther taxation, which would necessarily fall on natives (as the Europeans are assumed not to be here), so that the presence of Europeans, whom you call untaxed, nevertheless lessens the taxation on natives."

"Isn't that somewhat far-fetched?"

"Well, perhaps so; but now look at it in another way. What does an ordinary citizen pay taxes for? I suppose in exchange for protection against attacks on person and property; for maintenance of courts of justice for the prevention of such attacks; for the maintenance of roads; for certain advantages of public education; sometimes for the maintenance of a State Church. Now do you ask a resident Englishman to pay taxes on these grounds? If so, I say the Egyptian Government grants them no protection against attacks on

1.

person or property: the police were the leaders of the massacre of June 1882; the soldiers were the incendiaries of July 1882. They owe little to your tribunals, and until lately nothing; for they could only prosecute and be prosecuted in Consular courts, costing nothing to the Egyptian Government. Maintenance of the roads! Why, any that are made they have made themselves, and the Government refuses to keep them in repair. Public education! There is none in the country worth a shilling; certainly none of which any European could take advantage. State Church! They have each to maintain their own. Or does taxation go with representation? They have none."

"All that," said the Pasha, "is special pleading. You confuse what I will call imperial taxation and municipal rates. Europeans even indirectly pay little enough for the latter, nothing at all for the former; and whatever might have

been argued a few years ago, the payment of the indemnity claims to Europeans
and natives alike shows that the Government admits its duties to one as to the
other. But you can't mean to argue seriously that foreigners living in another
state should not be subject to that state's fiscal laws."

"Of course not. I only wanted to point out that there is something at least
to be said on the other side, and to point this moral, which the Egyptian Government seems disposed to ignore. By the taxation of Europeans you have undertaken certain duties towards them which they have a right to expect you to fulfil
—duties to which hitherto they had not the smallest claim, and which they
therefore performed among themselves. For instance, in no other country in
the world, so far as I know, is levied an octroi duty against a particular town,
the proceeds of which go to the national revenue. An octroi rate is a municipal
one, and if you levy it in Alexandria, Cairo, or any other town, the revenues of

Old Sakieh at Edfou.

that octroi should go to that town ; or if
you must take it, you are bound to give that
town sufficient for its ordinary municipal purposes."

"I don't admit," said the Pasha, "that a European, even when taxed, has any more right to interfere in
the disposal of the finances of the country than the equally taxed Fellah."

"Well, I daresay you're right in principle, but don't be led away by false
analogies. The European in Egypt is not, and never will be (until Egypt
becomes European), in the same position as a foreigner, say in France or England.
Numerically small, he is the life and backbone of the country. He is not helpless ; he gains less from Egypt than Egypt does from him ; and he won't stand
all that the Fellah stands. You had better learn to look upon him as a factor,
and the principal factor, for good or evil in your population. You may theorise
as much as you like, but you will have to rule Egypt by European ideas, not by
Egyptian ones."

"I quite admit that," said the Pasha, "only I want the European ideas of
the nineteenth century, not of the twelfth."

"Take the Egyptian ideas of the twelfth century," said the Scribbler, "and you will have a sufficiently good model. Have you ever read the first extant Capitulation of Saladin to the Pisan Republic in 1173? Listen to this, and give it as instructions to Sara there, and his colleagues. 'And in return for all these things (taxes), they (the tax-payers) must be treated with love, and they must be made to pay the tax in a kind way and amicably ; and they must pay nothing to any servant of the Government, be he great or small ; nor shall any wrong be done them, nor shall their goods be undervalued in such a way that they shall be sold below the price.'"

"When that ordered?" asked Sara, who had drawn near to listen, with suppressed feelings of contempt.

"1173," said the Scribbler, "by Saladin."

"Ah! Salah-ed-din! I thought you said 1873. Ismail not write rubbish like that ;" and he smole a relieved smile.

The Pasha laughed. "Poor Saladin! despised by Sara! Let's hear some more."

"Here is a clause that shows a sentiment next to godliness in the European of that day—'So also they prayed us for a bath, and we granted it to them ; and the custom-house was to pay all for them.'"

"False political economy," said the Nabob; "but it has its advantages. Go on!"

"'As to the church that belonged to them, and that we gave them, they shall have it, as they had it before ; and when they shall go to the church, they shall suffer no molestation whatever, neither on the way nor within the church ; and inside of the church no noise may be made that hinders them from hearing the Word of God, according to the precept of their law. But they may observe their law, even as the precepts of God and their laws ordain.'"

"Bravo! Anti-Crusader," exclaimed the Sketcher. "What are you reading from?" said the Pasha.

"Van Dyck's translation of Gatteschi; but the real point of it all is this. The proviso that the Pisans should pay nothing but the right duty—no baksheesh, that is—has been in successive Capitulations extended to mean that Europeans shall pay no other *tax* than duty ; and another clause, ordering that the Bajuli are not 'to occupy themselves with any litigation or matter between the merchants without their consent,' designed to protect them from what I suppose we should call to-day 'vexatious litigation,' has been similarly stretched until it has come to abstracting all Europeans from the jurisdiction of the country. Such was the return made for the generosity of Saladin to the suppliants at his stirrup."

"I'm glad to see that, in spite of your lecture just now, you're sound after all," said the Pasha. "Meanwhile I expect this is Koos, and I want to stop here to examine one of the few manufactures of the country."

For the *Cleopatra* had passed Coptos—where Isis was supposed to have heard of the death of Osiris; where Diocletian had wrought his fury against the rebelling Christians; the town which, some have it, has given its name to the whole land of Egypt—and was now, in obedience to the sudden orders of the Pasha, drawing to land at Koos, the site of Apollonopolis Parva, declared by Abulfeeda to have been in his time second in importance only to Fostat. An old monolith, now converted into a tank, and a few granite columns, are, however, the only remains of antiquity. Nor are they the object of the Pasha's visit. But the modern Koos is remarkable for one of the few

manufactures left in Egypt, long scarfs of many-coloured cottons, woven together not without taste. And the Pasha, who had begun to realise that his trip was partaking too much of the character of a royal progress, determined to stop at least in one place where he was not expected, and where the answers should not be dictated from Cairo. Perhaps, after all, the experiment was not a success; the worthy Nazir, who represented the Government, was so appalled or terrified at the honour of the visit, that such wits as prolonged residence at Koos had left him were not at his command. Were the people prosperous? Yes; and profoundly honoured at his excellency's visit. Were the crops good? They would doubtless improve after his excellency's visit. Were the people in debt? No; only to his excellency for his condescension in visiting them. Were the taxes high? No charge was too great in exchange for the pleasure of seeing his excellency; and so forth, as he stood with bent head, downcast eyes, and clasped hands. As there was little to be made of him, the Pasha ordered in majestic tones, "Bring the Sheik el Beled!" "Bring the Sheik el Beled!" echoed Sara. The Nazir looked round, and the small crowd on the bank at once slouched off. Then there were whispered conferences between the Nazir and his myrmidons, and an evident desire on the part of the villagers to avoid having greatness thrust upon them. Who could tell what the Sheik el Beled might be wanted for. It was not for nothing that Pashas and Beys from Cairo came to the village of Koos. Perhaps they were come for soldiers, and would seize the Sheik as a hostage. There was evident safety in flight. Still the Sheik el Beled had been asked for by the not-to-be-despised Sara, and he or a substitute must be found.

One venerable old man seemed preternaturally deaf to all shouts, threw his leg over a donkey, and ambled away; another loudly expostulated; and a third descended to abject entreaties. At last, one more servile or more courageous than the rest was found, and he shambled on board with an air of pious resignation to the will of fate; while the crowd, feeling the god appeased, gradually drew nearer to watch with selfish indifference the horrible fate of their sacrificial lamb.

A respectable-looking old Fellah he was, enveloped in a long white Bedouin blanket, perhaps the toga of his assumed office, leaning on a stick, and peering with anxious eyes at his supposed tormentors. Examination of them seemed, however, to reassure him. The Pasha smiled benignly; the Scribbler offered him a cigarette; even the great Sara placed his awful hand of authority gently on his shoulder as he said, "M'at avsh!" (Be not afraid). So he took the cigarette, and squatting himself on the deck with the ejaculation, "Allah Akbar!" (God is great), awaited his doom. At first the answers were something like those of the Nazir; but gradually, under the soothing influence of coffee and tobacco, he came out of his shell. "Times were bad," he said; "very bad; always had been bad, and generally worse; still he lived, thanks to God and in spite of the Government!"—terms which, in his mind, appeared naturally to represent the spirits of good and evil. "His father was here before him, and *his* father too, and, so far as he knew, his father's fathers ever since the world began. He had forty acres, which he supposed had belonged to his family for the same time; he, at all events, had inherited them, had not bought any." "Why?" "Well, because he had no money, and wouldn't have done so if he had had. The money went from the land to the tax-collector, of course; where else should it go?" "What is his land worth?" "Well,

R

perhaps £6 a feddan, or £250 altogether." "What does it give?" "Well, nothing!"

But here the accurate Crichton stops him, and in fluent Cymric Arabic extracts details.

"What is his family?" "Well, twenty-seven, if you count women." "And they all live on the land?" "Of course they do;" and the old patriarch expatiates at length on the uselessness of women, from whom evidently he suffers much; "useless to keep, and expensive to get rid of," is his unchivalrous verdict on the sex. "And what do they eat in a year?" "Much," says the unwary Sheik; "great as God's goodness is a woman's appetite!"

With much patient inquiry, Crichton extracts the following as the net result of the farming of this forty acres. First, the farmer has no money and no debts; second, he has kept his family of twenty-seven from the produce; third, he spends about a further £36 per annum in clothes and tobacco; fourth, he pays the Government £52 in taxes; and all this paid, he had last year a balance of about £7, or say three per cent. on the value of his land. This year, however, prices are low; times are bad; and he will not do more than cover expenses. Still, evidently, here is no over-taxed trodden-down Fellah. The old gentleman has got quite genial while talking over his household circumstances, and has abandoned the despondent tone which marked the beginning of his conversation. "If he could only get rid of the daughters," he says, "all would go well;" and he looks wistfully round as if inviting offers. As he leaves, he holds the Pasha's hand, and, with a benevolent and fraternal smile, assures him he is a very intelligent man. Then he returns, the hero of the village, to recount his marvellous experience; and the *Cleopatra* glides still southward.

"It strikes me," says the Nabob, "that if that is a fair specimen, your Fellaheen are not only more intelligent, but generally much better off than our ryots."

"Better off, for that matter," said the Scribbler, "than most landowners anywhere else."

"Yes," said the Pasha; "there's been plenty of rubbish written about the over-taxation of the Fellaheen. Of course it would be absurd to judge from a single instance like that; but still here we are in one of the poorest parts of the country—in Upper Egypt, where they can only get one scant crop—in a bad year, with prices exceptionally low, and you have the worst of it; a man, owning only forty acres of very poor land (he only values it at £6), and evidently disposed to make the worst of it, is still, when brought to the point, compelled to own that he makes a living for twenty-seven persons out of it; and that after paying taxes at a rate about equal to the average tax of the whole of Egypt. Yet Pashas with lands in the Delta, growing two or three crops in a year, try to make us believe that they are unable to make it pay."

"That," said the Scribbler, "in nine cases out of ten is pure rubbish. There are undoubted cases where the land is over-taxed; there are at least as many where it is under-taxed; but the vast majority of land, properly cultivated, will pay the existing taxation and leave a small return on capital."

"Then you mean," said the Nabob, "that there is a conspiracy among the landowners to misrepresent their earnings, in order to get a reduction of taxation?"

"No, not quite that. In many cases the landowner *is* unable to pay his way, but it is nearly always his own fault. The fact must be admitted that the Egyptians, whom Mr. Blunt and others think capable of governing their own country, are not only unable to run a factory or a shop, but are only very imperfectly capable of cultivating their own land—I should rather say of managing it. Here is the evil. An Egyptian, in some way or other, becomes possessed of say £1000, and at the same time of a desire to become a landowner. Not only does he wish to be a landowner, but he wants to get hold of as many acres as he can. Instead, therefore, of paying say £700 for land, and keeping the £300 as a reserve capital for working it, he buys £1500 worth of land, and borrows £500 to pay for it, possibly at 10 or 12 per cent. interest. What is the consequence? He has no capital to spend on his land, which deteriorates year by year; and he has to find not only the land-tax, but £50 or £60 a year for interest. Naturally he has to borrow more money for daily expenses; and his security being already mortgaged, he has to pay 15 to 18 per cent. His debts pile up, his interest charges get higher, and the revenue of his starved land naturally gets lower; in the end, his land has to be sold to pay taxes or interest, and he is quoted as another proof that land cultivation in Egypt does not pay, and that the Fellah is over-taxed."

"And is the debt of the Fellaheen to the usurer so colossal?"

"No; there has been exaggeration about that too. All sorts of ridiculous estimates were current in 1883; and Dufferin, who very wisely took them under very considerable discount, even then over-estimated them. It's impossible to get at them accurately, but they probably then did not exceed eight millions, and to-day are certainly under five. But all estimates are guess-work, for the Fellah himself can seldom tell you what he owes."

"Do you mean," asked the Pasha, "that he owes more than he knows of?"

"Sometimes that, but sometimes the reverse. I will give you an actual

instance, which will show you what I mean, both as to their ignorance as to
their own indebtedness, and the reasons of their failure to make land pay. An
English friend of mine wanted to buy some 140 acres of land from a native.
The native was largely in debt, both to the Credit Foncier and to the Government, for unpaid taxes. My friend went to see the land, found it in a deplorable
condition, and was told by the proprietor, who did not know he was a purchaser,
that the land was bad, and could never pay its heavy tax of 22s. ' How much
do you owe?' said my friend. 'About £1900,' announced the other, naming,
however, an exact sum. ' What interest do you pay?' 'Twelve or 13 per cent.'

Interior of a Fellah's House.

Now the Credit Foncier is supposed to charge 8 or 9 per cent., and the rate
seemed 'excessive. However, my friend thought well of the land, and offered
£15 an acre for it. With a little bargaining, of course, the matter was con-
cluded. The exact sum to be paid was estimated, and this sum, according to
the estimate of the seller, would just suffice to pay off the Credit Foncier, and
leave him £200 or so; so it was agreed that my friend should pay off the
Credit Foncier their £1900, get the title-deeds, which they held, transferred, and
then pay the seller the odd £200, which, he said, was all he would have in the
world. My friend goes to the Credit Foncier, and finds that they ask only
£1400. Being an honest man, he does not pocket the difference, but gives the

astonished proprietor £700 instead of £200. Now, how had the mistake arisen? Simply thus. The Credit Foncier had been charging only 8 or 9 per cent. interest, and the other 4 or 5 per cent. which the fellah had been paying had gone towards the extinction of his capital debt. He therefore was ignorant, not only of what he owed, but of the rate of interest and very terms of the contract he was fulfilling! He exaggerated, perfectly innocently, his debt by 30 per cent., and the rate of interest by 3 or 4 per cent.; and yet men like Villiers Stuart accept the evidence of him, and other men who exaggerated perhaps less honestly."

"Well, and how did your friend fare with the land?"

"That is precisely what I am going to tell you. My friend had paid £2100, and the first thing he did was to spend £1500 in bringing it back to cultivation, from which it had lapsed solely because the former proprietor had only debts instead of capital. The result to-day is that the land costs him about £25 per acre; he lets it at £3, 10s., pays taxes £1, 2s., and nets £2, 8s., or nearly 10 per cent.; and this on land that the proprietor told him would never pay its taxes."

"And has he no trouble in getting in his rents?" asked the Pasha.

"Hardly any," replied the other. "There is an Arcadian simplicity about the system. The proprietor provides seed; purchases cattle for them as they want it; acts, in fact, as their benevolent banker during the season; receives their crop from them into a common store; sells it; repays himself from the proceeds for rent and advances, and hands the balance to the tenant."

"And suppose the balance is the other way?"

"Well, that happens occasionally, but very rarely, and proves the tenant to be a careless cultivator; in which case he has to go, and a better cultivator takes his place."

"I wish," said the Sketcher, "that, instead of discussing political economy, you would explain to me why the sun is setting in the south."

The *Cleopatra* was running with her bow pointed full at the setting sun, which was about to dip into the river ahead of them.

"We have made a curve to the west," said Crichton, examining the map, "and are close on Luxor."

"And you have no idea what you've missed," said the Sketcher, who had been busily sketching, and handed his attempts to the Scribbler.

"And are not likely to have from these," said the other surlily, as he returned them; for the Scribbler was a man who loved the sound of his own voice, and did not tolerate interruption.

The Sketcher was equally zealous for the honour of his sketches, and for a moment the *entente cordiale* between Damon and Pythias was imperilled. But the first sight of Karnac burst on their view at the critical instant. Within the sight of those "temples, palaces, and piles stupendous," which even Horace Smith's doggerel cannot make ridiculous, all wrangle was hushed. Impatiently they listened to Crichton, who, conscientiously anxious that they should miss nothing, was laboriously explaining that Medamot, which they were passing,

was Maximianopolis. Hardly a glance could they spare for the ruins of Ptolemy Euergetes, against a column of which a buffalo was lazily scratching its back, nor for the fields blooming in all the glory of an Egyptian spring. Who has eyes for anything else when Karnac is in sight? or who can think of the pigmy Ptolemies in the presence of Ramses? And Karnac is the great Ramses personified—an epic in stone. Description of it is almost an insult. We may gaze on it with awe, and perhaps carry away some feeble impression of its majesty, but the writer or artist who can reproduce it is yet unborn.

CHAPTER XIV.

COMPARED with either Thinis or Memphis, Thebes is an upstart city, for it is only in the eleventh dynasty that she makes her first appearance. We have seen [1] how Egypt, during the seventh, eighth, ninth, and tenth dynasties, fell into comparative obscurity, under kings reigning both at Memphis and Elephantine. It is tolerably certain that at this time there existed internal dissension, aggravated by foreign aggression. We may perhaps assume that the Pharaohs at Memphis were occupied in repelling the already commencing invasion of the Shepherd tribes, and so, losing control over their southern provinces, allowed the Ethiopian invader to come down the river and establish himself at Elephantine. The attacking Hyksos and the defending Memphite monarch would both be weakened, and become eventually the easy conquest of the Elephantine Pharaoh, who established the eleventh dynasty at Thebes. Such at least is a probable explanation of the otherwise singular fact, that we find the eleventh dynasty established at Thebes, a powerful and prosperous state, immediately after a period when the fortunes of Lower Egypt were at a low ebb. During the eleventh dynasty, however, it is probable that Thebes extended little beyond the temple of Karnac. At the Necropolis of Drah Abou 'l nezzah were found the mummies, now in London, of the kings Entep of this dynasty, the sarcophagus of Aah Hoteb, with its collection of jewels at Boolak ; but much of the luxury of the period was expended on the mummies, and the tombs themselves show nothing of interest. We have seen, also, how the brief glory of the eleventh dynasty was overthrown by the Hyksos, and how, after 1200 years, Sekenen Ra had lost his life in expelling them.

[1] Chapter ix.

With this amount of necessary recapitulation, we resume the thread of Egyptian history where we left it, at the establishment of the eighteenth dynasty under Aahmes I., independent sovereign of all Egypt, ruling from Thebes.

With this dynasty begins the glorious period of Egyptian history, and Thebes rises to its unrivalled grandeur, warranting the description of the Prophet,

Necropolis of Drah Abou 'l nezzah.

"Populous No, that was situate among the rivers, that had the waters round about it, whose rampart was the sea, and her wall was from the sea : Ethiopia and Egypt were her strength, and it was infinite" (Nahum iii. 8, 9). For the long war of independence had turned the kingdom into a huge camp, and the B.C. 1703-1653. first of the restored Pharaohs, Aahmes, Amenhoteb I., and Tutmes I., probably regarded war not only as a source of profit, but as a necessary measure of policy;

A Portion of the Temple of Karnac.

and thus the expansion of Egypt commenced. To their already famed infantry the Egyptians had learnt from the Hyksos to add cavalry and chariots. Their armies invaded Asia, overran Syria, Judæa, and Arabia, advancing as far as Mesopotamia.

And commerce followed their flag : the emerald mines of Berenice and the gold mines of Midian enriched the capital of the Pharaohs ; white and yellow alabaster, red porphyry, and green diorite were brought from the hills beyond Rohanou and from the Wady Hammamat. The labour of establishing their authority, and thus extending their empire, left little time to these three first Pharaohs of the eighteenth dynasty to devote to the arts of peace ; but Amenhoteb I. constructed a portion of the temple of Karnac, and Tutmes I. built in front of its sanctuary those halls, pylons, and obelisks which adorn the southern side.

The death of Tutmes I., followed in a very short time by that of his son, B.C. 1630. Tutmes II., placed Egypt under the rule of a female sovereign, who had already acted as regent, the Queen Hatasou, whose reign perhaps marks the period of Egypt's greatest material prosperity, if not of military splendour. Her efforts seem to have been mainly devoted to the extension of commercial relations with neighbouring states, and more particularly with the coasts of the Red Sea. The temple of Deir el Bahari was raised to commemorate her successful expedition into Pount (Arabia Felix). On the walls we see her sending her troops to collect such treasures as could be found in the land of spices ; we see them successful, the soldiers drawn up on the coast of the Red Sea, the water of which is apparently so transparent that the fishes are visible ; the inhabitants of Pount leave their cupola-roofed dwellings and bring the scented gum in heaps ; the Egyptian fleet is receiving the valuable cargo, consisting of bales of goods, earthen jars, and live

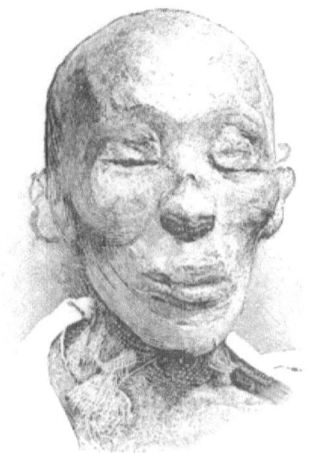

Mummy of Tutmes II.

animals ; journeying with sail and oar, they reach Thebes, and the different items are counted out at the feet of the Queen, in the presence of the god Ammon, who congratulates her Majesty.

At this time the nation seems to have returned to the luxurious habits which had been prevalent prior to the invasion of the Hyksos. Sumptuous feasts were apparently the order of the day; singers, musicians, and dancers contributed to the entertainment, while slaves handed the guests the different dishes crowned with flowers. Enormous sums were consumed in funeral ceremonies; the funeral barge was hidden beneath the luxurious offerings; professional mourners and slaves stood on the decks; and the embalming art, assisted by the spices and aromatic perfumes from Arabia and the Sommali Coast, reached its perfection.

B.C. 1600 (?).   The Queen Hatasou was worthily succeeded by her second brother, Tutmes III., who is said to have undertaken thirteen campaigns in his reign of fifty-four years. His conquering armies reached Cape Guardafui and the Indian Ocean; Babylon, Tyre, and the Lebanon paid him tribute; and large numbers of prisoners were employed to till the fields in place of the children of the soil, enrolled as soldiers. Nor did the glories of foreign conquest prevent him from adding to the treasures of his capital; he erected a temple on the left bank, adorned several Egyptian towns with the obelisks which now disgrace the principal cities of Europe; and he enlarged Karnac, of which he sketched out the general plan. Upon its walls we find a list of 115 cities subdued by Tutmes, possessing peculiar interest because they furnish a table of the Promised Land, made 270 years before the Exodus. Among the cities are Kadesh, Megiddo, Damascus, Beyrout, Acre, Jaffa, Migdol, and Rehoboth. An authority who cannot be suspected of sectarian prejudice, the late Mariette Bey, says: "No doubt whatever can exist. If these limits are not precisely the same as the tenth chapter of Exodus assigns to the land of Canaan, at all events these hundred and fifteen names carry us to the very centre and heart of that far-famed country. The data are certainly very precise with regard both to chronology and geography."

B.C. 1546 (?).   At the death of the great Tutmes, the Syrians seem to have thought the opportunity favourable for a revolt, which was suppressed with considerable severity by his successor, Amenhoteb II. Of his successor, Tutmes IV., we know little beyond the legend on the Sphinx, telling of his good intention to restore that monument. He was probably a mighty hunter, like Amenhoteb III., who succeeded him, and who is reported to have killed a hundred lions with his own hands during his reign. But the third Amenhoteb was more than a shekarri; he carried his victorious arms far into the Soudan, and continued to exact tribute from Mesopotamia. He built also the whole of the southern portion of the temple of Luxor, the northern temple of Ammon, the temple of Mout, the alley of Sphinxes leading to the temple of Khons, and the imposing edifice which stood behind the two Colossi on the west bank, both of which represent himself seated in the hieratic posture. The upper part of the more northerly of the two was destroyed by an earthquake twenty-seven years before Christ, and the accident added a spurious celebrity to its deserved fame. From the headless trunk came forth, with the first rays of the morning sun, a ringing sound like the human voice. Hard science may now explain it as due to the cracking of the stone, wet by the morning dew and heated by the sun, but the more imaginative Greeks and Romans heard in it the voice of their favourite Memnon appealing to his divine mother, Eos, the Dawn. There came from all parts of the known world pilgrims to behold the miracle, and to write their testimony to its truth at the foot of the god. Among other autographs is that of Sabina Augusta, consort to Cæsar Augustus, and of Vitalinus Epistrateges of the Thebaid, who brought his wife, Publia Sosis, and of two poetical gentlemen, an Italian, Petroniamus Dillius, and one Gamella, who, as a good *père de famille*, brings also his "beloved spouse Rafilla and his children." Alas! the miracle only lasted two centuries; for Septimius Severus thought, as others have thought since with equal success, that he would work a great reform in Egypt. He would improve on Memnon; he would impart beauty and clearness to the voice. What could be easier? A few blocks of sandstone, and it was done. The reform was effected, but the sound was effectually smothered, and the god remained for ever silent. O Septimius Severus, first of occidental reformers! thy successors exist in the nineteenth century!

Of Amenhoteb IV. we only find traces in a singular religious revolution at the instance of his foreign mother, Aten. He seems to have returned to the more primitive sun-worship of his forefathers, and changed his name from Amenhoteb, Peace of Ammon, to Khuenaten (Reflection of the Sun), to have effaced the name of Ammon, and substituted that of Aten on the monuments, and to have transferred the capital some 150 miles north to a city he founded and called Khosaten, now Tel-el-Amarna, where he and two or three successors reigned. But Horus or Horemheb, last of the eighteenth dynasty, re-established the cult of Ammon at the capital of Thebes, building the two southern pylons and the avenue of Sphinxes, which connects the first pylon with the temple of Mout.

Still the authority of the eighteenth dynasty seems to have suffered a shock, and the people, tired of their rulers for nearly 250 years, appear to have made an internal revolution, which resulted in the accession of the great family of Ramses and the nineteenth dynasty.

CHAPTER XV.

B.C. 1452 (?). OF the Ramses who established the nineteenth dynasty, little is known beyond the fact that he was the father of Seti I., Merenptah (Beloved of Ptah), and that he probably designed, though his son completed, the famous hypostyl hall at Karnac. Upon its walls are recorded the campaigns of Seti against the Armenians, the Arabs, the Assyrians, and the Hittites. The Armenians are depicted felling timber for the conqueror, who drives in his chariot a horse named "Strength of the Thebaid." Here he pursues and pierces with arrows the flying Arabs, who take refuge in a fortress; and here, returning victorious from his campaigns, he is receiving on the banks of the Nile the principal functionaries of his kingdom, who have come to welcome him. Seti was the first who appears to have conceived, and even probably carried out, the idea of connecting the Red Sea and the Mediterranean. He gave particular attention to the education of his son, the great Ramses, whom he caused to be instructed with other young Egyptian nobles, and possibly with Moses; for we may assume that the princess who adopted the future lawgiver was a daughter B.C. 1420 (?) of either the first Ramses or his son Seti. Ramses II., the Great, the legendary Sesostris of the Greeks, succeeded his father, probably about 1420 B.C., and reigned for sixty-seven years. If other periods were equally prosperous, this at least must be considered as the reign during which Egypt reached her highest military renown. Throughout Egypt, and beyond it, we meet the records of his victorious arms. The empire stretched to Dongola in the south, to the Tigris in the east, and to Asia Minor itself. Probably little of his long reign was spent in his magnificent capital, but he completed the temple of Goornah, the hypostyl hall of Karnac, built the surrounding wall of the temple, added something to Luxor, and left in the Ramesium a monument not unworthy of the glorious son of Seti.

The walls of Karnac and of the Ramesium are covered with the records of his exploits. Here, in the Ramesium, we find him engaged in battle with the Hittites on the borders of the river Orontes, near to Kaderu. The Egyptian generals do not exactly appear to have distinguished themselves, unless, indeed, they were conspiring to assure the renown of their sovereign. At all events, they have left him alone, even deserted by his escort, and surrounded by his enemies.

Nothing daunted, he charges alone the chariots; the enemy fly in terror; some are crushed under the wheels of the chariot and the feet of his horses; others are killed with arrows from the king's own hand, among them "the chief of the vile Hittites," and the rest are drowned in the river. On the opposite side of the bank is the scene after the battle. Ramses is seated on his throne, none the worse for his single-handed fight against a host. His officers, showing some moral if not physical courage, come to tender him their congratulations, and are received with a reproach which we cannot deem too strong for the circumstances. "Not one among you," he says plaintively, "has behaved well in thus deserting me, and leaving me alone in the midst of the enemy. The princes and captains did not join hands with me in fight; by myself have I done battle; I

Bazaar in Luxor.

have put to flight thousands of nations, and I was all alone." Ramses appears to have been very proud of his exploit, as well he might be. To put to flight a nation is something; but to put to flight thousands of nations is not, he fancies, an everyday exploit; so he reproduces it again upon the second pylon, and at Luxor, at Karnac, and at Ipsamboul. And that there may be no doubt as to the accuracy of the narrative, a poem on the subject by the great Pen ta Our is inscribed in the hypostyl hall, and near it the treaty of peace which followed with Khetu Sar, king of the Hittites, in the twenty-first year of Ramses's reign.

B.C. 1353 (?)   Seti II., also called Merenptah, succeeded his great father, of whom he was the thirteenth son. The monuments of Egypt give us few records of the reign, which perhaps possesses for the modern historical student more interest than any other period of Egyptian history. For while Ramses II. had been gathering for himself and his nation glory and extended territory abroad, there was growing up nearer home a difficult social problem, such as exists in some

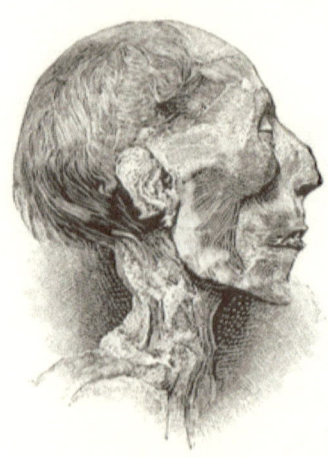

Mummy of Ramses II.

parts of Europe at this day. The seventy Hebrews, forming the family of Jacob, who had settled in the land of Goshen during the reign of the Hyksos, had rapidly increased and multiplied during the 400 years which had elapsed. We need not waste time in statistical calculations as to whether the seventy souls could increase in that space of time to the 600,000 men, exclusive of women and children, who, according to the Scriptures, left under the guidance of Moses. It is at least highly probable that other families from across the border gradually amalgamated, by marriage or otherwise, with the tribe of Jacob. What is certain is, that the industrious, saving, and even then comparatively intellectual Hebrew, had gradually acquired not only the best of the land, but some of the most lucrative appointments in the land, where they still regarded themselves only as sojourners. History repeats itself; and we have only to realise the popular prejudice regarding their descendants entertained to-day in Russia and Germany to understand the similar position which they held more than 3000 years ago in the Valley of the Nile. Nor was the order given by the great Ramses to the Egyptian midwives more repugnant to humanity than the proceedings of anti-Semitic court-chaplains of our own day. The order, at all events, was not obeyed; a future leader was saved for the chosen people by the interposition of one of the royal house itself, Moses the scholar, at On, or Heliopolis, near Memphis. Clemens of Alexandria and others tell us that Moses rose high in the service of Ramses; actually commanded an army

A Portion of the Temple of Medinet Abou.

T

sent to the Soudan, and founded on the Nile a city which he named Meroë, after the daughter of Pharaoh, to whom he owed his life, and for whom he still maintained a grateful affection. Whatever foundation of truth there may be in the legend, it is certain that when the great Ramses died he left his successor a difficult problem. The chosen race were still a great and prosperous people, and now led by a chief of ability and experience. The well-known biblical story of the Exodus it is needless to repeat; the partial confirmation that exists of it in the Egyptian records is less generally known. It is certain that Seti II. (Merenptah) was engaged in war with the Libyans, and was at the same time exposed to considerable danger from Semite tribes in Asia. The request of Moses to lead his people into the desert would very naturally alarm the Pharaoh, an essential part of whose policy it would be to prevent the union of the Israelites with other cognate tribes; but the records give an account of the expulsion of lepers, which is undoubtedly the Egyptian account of an event which reflected no glory on their history. The defeat of Pharaoh and his host probably combined with other causes to shake the power of the nineteenth dynasty; its history becomes obscure until, in the year 1288, the twentieth B.C. 1288. dynasty opens with the accession of Ramses III., who, if he could not surpass the warlike fame of his great ancestor and namesake, was successful in several campaigns, and endeavoured to excel him in the magnificence of his buildings and the decoration of his capital. He finished the temple of Khons, excavated the tomb now ridiculously known by the name of Bruce, and built Medinet Abou. On the walls of this last temple it is that we see so much of the life of Egypt under this the last of her warrior-kings. In the private palace we see the great monarch at home, surrounded by his family. One of his daughters brings him flowers, with another he plays draughts, and a third, who is offering fruits, he caresses by way of thanks. Little scenes like these are perhaps as interesting as the more glorious exploits which are also recorded. Here are portraits of his captives, apparently drawn from life, " the vile chief of the Hittites," a people for whom the Ramses seem always to have reserved their choicest epithets; another "vile chief of the Amorites;" the chief of the Teucrians from Asia Minor, those of the "country of Sardinia, which is in the sea;" the chief of the Arabs from the frontier along the Isthmus to Suez, the country of Tuscany, which is in the sea; the chief of the vile race of Negroes; the chief of the Libyans, and others who are less easily identified. Here, too, are representatives of various glorious expeditions against the Libyans, Pelasgians, Siculi, Dannians, Oscans, and others; and here he returns from battle, preceded by his prisoners in chains, whom he offers to the gods of Thebes. On one wall we may see, in a series of ten pictures, the whole history of a campaign against the Libyans and Teucrians, in the ninth year of Ramses. Only the necessities of space compel us to abbreviate Mons. Mariette's description. First goes the king, with his troops in marching order; in a large battle, in which he personally commits fearful slaughter, the Libyans are vanquished 12,535 of the enemy are killed, and the prisoners brought before the king. The king addresses the army under arms, who are again marching out to battle. This time the Teucrians are overthrown, the women and children flying in chariots drawn by oxen. The march is renewed through one of the fastnesses

of the Lebanon infested by lions, one of which the king kills. Then takes place the one Egyptian naval battle of which we have record. The scene is at the mouth of a river. Teucrians and Sardinians attack the Egyptians; Ramses stands on the shore, and his archers contribute to the Egyptian victory; one of the enemy's vessels is floating keel upwards. The army returns back to Egypt, and stops at Migdol, where the dead are counted by the number of hands cut off on the field of battle, and the prisoners pass before the king, who harangues his sons and generals. Then triumphal return to Thebes and general speech-making—"speeches from the gods, speeches from the king, speeches even from the prisoners themselves, who entreat the king to spare their lives, that they may long celebrate his courage and valour."

B.C. 1110.   Of the long line of Ramses who composed the twentieth dynasty, none, with the exception of the first of them, seem to have inherited any of the glory which attached to the name, and after a hundred years we find that they have given way before the priestly twenty-first dynasty of San : the military prowess of the Ramesides has been replaced by the priestly craft of the Tanis hierarchy. How did the change come about? Here, on the walls of the temple of Khons, we discover something of the history of the increasing usurpation of the priests of Ammon. In the hall of eight columns we see the high priest Her Hor, not yet indeed arrogating to himself the regal titles, but from the place reserved for kings alone addressing the god in the joint name of himself and the weak king by his side. And in another hall we see the next step : all disguise is thrown aside, and Her Hor appears with the urӕus, or sacred asp, on his brow, his name enclosed in the royal double cartouche. On the pylon we see his priestly successor, Pinotem, soon also to become king. From this point the sun of Thebes began to decline. Unable to rule, the priest-kings attempted to conciliate, and had to give way to Sheshonk, the Shishak of Scripture, who founded the twenty-second or Bubastite dynasty, who built the outer court of Karnac, where we find the record of a victory gained by Shishak. The gods bring

Mummy of Pinotem II.

him the towns which he has conquered. The twenty-ninth cartouche was read by Champollion as Joudah Melek (king of Judah), and until recently was recognised as a portrait of Jeroboam, though Brugsch has since maintained that there is nothing to justify this supposition.

During the twenty-third and twenty-fourth dynasties Egypt was hard pressed B.C. 810-715. by the Assyrians from the north and the Ethiopians from the south. Seven hundred and fifteen years before Christ, the Ethiopians under Piankhi, who had previously taken Memphis and returned south, effected the conquest of Egypt, and established the twenty-fifth dynasty.

For only fifty years, however, were they able to hold their throne, and during B.C. 715-665. that period the valley of the Nile was the bone of contention between Ethiopia and Assyria, the former continually trying to effect a coalition of its neighbours against the latter. Marching to the aid of Hezekiah, the Pharaoh Shubataka was defeated by Sennacherib ; a few years later, in Egypt itself, his successor, Tirhakah, was defeated by Esarhaddon. An unsuccessful revolt was followed by the complete annexation of Egypt to Assyria, and Thebes, the glory of Egypt, was pillaged. "Yet was she carried away, she went into captivity : her young children also were dashed in pieces at the top of all the streets : and they cast lots for her honourable men, and all her great men were bound in chains " (Nahum iii. 9, 10).

But Egypt was not destined to remain to Assyria longer than to Ethiopia. The conqueror had divided the county into twelve provinces. Psammetik, one of the twelve governors, allied himself by marriage with the family of Shabako, the legitimate heir of the Ethiopian dynasty, and, assisted by Ionian and Carian mercenaries, assumed the crown of Egypt, and founded the twenty-sixth or Saite dynasty.

B.C. 665-527.   Under the Saite dynasty, the star of Egypt seemed for a moment to rise again from obscurity. Greek mercenaries were established near Bubastis ; and encouraged by the decline of Assyria, Psammetik attacked the wealthy seaports. Necho, his successor, also attacked Assyria, defeated Josiah, king of Judah, the ally of Assyria, at Megiddo, but was himself defeated by Nebuchadnezzar at Karkemish. Necho is perhaps still better known by his attempt to join the Red Sea, not with the Mediterranean, but the Nile. Warned by an oracle that it would only benefit strangers, he desisted. Perhaps if his successors of some 2500 years later had also obeyed the oracle, it would have been better for Egypt, if not for the world. Hophrah, of the same dynasty, felt strong enough to attack the growing power of the Babylonians, tried to raise the siege of Jerusalem for Zedekiah, and when his efforts failed, accorded hospitality to the exiles. Defeated by the king of Cyrene, his mercenaries revolted and pro-claimed as king Amasis, who further encouraged Greek colonisation, gave to the adventurous colonists the port of Naukratis, and died, to be succeeded by his son, whose defeat placed Egypt under the domination of Persia.

B.C. 527-406.   The Persian rule of over a hundred years, under Cambyses, Darius, Xerxes, and his successor, is known as the twenty-seventh dynasty—a history of con-
B.C. 406-340. tinual revolt, finally successful, followed by a rapid succession of various conquerors and pretenders, who alternately displaced each other. This period
B.C. 340-332. is mainly remarkable for the visits of Herodotus and Plato. In B.C. 340 the Persians again recovered their authority, and eight years later Egypt fell, with the rest of the Persian Empire, under the authority of the great Macedonian.

Although the temple of Deir el Medinah and the two grand portals of Karnac mark the care of the Ptolemies for the old capital, the glory of Thebes, "the princely No of the waters," had long departed. Thebes was, above all, the city of Ammon and his triad—Ammon, the visible, tangible form of the creative force in nature, the symbol of that hidden force which presses all things

Temple of Luxor.

forward towards life and light, aptly symbolised by the sun ; and with him were associated, first, Mout, the eternal mother, the recipient in which is accomplished the mystery of creation ; and then, to complete the triad, Khons, who is Ammon himself in another form—Ammon Khons, the son of Ammon the father and Mout the mother, God of the rising life, representing the operation of divine intelligence in the outer world—his own father, his own son, without beginning or end, uncreate and eternal.

At Prayer.

CHAPTER XVI.

THE party would willingly have spent at Thebes as many days as they were allowed hours, but the *Cleopatra* was quickly under weigh, scudding past the lively little port of Luxor, and waving a farewell to the genial old Mustapha Agha. For the Pasha was inexorable ; the romantic associations of the past must, he insisted, give way to the financial exigencies of the present, and, as a conscientious servant of the Khedive, he could not afford the time to trifle with the Pharaohs. And though the Pasha spoke lightly, the rest had had ample experience that, if he took care that the journey should be one of pleasure to them, it was one of hard work for himself. The others might study Ramses ; Crichton himself was apt to groan at the restless energy of his chief, his insatiable appetite for the minutest details, the most intricate statistics extracted by cross-examination of fellaheen ; while Sara was unable to settle in his own mind whether the information of the one party or of the other was least valuable or most inaccurate.

"Both tell lies," he argued meditatively ; "Egyptians told them 15,000 years ago. You believe them monuments, and Pasha believes them Fellahs : I don't believe nothing," he added solemnly.

"But," said the Sketcher, "you can't be continually seeing these ruins and have no respect for them ; you must admire their size at least ? "

G. MONTBARD.

BAPARD

Arab School in an Old Temple of Luxor.

"I 'sure you, sir, I never saw 'em before, 'cept passing by in boat. I don't stop here ; ain't no taxes to be got out of ruins," said Sara contemptuously.

"Is it possible ? Well, but now you have seen them, you must have some opinion about them. How were they built ? "

"I ain't got no opinion at all of ruins," persisted Sara ; "never found 'em of any use. How were they built ? I tell you," he said confidentially, "with the kourbash ; same way as Ismail get taxes. You think it not more difficult get money out of Fellah than build up them stones ? " he added contemptuously.

"Ismail seems to have left some admirers, at all events," said the Nabob. "I suppose the secret is that he had a strong hand, and all Orientals, like children, would rather be bullied than spoilt."

"I don't know that there was much liking in it," said the Scribbler. "The days of Ismail were the days of high interest, the days of licensed peculation, of unjust privilege to those who could pay for it. That is sufficient to form an Ismailite party among all those who, having either money or position, were anxious to make the most of it. As for those who had neither one nor the other, nobody cared for their opinion, even if they had any, and, as a matter of fact, it always follows that of the others. One of the greatest blunders we can make in Egypt is to suppose that any material improvement in the country will make us popular. It is the exact reverse ; and if I wanted a proof that we were doing some good, it would be the fact of our unpopularity."

"That's rather a disheartening prospect."

"Possibly, but it's perfectly natural, and it's well to face it. The poorer and less educated classes, comprising at least six and three-quarter millions out of the total population of six millions eight hundred thousand, are, if not absolutely without an opinion of their own, utterly unable of giving expression to it, except in accordance with the will of the remaining wealthier, and possibly better educated, fifty thousand, or the majority of them. I believe that you may accept that as an axiom ; and I believe there is no country in the world where a very small minority hold, if they choose to use it, such an enormous power over public opinion. And now for the composition of that minority. A portion are wealthy proprietors, who were able formerly to avoid full taxation, to use the *corvée* for the cultivation of their fields, to get water at the cost of smaller proprietors, who got none, and who were nearly all proprietors of slaves ; another portion are officials in responsible situations at small salaries, with very large illegal perquisites ; another portion, officials with rather larger salaries, holding absolute sinecures ; another, contractors, who could make contracts with the Government at exorbitant charges, and perhaps by falsification of their accounts, accompanied by baksheesh, get paid even more than their originally exorbitant charge; others were capitalists, who, owing to the financial disorder, were able to get exorbitant interest on their money, and thus either make large profits or live on the interest of a very small capital; and others were religious fanatics. Now, note how every single possible reform must touch one of these classes. You insist on getting in taxes from the wealthy proprietors; you refuse the use of the *corvée;* you distribute equally the water; you prohibit purchase of slaves and destroy their value; you refuse to wink at baksheesh, and practically reduce an official to beggary, for they are unable to earn a penny; you dismiss the sinecurists; you make your contracts by public tender at lowest price, and introduce competition from Europe. By all this, you so improve the finance, that a man gets five per cent. where he used to get twenty, and the small capitalist is no longer able to live. And then you are surprised that you are not popular."

" But do you mean that all this has been done?" asked the Nabob.

" No," said the Pasha; " if it had been, we should have made the country too hot to hold us. We can't, for instance, get rid of all the sinecurists, and if we did, they would be at our charge for pensions; but we have done a good deal of it, and what the Scribbler says is true. The nearer we approach to perfection, the more certain we are to be disliked; and the fact that we are disliked is a proof that we have done much good."

" But surely the poorer cultivator, the man who had previously to pay for all mismanagement, corruption, &c., who didn't get his water, and who had to pay baksheesh, must find the difference, and prefer the new state of things?"

" Not in one case out of ten thousand," said the Scribbler. " Nor is it quite so extraordinary as it seems. In the first place, the difference to him has not been so apparent as you might suppose. In Ismail's time he had the high range of cotton prices of the American war; it gradually came down long before his deposition, of course; but there were always the reserves of the enormous profits made at that time, when, as it is popularly said, every dollar's worth of cotton fetched a sovereign, and prices of grain were high compared to now. Had Ismail had to do with the prices of produce we have had to deal with, it is impossible that he could have got on. In such a case, the Fellah would have been absolutely destitute, irredeemably ruined. But all this he does not see. He recognises that he has only now to pay his regular taxes instead of taxes *plus* exactions; but the price of his produce having gone down, the result to him is not so much better. The benefit he would have received from the reforms has been to some extent neutralised by other circumstances, and so he doesn't see it.

What he does see is, that the produce of his land produces less cash sterling, and, like more intelligent farmers, he abuses the Government for low prices. Another thing is, that, with rare exceptions, a Fellah does not save, does not look ahead, and only regards his debt as an unfortunate circumstance involving a yearly payment. If he has a good result in his year's farming, he spends it; if he has not, he tries to borrow, and spends that. Under Ismail, at some rate or another, he could always borrow, and so could always spend. Now he cannot borrow so easily, so he seems to have less money. He undoubtedly lives better, is housed, clothed, and fed better than he was twenty years ago; but he disregards this, and tells you that living is dearer, instead of admitting that he lives more extravagantly. Add to all this the fact that, as I say, he takes his opinions from the fifty thousand who suffer by our interference, and that his fanatical feelings are kept alive, and you will understand why the opinion of the majority is not pronounced in our favour."

"But are the bulk of the people really so hostile to us?" said the Pasha. "I doubt it."

"Remember that my whole argument is that the bulk of the people have no opinion of their own. Still, if you were to poll the people to-day, you would certainly find nine against, for every one in favour of, our remaining. And yet who can say? for when it came to the critical moment, I expect you would see singular hesitation. Those who have to gain by disorder, those who, as in Arabi's time, hoped to get clear of their debts, would welcome it in the hope of a disturbance; and the prevalence of the feeling would so alarm the men who have something to lose, some of the very classes who now want us to go, that you might see a complete change. You must remember that the leading characteristic of the Egyptian throughout all time has been to be 'agin the Government.' So long as we are here, we are the Government, and are hated. The moment we were gone, and perhaps before, our virtues would be sung in every village to the detriment of our successors."

"And when will the English troops leave?" asked the Sketcher.

"Bah!" said the Nabob; "who would venture to fix the date?"

"I will," said the Scribbler quietly; "I will fix it with extreme precision. Do you remember that man at Luxor who tried to sell us a coin with the date legibly marked 1156 B.C., and who couldn't be got to see the absurdity of a date which must have implied a gift of prophecy? Well, I will fix the date in the same way. The English troops will leave Egypt in the year 2 B.A., that is, 'Before Annexation!'"

"You mean"——

"I mean that within six months of our departure there will be a riot, anarchy, and financial collapse. The Powers who have guaranteed the last loan will insist on the restoration of order. England, allowing no one else to interfere, will have to return, and, giving her eighteen months to decide on a step which will then be inevitable, will annex Egypt, or, what is the same thing, assume the Protectorate."

"To look at that village, you might almost have annexed it already," said the Sketcher, as they passed the pretty little town of Erment. "You only want a spire instead of that minaret, and you have a Thames village. That house there would do excellently for a parsonage. There's the manor-house, with its garden running down to the river; and absolutely that's the village pub, with its signboard at the side of the main street."

The background of desert somewhat destroys the accuracy of the comparison, but there is certainly an un-Egyptian air in the neat little town near the site of the old Hermanthes, and Cleopatra seems to have left some of her beauty in the neighbourhood of the little temple, where she is represented adoring the local Apis of Hermanthes. Opposite is the minaret of Tuot, showing the site of the ancient Tuphium, and beyond the singular cliffs of Gebel Ayn; passing under which, the Pasha gave the order to halt at Esneh. Satiated with Karnac, the Nabob declined to accompany the Sketcher to the temple, declaring that he had not come to Egypt to examine a temple of the Caesars, with sculpture pronounced by the best authority to be "of the very worst execution," and defaced with vulgar puns and *double entendres* in hieroglyphs. Compelled to rely on his own resources, the Sketcher wandered aimlessly through the

An Arabian Singing Girl of Esneh.

modern town, and was rewarded by the sight of one of the prettiest bazaars in Upper Egypt. At first sight, it seemed as if the white houses and streets of Esneh were mainly inhabited by pigeons; rows of narrow streets afforded a shaded desert, with singular absence of life; but suddenly he found himself at what he first mistook for the entrance to a private house. A respectable old Sheik, however, invited him to enter, and the narrow covered gateway, lit by sunbeams that broke through the imperfect roof, gradually widened out into a bazaar, where seemed congregated all the life of the province. Through it rode leisurely swarthy negroes on camels, bringing in produce of all kinds from the adjacent villages, as well as more rarely a few bales of merchandise from the Soudan. Here was the shop with the invariable Man-

Bazaar of Esneh.

chester goods, and a stately Ghawazee wandered listlessly among the crowd, shaking her tambourine

Bazaar of Esneh.

in hideous coquettish fashion at the most respectable elders of the city. Moslem, Copt, and Jew mixed in friendly gossip; and the Sketcher, who, as we have said, was apt to generalise, returned with elaborate theories on the manners and customs of the inhabitants. In particular, he desired it to be recorded, for the benefit of the future historian, that the principle of religious toleration was carried to the extreme; for he averred that the chief Rabbi, to whom he had been introduced, wore a costume which combined the Islamic slippers with an Evangelical Geneva gown, and a turban folded in palpable imitation of the Papal tiara.

The Pasha's business finished in a few minutes, the *Cleopatra* was off again with all speed to reach Edfoo, and soon left behind the dilapidated pyramid of El Koola, the red mound of Hieraconpolis, the not tempting-looking ruins of

El Kab, coming at sunset in view of the portico of the Ptolemaic temple with its porpylon towers. Begun under Philopater, it took ninety-five years to build, and nearly as many more to decorate. Constructed on the same plan as Denderah, it was evidently adapted for the same purposes. Four masts, nearly 150 feet high, and decorated with long pennants, rose from the pylon, which apparently served no other purpose than to signal from afar the edifice. We may dismiss it with the words of Mariette: "The temple of Edfoo is one of those monuments which speak for themselves, and to which no description can do justice."

"That," said the Sketcher, when they got on board, "is a sentence worthy of Herodotus. Nothing is so delightful in the Father of History as the way in which he conceals his ignorance; he would have been the *beau idéal* of a newspaper correspondent. The Egyptians," he says, "represent Pan with the face and legs of a goat, as the Greeks do, 'but why they represent him in this way I had rather not mention.' He knows all about the most expensive manner of embalming, 'the name of which I do not think it right to mention.' He knows, omniscient man, why they sacrifice swine to Bacchus and abhor them at all other festivals, 'but it is more becoming of me not to mention it.'"

"Perhaps," said the Scribbler, "the old Egyptian found some connection between swine and the worship of Bacchus. But say what you will, the more I know of Egypt, the more convinced am I of the value of Herodotus. There's a singular passage in which he tells how the Nasamonians followed up the river, and bending to the west, came

Chief Rabbi of Esneh.

upon a diminutive race, 'less than men of middle stature,' describing accurately the Niam-Niams, who exist to this day. He gets horribly mixed up with the Ister later; but then he admits this to be only the conjecture of Etearchus. The actual report, though only at second-hand, is proved correct. About the rise of the Nile, again, he has got the right explanation, though it's true he scoffs at it. But where he shines as an observer of mankind is in his recognition of what I will call the contrariness of the Egyptian. 'Other nations in weaving throw the wool upward, the Egyptian downward; women attend markets and traffic, but the men stay at home and weave; others feed on wheat and barley, but it is a very great disgrace for an Egyptian to make food of these. They knead the dough with their feet, but mix clay and take up dung with their hands; other men fasten the rings and sheets of their sails outside, but the Egyptian inside; others write from left to right, the Egyptian from right to left.' In this last he was not quite correct, for they wrote both ways, but it is singular that the introduction of Arabic has justified his prophetic assertion. To this day, if a man is badly off, he is spoken of as eating wheat. The observer of to-day may mark that the men walk in the road and the donkeys on the footpaths; while in parts of the country you may see them sowing first and ploughing afterwards. Ask an Egyptian where his ear is; he will take up his right hand, pass it all round his head, and hang on to his left ear. The Egyptian people were created upside down."

Arab Scribes.

CHAPTER XVII.

THE *Cleopatra* sped onwards next morning, and passed through the narrow cleft of Silsilis. The low mountains here on either side seem to have been willing to combine in an effort to close the magnificent stream, which disdains their efforts and rushes noisily by. Here is a monument, one of the few of Horus, last king of the eighteenth dynasty, with a picture of Horus nourished by the goddess, and then too the well-known picture, the triumph of Horus—the king borne by twelve officers of his army, two other officers bearing the flabellum over his head, returning after his triumphant expedition against the Kouch, &c., led as trembling captives behind him.

On sped the *Cleopatra ;* passed Ombos with its Ptolemaic temple, destined to become the prey of the river, rushing from the Cataracts, now so near ; for soon appears Assouan itself, a fertile oasis in a desert, with the island of Elephantine beyond, "a mosaic of vivid green, golden sand, and black syenite." The view of Assouan is singularly effective as one approaches from the north ; the town lies below, bending down to the river from a rich slope of green, and beyond and all around the bleak desert, and overtopping all the desert crags, surmounted by the town of Syene. Those who have passed through the fertile valley of the

View of Aschuan.

Nile, who have seen the desert with its fearful waste hungrily bordering on the verdure and standing thirsting before them, can realise the terror of the prophecy, " I am against thee, and against thy rivers ; and I will make the land of Egypt utterly waste and desolate, from the tower of Syene even unto the border of Ethiopia " (Ezek. xxix. 10).

There are Egyptian troops still here, and the English Colonel comes down to welcome the glad sight of Anglo-Saxon faces. Truly the British officer is a wonderful man, and a martyr to his uniform. The heat of an Assouan sun cannot make him dispense with the regulation tight-fitting jacket, and the gallant officer comes on board as if dressed for parade. Alone with one other compatriot English officer, he takes his daily meals off tinned meats, bully-beef, and dry bread, in a miserable hut, with the same stately solemnity as if at his own regimental mess-table. Every night the glass of *vin ordinaire* is solemnly raised, and the health of the Queen drank in silence, followed by that of the Khedive. But let it not be thought that only in this observance of form does Colonel ———— maintain his English habits in the far desert.; His men, Egyptians though they be, are as smart as if liable at any moment to be called out for inspection ; and at any and every moment they are liable to be called to man the forts, and to prepare to receive an imaginary enemy. For the benefit of the party the alarm-gun is sounded, and in a moment every man is at his place, every gun loaded and run out, waiting the command to fire. But from the bleak hills away to the south there is nothing but silent desert, the Nile rushing beneath, and a sight of the lovely island of Philœ. Riding round the fortifications, the gallant Colonel, whose face is so well known in the neighbourhood of Piccadilly and Pall Mall, has yet an eye for every weak point, every defect in detail, and a kind word of approval for the young subalterns, who have none of that sullen, discontented appearance which was so striking in the days when they were under Egyptian or Turkish officers. Not a word of regret has the Colonel for the time which some men might think he is wasting here. Perhaps, it is true, he has a shrewd idea that his service in Egypt may help him with the constituency whose votes he hopes to win at the next general election ; but none the less is his heart and soul in his work. Juvenal, he thinks, made much too much fuss about his exile to Syene ; his liver must have been out of order when he indited those terrible Satires. Assouan is charming ; he finds the Egyptian climate and Egyptian troops equally perfect. One grievance only has the gallant Colonel, and that is against the well-meaning old ladies who write to remind him that "they also that uphold Egypt shall fall ; from the tower of Syene shall they fall in it by the sword." That quotation, as the tower of Syene is his messroom, he thinks in bad taste; but he lets out an extra length to his waistbelt, pats himself comfortably thereon, and says cheerfully, "But I never felt less like falling in my life."

"But will your men fight, Colonel, as well as they look?" asked the Nabob.

"That's the question that every one asks, and every one answers differently," replied the Colonel, "forgetting that 'fight' is a relative term. They'll certainly not bolt, as they did at Tel-el-Kebir; nor will they perhaps ever carry entrenchments as we carry them. But remember that the Egyptian soldier is a perfectly new experiment; you can't expect a people who have been treated as curs for several thousand years to suddenly develop the qualities of lions. You can't expect men dragged unwillingly from their homes, ill-fed, ill-clothed, and unpaid, to develop any of the *esprit de corps* which is the first quality of a soldier. But treat them well, pay them regularly, and above all, feed them well, and I am much mistaken if in time you don't make good soldiers of them, so long as you have good officers to lead them. Without that, your Indians are useless, and so will these men be."

"But in five years or so the army is going to be handed over to the Turks," said the Sketcher.

"Then in six years or so," said the Colonel, "the army will certainly be worthless, and probably a danger. Whether you might have made a native army with Turkish officers five years ago, is a question; but, without suppressing another rebellion, you certainly will not do it now. However, here we are at the station, and there's your train."

The station was indicated by a pile of luggage and merchandise, on which was lying the Pasha, surrounded by a crowd perhaps the most varied and picturesque that could be gathered even in Egypt. The Fellah, the Barabras, and the Nubian, to which one has become accustomed in the journey up the river, here mix with tribes from the interior and from the far Soudan; Bishareens who have come from Berber, Ababdehis, and even a few Hadendowa, mingled with Abyssinians, Turks, and Greeks; and here and there the Nabob found a few Indians, to whom he graciously condescended to speak in an apparently unknown tongue.

Loaded camels were seated lazily munching from their burdens of fodder with grumbling content; a few packets of gum, ostrich feathers, and ivory lay on the ground; anxious traders squatted around, eagerly scanning the countenance of the Pasha, and trying to gather from it some faint hope that commerce would re-open and the river be available for traffic; in little groups some new-comer from the south was relating his unhappy experiences to eager listeners; and the whole appearance of Assouan was one of depression. Drawn up against a tumbledown building dignified with the name of station was a train of a few trucks, a dilapidated carriage, and a worn-out engine, looking as if they had been dropped there some years before, and were utterly incapable of motion.

"We've not," said the Sketcher, "to travel in that thing, have we? You're not going to blight my last hopes, and send me across the desert in a locomotive, are you?"

"I'm afraid I'm going to blight your hopes even more effectually than that," said the Pasha. "Here's a telegram calling me back to Cairo. I've tried hard—assisted, I must admit, by a telegraph clerk—to misunderstand it, but I couldn't manage it. It's too fatally clear even for an Egyptian to muddle, and back I must go."

"What! at once?"

"Well, luckily for you all, the steamer has got to take in supplies, and won't be ready to leave till to-morrow; that just gives us time to get up to Philœ, and shoot the cataract on our way back. Sara here has arranged everything."

News from the South.

"And we miss Korosko and Wady Halfa?" said the Nabob.

"And Abu Simbel?" wailed the Sketcher.

"Well, as far as I'm concerned, yes; but of course you are not bound to return with me. You may take your chance of Cook's boat in a week, or any postal-boat, for that matter."

"I have travelled with a Pasha," said the Sketcher, "and will descend to nothing meaner; but do you mean to say this wreck and skeleton is capable of taking us to Philœ?"

"We must give it a trial, at all events," said the Pasha, "for it's our only chance. The Mudir has the greatest respect for it, however, and assures me it will go as fast as a camel, and do the eight miles in less than an hour."

Into it the party got, and with much coaxing, groaning, and shrieking, the engine was got under weigh. Every single turn of the wheels was made as if with an effort, and with frequent pauses, as if to take breath. Its path seemed to be the trackless desert; but Sara said there was a man on the engine who knew the way, and so it proved; for finally stopping, as if from sheer exhaustion, there lay below the river, hurrying on to the rapids, and the beautiful isle of Philæ in its silver lake.

For the river, landlocked by sombre red mountains, looked, but for an occasional palm tree, more like a Scotch lake than an Egyptian river. Behind lay Elephantine, with its gentle slope covered with tumbledown huts, and all around the sharply defined mountain ranges closed in the view; while Philæ, like an enchanted isle, seemed floating in the midst. In spite of the weighty authority of the Tourist's Bible, it must be doubted whether anything to be seen in or from the island itself can compare with the view of it from the river. Other views in Egypt are remarkable for the magnificence of the panorama which they afford or the historical associations which they evoke; but the view of Philæ is nothing but one of pure beauty. Perhaps even one loses by going on shore; for Philæ excites no feelings of grandeur to swamp those of irritation to which the vulgar records of tourists give rise. The temple of Karnac is the embodiment of the majesty of Egyptian art; Philæ is the point at which we see that majesty blending with the pure beauty of Greece. The scene of ruin almost heightens the effect of Karnac; it jars with the beauty of Philæ. We look away from the black rocks; we hear the distant roar of the Cataracts, speaking of rage and strife; and we recognise in the lovely island the abode of Peace. We care not to see the records of triumphant monarchs, still less of such as Tiberius, Caligula, and Claudius; nor the vandalic record of Desaix; let us rather regard it, correctly or not, as the abode of Hathor and Isis.

The boat is waiting; the Pasha is stern, and will admit of no more delay. The Sketcher gives one last look southward, and to the cry of "Allah Illah Allah, Rasoul Allah," the boatmen send the little craft into the middle of the stream. The pace quickens, but by no effort of the oars; and Sara is seen in confidential talk with the Reis. Suddenly the boat pulls to shore.

"What on earth is the fellow at?" asks the Pasha.

"Stop! stop! never mind!" says the Reis; "very good donkey."

And then on the bank is visible a group of screaming donkey-boys urging their animals to the shore.

"What, in the name of Osiris, is the meaning of this?" says the Pasha; "put out into the stream at once."

But the Reis has jumped on shore, and Sara has followed him. "He

Elephantine Island.

say, your excellency," replied the latter, "that it's very dangerous; that no boat could do it at this time of year."

"Tell him to go on at once."

Then the Reis and the Mamoor fell on their knees; they begged and beseeched the Pasha to abandon the wild attempt. They were poor men; they were the slaves of his excellency; they would die for him, do anything for him, but not go down the Cataract with him.

The Pasha got exasperated. "This is all rubbish," he said, appealing to the others; "hundreds do it every year, and we must do it."

"Let's do it without him," said the Sketcher, airily seizing an oar.

"Thanks! no," said the Scribbler. "All this is merely a part of the usual business, to increase the merit of obedience. We've only to sit still and

it'll be all right; there's no danger whatever so long as the Reis is here; but if the Sketcher wants to take charge, I prefer the inglorious ease of mine ass."

"Look here, Sara," said the Pasha; "tell him I've no time to lose, and let him get into the boat at once."

Meanwhile Sara had been having an earnest conversation with the Reis, and having himself got on *terra firma*, which he had no intention of exchanging for the boat, seemed much more willing to support the views of those who were foolish enough to show less prudence.

"He say, your excellency, he very willing take all these other gentlemen, but dare not take you."

"And why on earth am I to be excluded?"

"Well, your excellency, he say not mind kill other gentlemen, if they give him certificate they don't mind; but he say that if he kill your excellency he be hanged!"

Sara gave the explanation with the air of one who felt that there was much in the argument.

"Tell him we have decided all to die together," said the Sketcher.

"Tell him he shall have four napoleons," said the Scribbler.

The eyes of the Reis twinkled. "Make it five," he said.

"You go at once, or you shall be hanged, whether I'm drowned or not," said the Pasha.

The Reis is convinced that his excellency means business. "It is the will of Allah," he says; but there are too many in the boat, and one Inglez must go with Sara to testify that the Pasha went to death of his own will. Crichton is made the Jonah, and the boat starts again. But before starting, every sailor strips, and displays a physique that would put to shame the weak-kneed Fellaheen of the Delta. At the last moment slips on board a coal-black little nigger, who takes the party under his protection. "You not be 'fraid," he says; "me, Homer, here—all right."

"Allah Illah Allah, Mahmoud Rasool Allah!" cries the Reis; "Issa el Nebbi!" shout the sailors.

Up the stream goes the boat, cautiously approaching the mid-current, a few inches at each stroke.

"Hold tight!" says Homer, and suddenly, with a swing, the boat's bow wheels round twice, and we are in full stream.

Very gently move the oars now, for they are not needed, and only kept near the water to steady her; quick flies the boat, and the whirl of water lashes angrily against the black boulders on either side.

"Bab ya Abu Bab! Bab ya Abu Bab!" cry the sailors in monotonous chant; and the old Reis sits grim and black in the stern, with watchful eye on his men and grim eyes ahead.

"Now he come!" said Homer, with a merry twinkle that was reassuring.

"Great Ammon! look at that rock ahead," whispered the Pasha.

The Sketcher made a movement as if to rise, but a hand was on his throat. "Sit quiet!" said the Reis, with a look that was positively demoniacal.

The big rock got nearer, and the Reis, apparently frantic with anxiety, screamed his directions at the top of his voice. Back screamed the sailors angrily, as if in mutiny. "Allah help us! great Bab help us!" rises in agonising cries.

"By Jove! we're into it," said the Pasha.

"Don't waste your strength fighting with the stream," said the Nabob quietly as he slipped his arm out of his coat.

A big wave seemed to lift the boat into the air and to be about to dash it on the big black rock. A look of horror came over the Reis' face with one despairing shriek, as, skimming on the very crest of the breaker, the boat gave a turn at right angles, passed the rock to starboard at a yard's distance, gave two rapid turns completely round, and was riding placidly in swift open current. Homer gives a wink and says, "All finish!"

The Reis looks solemn, and says, "Very clever; plenty baksheesh!"

"Confound the fellow! I was taken in," said the Nabob.

"Well, you kept your head wonderfully cool anyhow," said the Pasha.

"Never tell me the Egyptians are incapable of governing again," said the Sketcher; "I feel that fellow's hand round my throat now, and the raven-like look in his eyes, as he bade me sit quiet, makes me still shiver to think of."

The Scribbler for a while was silent, then he said solemnly, "I was in a towering funk, and the worst is that's the third time I've been taken in in the same way!"

A long row, which the previous excitement rendered doubly monotonous, brought the party to Assouan, exhausted, cross, and hungry. Only Sara was up to the mark, and he improved the occasion. "Never no need be afraid at all when with Arab," he said. "Arab nearly big coward as thief; he never go where there danger. I done them cataract often and I never afraid." And Sara strutted the deck as a hero of a hundred cataracts.

CHAPTER XVIII.

THE next morning, before daylight, the *Cleopatra*, under orders that everything was to give way to speed, was rapidly going down river with the
stream. One stoppage at Luxor only was to be allowed, and another day was
to bring them to Assiout. The weariness and excitement of the previous day
had been calmed by a peaceful slumber of the whole party on the broad deck.

Head of Sayce.

Sara had dreamt away his feeling of superiority,
and had again become the most submissive of
interpreters; the Pasha was hard at work dis-
secting figures with Crichton; the Sketcher was
filling his book with sketches from river and
shore; while the Nabob and Scribbler were
pacing the deck.

The conversation had begun on their experience of the day before, but had drifted into a
discussion as to the character of the Egyptian
of to-day.

"When," said the former, "you deny the
existence of any popular opinion in the country,
surely you ignore the Arabi movement."

"Please understand," said the other, "that
I do not ignore the existence of a popular
opinion. On the contrary, I not only admit it,
but define it. There is one, and one only; it is that of being 'agin the Government;' and I am not urging it as a reproach; it is perhaps the strongest characteristic of every race, except the Anglo-Saxon, and it is growing there. If I were
a Fellah, I should hold it myself; just as, if I were a Russian, I should be a Nihilist.
With the experience an Egyptian has had, it is unreasonable to expect him to be

anything else but what he is, 'agin the Government;' or to expect that by five years good legislation you can subvert the rooted and inherited idea of centuries. With that idea the Fellah has other personal ones; he is sensual and covetous of land. Arabi had that idea, but had nothing else. The history of all fads teaches us, that when a man is possessed of one sole idea, he can easily find converts, even among the indifferent; how much more so when that idea, in an indistinct form, permeates the whole community. The first people with whom Arabi came in contact were the soldiers. Naturally, then, the first to give expression to it was the army. They declared 'agin the Government;' so far it was a purely military revolt, furthered by individual dislike and jealousy of certain Turks. The authorities temporised with the officers, and the result was the soldiers got all they asked. Is it wonderful that the people, seeing this, went with them? They too had grievances; they had debts! 'Abolish all debts,' said Arabi, and the people cried 'A Daniel come to judgment!' If that is a popular movement, I give it you; only, is there any man who could not lead on such terms? Is there any people who would not be tempted? What about 'the three acres and a cow' in England? Well, Arabi's offer was all the acres and all the cows, and the people were, if possible, still more ignorant."

"You believe, then, there was no feeling but that of self-interest through the whole of it?"

"Stop a bit! there is no need to go so far as that. We have got to this point—a strong selfish feeling in favour of Arabi, the man of one idea. Now enter political intrigues of Europe. England shows a disposition to support the authority of the Khedive; that is sufficient to induce, I will not say the French Government, but the French colony in Cairo, to take the other side. The first people to give the movement any importance were Franco-Egyptian officials. If they could only get Arabi to act with them against the English, what annoyance they might cause! what a triumph for *la grande nation!* They held meetings of the colonels in their houses, they talked to them about the national sympathies of a republic, and so forth. Arabi began to feel himself a power, and enter a second idea—ambition; not, too, altogether an unworthy one, let it be said; only the ill-directed ambition of an ill-educated, not vicious man, led by others less ill-educated and more vicious. Why should he not do as Ismail had done, and play France against England. Still, I believe the Government of the Republic acted fairly, and straightforward common sense would have triumphed. Arabi was on the point of giving in; his movement had gone far enough to have compelled the two Powers to pay more attention than they had done to the internal affairs of the country—to the legitimate grievances of the

country, which Arabi had never pointed out, but to which public opinion had
been drawn by his movement. But, unfortunately for Egypt, there came on the
scene Mr. Wilfrid Blunt, a man to whom every subsequent wrong committed in
Egypt, either by one side or the other, must be attributed—upon whose head

Seller of Sticks.

must lie the full weight of all the blood and treasure
which has been poured out in the country since 1882.
And of course—is it necessary to say it?—is not the
worst evil done by well-intentioned men?—no man ever
came to Egypt or acted throughout with purer motives.
Consumed with an exaggerated idea of his self-import-
ance, not because of his talents, which were great, but
because he had some remote connection with Lord
Byron, the unfortunate man thought it his mission to
regenerate a fallen race. He looked for Greeks, and
found Egyptians, for Missolonghi, and he found Crabbet
Park and the constituency of Camberwell. His genuine
enthusiasm, ridiculous though it was, had its effect on
Arabi, and at first a good one. Even at this moment, I would not say that
he may not have aroused in the poor, ignorant, noisy Fellah colonel a glimmer
of some real patriotism. He recognised in Blunt all the real qualities he possessed—honesty, conviction, real singleness of purpose. He saw such a man as
an Egyptian has never conceived of—a man who was really not working for his
own pocket. He saw it and believed. But if Arabi saw and understood it, his
less scrupulous allies did not; to them this man, who came to them with
sympathy and money, was evidently a powerful Pasha in his own country. As he
could not have come for nothing, and as they could not see how he was to gain
anything in cash, it was evident to them that he was an emissary of his Government. Sir Gladstone was evidently jealous of Sir Malet, and was trying to
thwart him; such things daily happened among their own people, why should it
not be so with Englishmen. The obvious conclusion was, that England was not
in earnest, that she was afraid; and all this, poured into the ears of the simple
Arabi, smothered the better feeling that was perhaps rising in his nature, and
spurred him to further resistance. And as if to confirm the idea, the British
Government acted precisely as an Egyptian acts when he is afraid. First they
bullied, then they cringed; first they threatened, then they apologised. Fleets
were sent, but they were apologetically small; ultimatums got to be called pen-
ultimatums, so frequent were they; and all the time France was whispering, "We
will never permit it," and Blunt whispering, "England does not mean what she

says," till Arabi really became a power and the ruler of Egypt. Then he lost his head, became deaf to all control, and the brutal instincts of the Egyptian in power asserted themselves. Then began the persecution not of Christian and European alone, but of Copt, Jew, Berber, and of every race that was not plain senseless Fellah. No Turk, not Ibrahim himself, ever displayed the same unscrupulous, cold-blooded cruelty. The chiefs of the Inquisition were actuated by the highest motives ; so probably was he when he introduced tortures which would have done credit to their ferocious ingenuity. Then at last came the bombardment ; of which we may say it was a folly rendered necessary by previous folly, but too foolish in its method of execution for any folly to justify. There were fifty ways in which at one time we might have avoided it ; when it became inevitable, there were fifty pretexts we might have chosen, all more or less good, and fifty precautions we might have taken, all more or less efficacious. I defy any one," said the Scribbler, " to find a greater proof of imaginative genius than was shown by the British Government in avoiding every one of those different courses, pretexts, and precautions—in discovering a policy which rendered the bombardment inevitable, a pretext which rendered it ridiculous, and an absence of precaution which ensured it being fatal. I stand aghast even now when I think of the superhuman ingenuity which was displayed in committing every possible blunder. Let no man ever contest

Coptic Native of Egypt.

Mr. Gladstone's genius. His intellectual reputation may rest on his achievements in Egypt. We may deprecate the policy, we may deplore the results ; but as a mere intellectual effort, the discovery of a policy which should commit every possible blunder and avoid every possible advantage, it was unparalleled."

"But, 'returning to our sheep,'" said the Nabob, "you must admit that even after the bombardment, when England had shown she *was* in earnest, Arabi was still able to raise the country, and put some 60,000 men under arms."

"Your quotation is more appropriate than flattering. 'Poor sheep! they scattered you,' says the admiring Blunt, adding, from the vantage-ground of the Oriental Club, 'I care not if you fled.' You say Arabi raised 60,000 men, but you omit to say what he raised them for. Ismail, you, or any other man in power could raise five times that number of Egyptians to work day and night,

without tools, pay, or clothing, almost without food, at cleaning the canals.
What Arabi did was to get 60,000 men or more, who, in exchange for food,
clothing, and pay, undertook to do—what? To stand behind an earthwork with
a gun. Why, it was holiday for them on full pay; they had never had such
a good time before, and they were even willing now and then to help to make
an earthwork or to fire a gun ; but when it came to fighting—no, that was not
in their contract, and they bolted. No greater rubbish has been talked than that

Shoeblacks.

about Arabi's powers of organisation. As for his powers of
administration, take the three acts associated with his short
term of power—first, the lowering of the rate of interest by
decree ; second, a pension law which gave full pay to two
generations ; and third, a suggestion that the sentences of
the judicial tribunals should be submitted to the Minister
of War—that is, himself—for approval before becoming
executory. Myths always die hard, but the Arabi myth
seems destined to survive every shock. Lady Gregory did
much towards its creation. In a charming little paper she
represented the stern patriot in the bosom of his family,
with an adoring wife and mother, who hung on his lips, and
regretted that his high dignities absorbed his attention.
About three months later Arabi has to go into exile in
Ceylon. The adoring wife and mother refuse to accom-
pany him, and find other consolers, as does Arabi himself. Blunt paints
him as the pure-minded patriot, aghast at the cruelties of the age. He gets
into power ; becomes, outwardly, a fiend in human shape—inwardly, a
spiritual mystic ; sees dreams, and tortures his enemies by the direct command of Heaven ; is at once the tool and figurehead of all the scoundrels
in the country ; preaches resistance to death, and bolts before the first shot.
Comes crawling back to Cairo demoralised and abject ; delivers himself up
through sheer want of courage to resist ; cringes for his life, and will sell that
of all his companions to gain it—and yet the myth lives ! ' Ahmet Arabi, the
Egyptian !' he claims the title ; give it him ; it describes him better than pages
of rhetoric ; for when has the Egyptian ever been anything but the cringing,
lying, cowardly slave, or the cruel, rapacious, cowardly master?"

" Then it's needless to say you don't believe in Egyptian self-government,
or Egypt for the Egyptians ? "

" Egypt for the Egyptians certainly ; but Egypt by the Egyptians, no ; for
your only way to keep Egypt for the Egyptians is to give them a government

which governs for the Egyptians. If you could really leave the Egyptians to
govern themselves, the result in the future would be the same as in the past
—they would succumb to the Ethiopians, to the Soudanese; the weaker would
be sure to go down before the stronger rule. In no period of history has there
been an independent Egypt except under foreign rulers. Our mission in Egypt
is to see whether we can educate the people to self-government. We are more

An Egyptian Village.

likely to be able to succeed than any other foreign ruler; and those who, like
Blunt, believe in and hope for such a consummation, should be glad to see us
there. Once we go, the only question is whether the next conqueror shall come
from the north or the south—from Europe or the Soudan."

"But are we doing anything towards educating them for self-government?"

"Nothing, or next to nothing; and that is the real vice of our occupation.
We started with two false ideas, two totally incompatible promises,—the one

that we would reform the country; the other, that we would evacuate shortly. Either was possible without the other; the two together were impossible. To reform the country, we should ourselves have assumed the whole direction of the

government; we should have devoted much attention to education; we should have had responsible heads of each separate department, and have gradually trained up our successors. Little by little we should have been able to surrender to them the management under a general control, and at the end of one or two generations we might have made a self-governing Egypt. But we had promised to evacuate; time hung over us like a Damocles' sword; we would not touch this, we would not attempt that, because it would require too much time. We would employ Armenians, Syrians, or such ability as we could find in the country, because it was useless upsetting the old system for so short a time; and thus we have left untouched the greatest abuses, just because they were the greatest, and required the time we were unable to give. We talk of reforming the country, and we ignore the internal government, the administration of justice and education."

"Then you mean that we have done nothing?"

"By no means; we have done much; we have to some extent restored the finances, and we have improved the irrigation; we have controlled many arbitrary practices; we have lessened corruption and cruelty; we have organised a fairly disciplined and contented army. All this is much, and undoubtedly the lot of the Fellah is considerably ameliorated; but it is all temporary and evanescent. If we go to-morrow, it falls within six months. It is an excellent building, good, solid, and adapted to all existing needs; but it is a temporary one, without any foundation; and when we go, we carry it off on our back."

"What's that you are proposing to carry off on your back?" said the Pasha, sauntering up to the pair; "Philæ or Karnac?"

"Neither; but something between the one and the other," said the Scribbler; "a pretty edifice based on ruins."

"I'm weary with reading Arabic parables," said the Pasha, "so condescend to be less figurative."

"I was saying that when you go, you will carry your whole financial adminis-

Bedouin Sellers of Horn.

tration with you, that being the temple of Philœ, and that you will leave behind you the financial ruins of Karnac."

"Heaven forbid that I should carry off Sara," said the Pasha, laughing ; "I've left him trying to turn into Arabic Shelley's ' Ode to the Nile.'"

"I suppose it betrays consummate ignorance," said the Nabob, "but I never knew that Shelley ever wrote an ode on the Nile."

"Very few people do ; and though it sounds blasphemous, I don't know that one loses much by not knowing it ; but here it is :—

> " Month after month the gathered rains descend,
> Drenching yon secret Ethiopian dells,
> And from the desert's ice-girt pinnacles,
> Where frost and heat in strange embraces blend
> On Atlas, fields of moist snow half depend ;
> Girt there with blasts and meteors, Tempest dwells
> By Nile's aerial urn, with rapid spells
> Urging those waters to their mighty end.
> O'er Egypt's land of memory floods are level,
> And they are thine, O Nile, and well thou knowest
> That soul-sustaining airs and blasts of evil,
> And fruits and poisons, spring where'er thou flowest.
> Beware, O man, for knowledge must to thee
> Like the great flood to Egypt ever be."

"I'm going to be still more wicked than you," said the Scribbler, "for, Shelley's though the lines be, they seem to have every vice of poetry, with none of its redeeming features. The metaphor is involved ; floods are level in most places ; the atmosphere of Egypt is body-prostrating rather than soul-sustaining ; the floods do not bring poisons ; and the last two lines are rubbish. But listen to this, also Shelley's, on Ozmandyas :—

> " I met a traveller from an antique land
> Who said : ' Two vast and trunkless legs of stone
> Stand in the desert. Near them, on the sand,
> Half sunk, a shattered visage lies, whose frown,
> And wrinkled lip, and sneer of cold command,
> Tell that its sculptor well those passions read,
> Which yet survive, stamped on these lifeless things,
> The hand that mocked them and the heart that fed ;
> And on the pedestal these words appear :
> " My name is Ozymandias, king of kings :
> Look on my works, ye Mighty, and despair ! "
> Nothing beside remains. Round the decay
> Of that colossal wreck, boundless and bare,
> The lone and level sands stretch far away.' "

Or this of Keats, written in competition with Leigh Hunt and Shelley :—

> " Son of the old moon-mountains African !
>   Stream of the Pyramid and Crocodile !
>   We call thee fruitful, and that very while
> A desert fills our seeing's inward span :
> Nurse of swart nations since the world began
>   Art thou so fruitful ? or dost thou beguile
>   Those men to honour thee, who, worn with toil,
> Rest them a space 'twixt Cairo and Decan ?
> O may dark fancies err ! They surely do ;
>   'Tis ignorance that makes a barren waste
> Of all beyond itself. Thou dost bedew
>   Green rushes like our rivers, and dost taste
> The pleasant sun-rise. Green isles hast thou too,
> And to the sea as happily dost haste."

" Now, as we've nothing to do all this afternoon but watch the Eternal Nile, I propose that we should try and evolve something better than Shelley or Keats. The Scribbler, of course, will do it easily, as he criticises so freely."

"Excuse me, but that's illogical," said the Scribbler. " Because I criticise the cut of your tailor, it doesn't follow that I'm bound to prove my right to criticise by making a better pair of breeches ; but I'm quite willing to undertake finding you something better than those lines you've just read."

"Agreed !" said the Pasha ; "and I elect myself judge—competition verses to be read during dinner."

It is in descending the river that you see it at its best. The Gebel Silsileh stand out with a bolder front approaching them from the north than from the south. Edfoo breaks upon you at a sudden bend of the river, from which you see the long reach to El Kab, and then come sweeping down on Esneh, with its rows of palms. The north wind blowing fresh in one's face mitigates the oppressive heat of the sun, and curls up the river in dancing waves. At sunset the *Cleopatra* was approaching Luxor ; the sun setting behind her threw the long shadows of her mast on the water ; and ahead the spires of Karnac seemed to be apparent through a broad faint rainbow, which on the horizon spanned from desert to desert.

"That, if anything, ought to inspire poetry even in the Scribbler," said the Pasha. "Now, then, competitor of Shelley, strike the lyre !"

"My lyre has no pretence to originality," said the Scribbler. "I've heard the Nabob trying for the last half-hour to get an appropriate rhyme to 'face.' Let him begin."

"All true poets," said the Nabob, "require time to polish the efforts of their genius; but as I believe I'm the only one who has the moral courage to brave your sneers, I accept the challenge, and await annihilation. Read!" and he passed a paper to the Pasha.

"'Father of waters!' I knew every one would begin with that :—

> 'Father of waters! thou whose stream hath borne
> Earth's sons for ages past thy banks serene,
> So bear thou us ; nor visit with just scorn
> This land of noisy revellers, who, between
> Sun rise and set, with jest and laughter keen,
> Deride the beauties of thy classic face.
> Forgive our mirth ; nor yet for what hath been
> Invoke revenge, since now, with soberer face,
> In fear we move, and humbly ask for grace.' "

There was a pause, till, with an effort at appearing unconscious, the Nabob said, "What a splendid propylon!"

"I'm wondering why the banks are 'serene,'" said the Scribbler.

"If you were not possessed with a mean spirit of envy," said the Nabob, "you would recognise that it was the only available rhyme. But now, your own!"

"I've none of the divine afflatus, my dear fellow, and wouldn't dare to go into competition with you. It is merely over Shelley that I claim a superiority for Leigh Hunt. I knew these lines before I knew the Nile, and don't think that the river itself has made me know them better :—

> ' It flows through old hushed Egypt and its sands,
> Like some grave mighty thought threading a dream ;
> And times and things, as in that vision, seem
> Keeping along it their eternal stands,—
> Caves, pillars, pyramids, the shepherd bands
> That roamed through the young world, the glory extreme
> Of high Sesostris, and that southern beam,
> The laughing queen, that caught the world's great hands.
> Then comes a mightier silence, stern and strong,
> As of a world left empty of its throng,
> And the void weighs on us ; and then we wake,
> And hear the fruitful stream lapsing along
> 'Twixt villages, and think how we shall take
> Our own calm journey on for human sake.' "

"Yes, after that we may all be silent," said the Pasha; "it's a fitting preparation for Karnac by moonlight, and here we are at Luxor. I must go on shore here for at least half-an-hour, but you may as well drop down to the temple, and I'll join you there later."

An hour later the Pasha joined them in the hypostyl hall.

"Conceal your joy," he said; "I've found you a fellow-passenger. I came to the conclusion we were all getting tired of one another; the Scribbler has exhausted his politics, the Sketcher his block notes, and the Nabob his poetical genius."

"We're doing very well as we are," said the last-named. "Who on earth have you got?"

"A man of one idea, who is dying for converts. We've only got to stand him for a day; and he's original, if nothing else. He's generally known as the Professor, though he resents the title as derogatory, for he tells you that he has passed beyond the professing stage, and considers his theories so absolutely proved that they require no demonstration."

"But what is his particular theory?"

"I wouldn't tell you for worlds—first, because it would anticipate the intellectual repast you are going to have to-morrow; and secondly, because I've never been able to get to the bottom of it. He joins to-morrow morning before we start, and you'll have had more than enough of it before you get to Asyoot. So come on board, turn in, and prepare for a tedious day.

Types of Bedouins.

CHAPTER XIX.

The new arrival—Sleep a luxury—The sleepless Joseph—Joseph the creator of Egypt—A new theory—Fayoum and the Land of Goshen—The Bahr Jussef the work of Patriarch Joseph—Tradition of Murtadi—The creation of the Fayoum—An original derivation—The field of Zoan and the land of Ham—Israelite exodus—Did they cross the Nile ?—The blessing of Jacob—Jacob's will and testament—A new reading of an old text—Qualified approbation—Back to Shepheard's.

THE next morning the Nabob was awakened by a shrill voice—"Yes, that will do—that will do. Thank you—certainly—of course—of course. Throw it on board; don't make a noise, and on no account wake anybody ;" and a bulky carpet-bag came against the Nabob's head, and nearly rolled over the side.

"Are there many more coming ?" said the Nabob rising, and holding the first projectile as a buffer to ward off any further attack, "or may I fling this overboard ?"

"I beg your pardon a thousand times," said the other ; "I'm afraid I disturbed you ; but I cannot help looking upon your presence there as providential. But for your head, now, that might have rolled overboard," he said with a look which combined gratitude and an appeal for sympathy.

"I confess," said the Nabob, feeling his head, "I regard it in another light. The ways of Providence, at all events, seem to be one-sided in this case."

"Ah! yes; I'm afraid it may have hurt you; but if it had gone overboard the loss would have been irreparable—utterly irreparable; not to me—not so much to me—but to the world at large. The future of more than Egypt itself depends upon that bag," he said, taking his seat upon it.

"I'm glad it's safe then," said the Nabob; "but being so, perhaps, as it's early, you won't mind my going to sleep, again with a consciousness that for once my head has saved the world?" and he turned round in his rug.

"Certainly, certainly—of course, of course. I never sleep myself—never require it—never have done for years. Did you ever try to do without it?"

"I can't say I have," said the other.

"Oh, you should—you should; simplest thing in the world; purely matter of habit."

"But I can't say I've any intention of trying to contract the habit just yet; so I'll get a sleep first, and discuss it afterwards."

"Quite right—quite right; at least, no—quite wrong, quite wrong. Do you know now," said the new-comer, argumentatively, "that there's no evidence in the Pentateuch to prove that either Moses or Joseph ever slept; in fact, as regards the latter, it's conclusive that he didn't?"

The high tone of the speaker had now succeeded in awaking all the occupants of the deck. The Nabob gave it up as a bad job.

"And how on earth do you prove that?" asked the Scribbler.

"Because he could never have accomplished the work in Egypt that he did if he did so."

"I thought Joseph dreamed dreams," said the Sketcher.

"Precisely," said the other; "and that proves my proposition, for his brain never slept. So the evidence is conclusive on that point, even if we could assume it possible that he had time to sleep and yet achieve his work in Egypt."

"And what was that?" asked the Scribbler.

"What was that?" asked the Professor aghast; "what was that? Why, the making of Egypt. The evidence is conclusive that Egypt was the creation of Joseph, as I will prove to you."

"Well, before beginning, we'd better dress and have some coffee," said the Pasha.

The Professor was left pacing the deck and gesticulating to himself; he was evidently arranging an oft-repeated lecture; and hardly were they seated at table before he began.

"If you look at the first mention of Egypt in the Bible, you will find nothing to indicate that Egypt was a land of any more importance than Canaan, Sichem, Moab, and the other lands through which Abram journeyed. The dates are, of course, very obscure, but it is obvious that Egypt was then little more than a desert, blessed with a capricious river, which no one knew how to utilise. Even later, when Joseph is a servant in Potiphar's house, there is nothing to show that Egypt was a kingdom of any importance."

"But are you going to ignore all but the Bible records?" asked the Scribbler impatiently. "What about the records of stone?"

"Does your name happen to be Markham?" said the Professor; "because there's an interesting historical work by a person of that name, in which information is conveyed in the form of question and answer; and it occurred to me that you might be the lineal descendant of the sagacious Richard, the bold George, or even of the precocious Mary. You will have observed, however, that even in that work the conversations are deferred until the end of the chapter."

The Scribbler took his rebuke humbly, and the Professor continued—

"I have already said that the chronology is obscure. I know just sufficient of Egyptology to know that Egyptologists know nothing; and even if all their chronological theories were accurate, there is nothing to show that Joseph did not enter Egypt before the oldest existing relic of his greatness. Seeing that men like Bunsen and Lepsius differ to the extent of 1000 years in the date of arrival of Jacob's family, I may be permitted to go farther back than either. Or even, if I admit the pyramids as existing prior to Joseph's time, I am still correct in saying that Joseph formed Egypt, if I accept Bunsen's chronology, and date Joseph from the rise of the twelfth dynasty, when Egypt began to recover from the dark ages of the previous 400 years. The rise of Egypt began with the great famine mentioned in Scripture; that placed in the hands of the ruling Pharaoh the whole land of the country; he again placed the entire administration in the hands of the greatest administrative genius whom the world has ever seen. And Joseph introduced his own people; with their aid he raised the country to a position which it has never experienced before or since; and when the infatuated Pharaoh who knew not Joseph drove them out, he sealed the ruin of Egypt, which from that date began to fall. The early history of the Jews is the history of Egypt which they made."

"If the time for asking questions has arrived," said the Scribbler, taking advantage of a pause, "I should like to ask whether you have any proof of that beyond the imperfect one of assertion?"

The Professor loftily ignored the sneer. "The proof of it," he said, "is written in the land of Goshen."

"And where is that?" said the Pasha quietly.

The Professor drew himself together, as a man who feels that the moment of struggle has arrived.

"The land of Goshen," he said, "is the Fayoum; and what is the Fayoum?—the creation of Joseph—the Bahr Jussef."

"But, my good sir, there is not the smallest connection between the Patriarch Joseph and the canal of Jussef Salah el Din," cried the Scribbler.

The Professor smiled with lofty contempt. "The Bahr Jussef, you say, was named after our old friend, Saladin. Has it never occurred to you as somewhat

singular that this canal, which certainly existed 2000 years before the Crusades, should have been named after the hero of them? Are you prepared to say that it is probable that Saladin deliberately gave his name to a work which must then have been for 2000 years known under some other name which has completely disappeared? Such an act would only be paralleled by the ruins of Stonehenge being called the Victoria Temple in honour of the Jubilee."

"I admit there's something in that," said the Scribbler; "but the negation of one derivation isn't the proof of the other."

"Of course not," said the Professor, slightly mollified by the concession. "But now, why should you ignore early tradition, with considerable elements of probability in it, for a later tradition with no such elements in it? Whatever be Joseph's era, it is certain that he was nearer to the period of the Bahr el Jussef than Jussef Saladin. We know of no other Jussef, and tradition tells us not only that he made this canal, but the whole story of it, and adds, that prior to the removal of his bones by Joseph, he was buried by the side of it."

"And where is that tradition?"

"Here—everywhere—in the mouth of every dweller on the Bahr Jussef. Leo Africanus, writing about 1500, tells us that Medinet el Fayoum was built by one of the Pharaohs, 'on an elevated spot, near a small canal from the Nile, at the time of the exodus of the Jews;' and he adds, 'here, it is related, was buried the body of Joseph, the son of Israel.' So says also Masudi, writing about 930; and Murtadi, another Arabic writer, whose date I don't know, but whose work was translated in 1666, gives a circumstantial account of it all. The life

of Joseph Ibn Isaac fills volumes of Arabic literature; in nearly all, this work is directly attributed to him. On what ground is the tradition upset?"

"What are the details of Murtadi?"

"Unfortunately I have not the translation here, or I would read it you; but briefly it is this. When Joseph was well stricken in years, an intrigue was set on foot against him. The advisers of Pharaoh were jealous, and said, practically, 'He has doubtless been a very grand old man, but his day is past, and he is no longer what he was.' Pharaoh supported the man to whom he owed so much, and at last said, 'Well, name the thing which he cannot do, and if he fails to do it, I will dismiss him.' Then the courtiers took counsel together, and they went to Pharaoh and said, 'Bid him drain the swamp of the Reian and make it cultivable.' Then Pharaoh was sad, for he felt it impossible; but he went to Joseph and said, 'Thou knowest that I must marry my daughter, and I have no

portion to give her except the Reian, and it is a marsh.' Then Joseph said, ' I
will drain it and make it cultivable.' ' When ?' said Pharaoh. ' Now,' replied
Joseph. Then he set to work ; and here follows a long description of the existing
canals. And after some time he called Pharaoh, and Pharaoh went with his
courtiers, and the place was like a garden, so that they marvelled. And Pharaoh
said to Joseph, ' How long have you taken to do this ?' And Joseph said,
' Ninety days !' ' No other man,' said Pharaoh, ' could do it in a thousand days '
(Alph Yom) ; and so the place was called El Fayoum."

The conclusion of the legend was greeted with laughter.

"'Then Pharaoh spoke Arabic some 3000 years before Mahomet ?"

" I don't," said the Professor, "ask you to accept the legend as true in

details ; the derivation is of course fanciful and ridiculous, but so the legend has
existed from time immemorial."

" But I don't see," said the Pasha, " how it helps your theory. If the
Fayoum was only created when Joseph was an old man, it's evident that it
couldn't be the land of Goshen, where his brothers settled when he was still in
his prime."

" I repeat that the legend is only of value as showing the connection with
Joseph. Another point is worth noting—that Pharaoh had no dowry for his
daughter ; that shows that Egypt was a country of no great riches at the time
when Joseph made the canal, which was doubtless before the famine."

" You treat your legend rather freely," said the Nabob ; " you take an
isolated line, throw over all the rest, and then use the whole as a proof that
the land of Goshen was in the Fayoum."

" My point requires no proof," said the Professor ; "it is self-evident. What does all our knowledge of the settlement of the Jews amount to? Take the Scripture narrative. Instructed by Joseph, they tell Pharaoh, ' Thy servants are shepherds, both we, and also our fathers. . . . . For to sojourn in the land are we come ; for thy servants have no pasture for their flocks ; for the famine is sore in the land of Canaan. Now therefore, we pray thee, let thy servants dwell in the land of Goshen. And Pharaoh spake unto Joseph, saying, Thy father and thy brethren are come unto thee ; the land of Egypt is before thee ; *in the best of the land* make thy father and brethren to dwell ; in the land of Goshen let them dwell. . . . . And Joseph placed his father and his brethren, and gave them a possession in the land of Egypt, in the best of the land, in the land of Rameses, as Pharaoh had commanded.' All, then, that we know of the land of Goshen is, that it was (1) the land of Rameses ; (2) the best of the land of Egypt ; (3) a place for pasture. In view of the fact that we are afterwards told that the Israelites in the days of their affliction built the treasure city of Rameses, and that no place could have had such a name at the time, we must assume that the writer of the Pentateuch was using a name only given later to the place. Where was the pasture land, ' the best of the land of Egypt?' Certainly it was not in the barren desert around the so-called Tanis, as Rawlinson says ; nor in the narrow Wady Tumeylat of Poole ; nor near the sea-coast, as says Michaelis ; nor at the mouth of the river, as say Payne Smith and Wiedemann. The best of the land of Egypt given to Joseph's brethren, must have been that which was watered and drained by Joseph himself, the borders of the Bahr Jussef, that which is to this day called the garden of Egypt, recognised as Goshen by St. Jerome, by Jablonski, by myself, and by all tradition. And if farther proof were wanted, study the history of the exodus. We have got on safe chronological ground now, for it is the nineteenth dynasty, and where is the seat of government? At Tanis, say modern archæologists. What! Seti, and Ramses the Great, and Seti Menephtah ruling from Tanis ! The very idea is preposterous. And on what is it based ? On the poetical expression of the Psalmist : ' Marvellous things did He in the sight of their fathers, in the land of Egypt, in the field of Zoan . . . How He had wrought His signs in Egypt, and His wonders in the field of Zoan.' Therefore the miracles of Moses and Aaron were in Zoan, and Zoan, say the wiseacres, is San or Tanis. Now, assuming even the latter, which I am not quite prepared to admit, does the use of the word Zoan in such a connection have any geographical significance ? A few Psalms farther on we read, ' They showed his signs among them, and wonders in the land of Ham ;' and in the next

Psalm, 'Wondrous works in the land of Ham, and terrible things by the Red Sea.' So if geographical value is to be attached to such phrases, I might say that the miracles of Moses and Aaron were wrought in the land of Ham, that is, the land of Khemi, that is, the Fayoum. But I make no such argument ; the land of Zoan and the land of Ham are equally poetical expressions for the land of the Nile. But there is another reason why our sages of modern research will have it that Seti Menephtah abode at Tanis, because otherwise their land of Goshen will not bear criticism. Why, even if he were at Tanis, instead of at Memphis, where we know he was, what need had the Israelites to ask for three days' journey into the wilderness? In numbers they were stronger than the Egyptians ; and, if they were in the Wady Tumeylat, they were already in

the desert ; at all events, it barely required three hours to get there ! Ah ! but if they were in the land of the Fayoum, then indeed they were shut in, and could not pass to the desert but with Pharaoh's permission. Look at the map again, and you will see how the monarch who held the river had them in his grip. 'Memphis,' says Mariette, 'seems to have been shut in between the Bahr Jussef on one side, and the Nile on the other.' Look at your map again, and study the plague of locusts ; an east wind brought them, and a west wind swept them into the Red Sea. Why, at Tanis a west wind would have swept them into the Mediterranean or into Syria. Note, too, a singular fact, the pyramids of the Fayoum, Illahoon, and Dashour are brick pyramids ; and even Murray will tell you how some of the bricks are made with straw, and some without."

The Professor closed as one who had silenced all discussion.

" But surely," said the Scribbler, " you've shirked one great difficulty. From

The Bahr el Jusef.

the Fayoum they must have crossed the Nile, and would have wanted a special miracle to accomplish it."

"That's a fair objection," said the Professor, "but by no means insurmountable. It's more than probable that there was then, as now lower down, a bridge forming part of Joseph's irrigation works. If so, there was a good road, a golden bridge ready for them. Artabanus, an Alexandrian Jew (and Jews have always been tenacious of their own history), writing 100 years before Christ, says, 'The Jews borrowed of the Egyptians many vessels, and no small quantity of raiment, and every variety of treasure, *and passed over the branches of the river* towards Arabia.'"

"That," said the Scribbler, "tells rather against you than in your favour, for

from the Fayoum they would only have had to cross the main stream. From Tanis Zoan, on the other hand, they would have had to cross the branches."

"Then, if so," said the Professor, "you need make no difficulty about the absence of any mention of crossing the Nile. If they were where I assert, they had one main stream to cross; if they were where others pretend, they must have had at least one, and probably more branches to cross. Of neither is there any mention in Scripture. The fact is, we must not look to Scripture for detail; we find there the statement of a few bare facts; the Israelites settled in the best of the land of Egypt; they increased and multiplied to an extent which alarmed the rulers; they were intellectually superior to the race which Pharaoh governed, probably to Pharaoh himself; they became the intelligence of the nation; with their superior intelligence they were a standing danger to a despotism which can only exist with ignorance; then began the first recorded Judenhetze, continuing to this day in Russia and Germany, and wherever there is a despotic Government. Now, where did this people of 600,000 able-bodied men, probably nearly two and a half million souls, live? Do you want to make me believe that they existed in the little Wady, which is popularly identified with the land of Goshen?"

"But surely," said the Pasha, "there's nearly the same difficulty with regard to the Fayoum, the population of which to-day is barely 170,000?"

"The Fayoum to-day!" said the Professor impatiently; "but what is the Fayoum of to-day? Possibly 500 square miles; but the Fayoum of Joseph's day extended beyond the Birket el Korn, was cultivable where now it is a morass, and must have covered 1500 square miles of the richest land in Egypt. It was the only place where the olive and the vine flourished; even now it is the garden

of Egypt; and then it had 366 towns. But of course, I do not mean to say that the Israelites confined themselves to the Bahr el Jussef. The blessing of Jacob shows that they extended down both sides of the river."

"The blessing of Jacob?" asked the Scribbler.[1]

"Ah! you probably associate the blessing of Jacob with a map of Palestine nicely divided into tribes, with imaginary boundaries which never existed. We are so apt to adopt the first mystical explanation given us of anything that we don't understand, that we neglect to try and find a reasonable explanation for ourselves. Remember that Jacob died in Egypt; that he had certainly never explored the whole of Palestine; and if you accept the theory that he was

[1] To avoid any charge of "literary coincidence" or of exaggeration, let me at once admit that neither the theory of the Professor nor even the words in which it is given are original. They are to be found in a very learned paper read by a very learned man to a very learned society. I have to apologise for placing them in the mouth of the Professor. (The Scribbler's Note.)

speaking solely with the spirit of prophecy, can you give that prophecy any rational geographical fulfilment? I doubt it; and seeing that there is nothing in Scripture to show us that it was intended for a prophecy, surely we may try and find a simpler explanation of it. The Patriarch was dying in Egypt; he had seen his descendants spreading throughout the land, increasing in their possessions; and what can be more natural than that he should wish to guard against any quarrels among them by apportioning to each their territory, in the distribution of which he, under the Hebrew patriarchal system, would have full power. True, their position was due to the all-powerful Joseph; but no authority was allowed among the Jews to supersede that of the head of the clan, and we need have no difficulty in assuming that, with Joseph's consent, the old Patriarch made, as it were, his last will and testament. Now, with this in your mind, read the blessing of Jacob again :—

Jewish Native of Egypt.

' Reuben, thou art my first-born,
　My might, and the beginning of my
　　strength,
　The excellency of dignity, and the
　　excellency of power.'

"The Beni Reuben, or tribe of Reuben, were situated in that part farthest north which lay nearest to the seat of government; but the river here divided into streams.

' Unstable as water, thou shalt not excel.'

"The Beni Reuben followed the waters of the Nile, and intermarrying with the natives, tainted the ancestral blood. So far as his descendants by Reuben were concerned, the efforts and sacrifices of Jacob to preserve the purity of the race of Abraham were nullified.

　　　' Judah, thee shall thy brethren praise;
　　　Thy hand shall be on the neck of thy enemies;

2 C

Thy father's sons shall bow down before thee.
Judah is a lion's whelp:
From the prey, my son, art thou gone up:
He stooped down, he couched as a lion,
And as a lioness; who shall rouse him up?'

"Judah Jehudah—the Andro Lion—the Sphinx, or Strangler—Abu Haul, the Father of Terrors, stooped down and crouched as a lion, with his paw on the neck of the Nile, and on the Fellaheen of the Delta.

'The sceptre shall not depart from Judah,
Nor the ruler's staff from between his feet,
Until Shiloh come;
And unto him shall the obedience of the people be.'

"The temple between the feet of the Sphinx, and the broad terrace paved with basalt in front of the pyramids, survive to mark the judgment-seat of all the tribes to the north of Beni Sonef; or, in other words, until one came to Shiloh; for here Moses was born.

'Zabulon shall dwell at the haven of the sea;
And he shall be for a haven of ships;
And his borders shall be upon Zidon.'

"Zayat el Aryan marks the abode of Zabulon; Saida or Zidon, below Memphis, was the haven of ships.

'Issachar is a strong ass
Couching down between the sheepfolds:

And he saw a resting-place that it was good,
And the land it was pleasant ;
And he bowed his shoulders to bear,
And became a servant unto taskwork.'

"Issachar—Sachar—Saqqarah, near Memphis ; Men-nefer, 'the resting-place.' Within the white-walled fortress the tribe of Issachar found employ-ment, and ate the bread of industry from the lords of Memphis. Some others," continued the Professor, "are more doubtful ; but Ashur we find in the pyramids of Dashur ; and Benjamin, the wolf that ravineth, we identify with Lycopolis, the city of wolves, Assyoot. Of course, however, the conclusive proof of the whole we must expect to find in the blessing of Joseph, whose two sons, Manasseh and Ephraim, let me remark in passing, have given their names to Minieh and Beni Suef (son of Joseph)—

' Joseph is a fruitful bough (the Bahr Jussef, a branch of the Nile) ;
A fruitful bough of a fountain (the reservoir of Middle Egypt, Lake Moeris) ;
His branches (waters) run over the walls (of the valley):
The Archers (of the Sun) have sorely grieved him,
And shot at him, and persecuted him.'

"(The conflict between the Heracleopolitans and the inhabitants of the Arsinorte nome or Fayoum inflicted, as we know, irreparable damages upon the Labyrinth.)

' But his bow (the lakes of the Horns) abode in strength,
And the arrows of his hands (the canals) were made strong
By the hands of the Mighty One of Jacob
(By the Hyksos, the allies of Jacob) ;
From thence is the Shepherd (race), the stone of Israel.
Even by the God of thy father, who shall help thee ;
And by the Almighty, who shall bless thee
With blessings (i.e., pools) of (rain from) heaven above,
Blessings of the deep (Moeris) that coucheth beneath,
Blessings of the breasts (the bosoms of the Nile),
And of the womb (the bread-fields of Beni Suef):
The blessings of thy father have prevailed above the blessings of my
        progenitors
Unto the utmost bounds of the everlasting hills (Libyan range):
They shall be on the head of Joseph,
And on the crown of him that was separate from his brethren.' "

The Professor paused. "I ask you," he said, impressively, "whether that is not conclusive? You hesitate to reply. I can well believe that you are astounded; but I have not given you half my proofs yet."

"I assure you we're all satisfied with those you have given us," said the Pasha hastily; "the evidence is—well—abundant," he added, after some hesitation.

"But I have more, much more," said the Professor eagerly, foreseeing easy converts. "Are there any of you who are unconvinced?"

There was an ominous silence as the Pasha gazed inquiringly at each one. They were truthful men, but also considerate of the Professor's feelings, and doubtful of their own powers of endurance. At last, the Nabob, seeing that the Professor was hurriedly preparing fresh proof, said solemnly, "Professor, I feel convinced that, if what you have said has not convinced, nothing will."

"Sir," said the Professor, grasping his hand warmly, "I thank you for your encouragement; you shall not go unrewarded. I have this bag *full* of further proofs. I have given you only the most obvious—those, in fact, which hardly require explanation; but you shall have all the rest, which require a little more elucidation, before we get to Cairo."

"What do you all think of my guest?" said the Pasha, laughing, as the Professor walked to the fore part of the *Cleopatra* in search of further possible converts.

"His ideas are not more ridiculous than the Lost Tribe theory," said the Nabob. "I have met many such; only, as I saved you by my last speech, I rely on your sense of honour to save me from the farther proofs which he has threatened."

"Men with such theories are to be esteemed and avoided," said the Scribbler oracularly.

"And you, Sketcher?" asked the Pasha.

"I could not follow him entirely," he replied; "there were some very long quotations; but I think he said something about there being an ass at Sakkarah, bowing his shoulders to bear, and becoming a servant unto taskwork. Did he not?"

"Well?"

"Ah! well, I saw that ass; he was carrying the Scribbler to the tomb of Ti; that was a true description, but I couldn't understand the rest."

The Scribbler would have resented the reference to his sixteen stone, but the sight of the Professor coming aft caused every one to show an intense interest in the scenery, and to examine with absorbing curiosity the Sketcher's portfolio.

Late in the evening the *Cleopatra* arrived at Asyoot; a special train was waiting to carry the Pasha to Cairo ; and in a few hours our two travellers were again at Shepheard's.

From Sakkara.

CHAPTER XX

History —Egypt under the Persians, Macedonians, Ptolemies, and Romans—Bablun— Ezra and Elijah—The Mosque el Amr—A kourbashed pillar—A strait gate— The Ommiades—The Abbasides—Tûloonides—Mosque el Tûloon—Egypt the seat of the Khalifate—El Kahira—Mosque el Azhar—Mosque el Hakim—Saladin —Ayubites—Mamluk period—Mosque el Kalaun—Mosque Sultan Hassan— Legend of the Bloody Mosque—Mosque Kait Bey—Mosque el Ghoriya—Egypt a Turkish Pashalic—The generous Egyptians—Rise of Mohamed Ali—Europe in Egypt—Ibrahim—Abbas—Said—Ismail—Tewfik—French intrigues—Arabi revolt—England in Egypt—Three policies.

WHEN Egypt, with the rest of the Persian empire, had fallen under the dominion of Alexander, the days of the great conqueror were already numbered. The Ptolemaic Greek dynasty which succeeded to this portion of his empire is known as the thirty-third dynasty. Lasting nearly three hundred years, it established Alexandria as the capital of Egypt, and for a time of half the known civilised world. What we owe intellectually to this period has already been noted —the museum and library of Alexandria, the revival of learning, the Pharos, the cities of Berenice and Arsinoe, the Septuagint, the History of Manetho, the collection of Homer. From an antiquarian point of view, we have the Rosetta Stone (173 B.C.), the key by which was unlocked all our knowledge of past Egypt; the decree of Canopus (247 B.C.), the temple of Edfoo (217 B.C.), the Pharaoh's bed at Philæ (B.C. 132), the temples of Kom Ombos, Esneh, and Denderah. The battles of Philippi and Actium threw Egypt from one foreign ruler to another, and she became a province of the Roman empire (B.C. 30). Her history for the 650 years of Roman and Byzantine domination is absorbed in that of Rome and of the early Christian Church. Even a sketch of it here would be out of place. All the signs that remain of it near the not then founded city of Cairo is the fortress of Bablun at Fostat. Here was stationed one of three Roman legions, with another on the opposite bank at Ghizeh, connected by a bridge. The long dusty drive to the Roman fortress is perhaps scantily repaid by the remains visible, but those who are disposed to believe in tradition may think it worth while to visit the crypt of the Coptic church of St. Mary, where within its walls, the priests will tell you, rested the infant Messiah and his mother; or other churches and synagogues, where you may see an alleged scroll of the Thorah written by the hand of Ezra the scribe; the spot where Elijah appeared, and where Moses is said to have prayed for the cessation of the plague of thunder and hail (Exod. ix. 29). But unless it be for some carvings in wood and ivory, there is nothing of either historic or artistic value.

Within half a mile, however, we may rightly commence our survey of Saracenic Egypt with the Mosque el Amr. The quarrels of the different sects of Christian Egyptians had, as usual, facilitated the invasion of the Persians under Chosroes (610 A.D.), and similar quarrels facilitated that of the Arabs; for the Egyptians, whether followers of Ammon or Serapis, of Christ or Mohammed, were always willing to betray the existing ruler to a new conqueror. Amrou, the general of Omar, entered Egypt by Pelusium (Isthmus of Suez), went up the country to Memphis, took Bablun, and then Alexandria after a siege of fourteen months. So terminated, on the 10th December 641, and the first day of the year 21 of the Hejira, the Roman dominion in Egypt; and building Fostat, the victorious general built this, "the crown of the mosques," now called, after him, the Mosque el Amr. The greatest authority on Saracenic art[1] tells us that the mosque "has been so repeatedly restored that it is not safe to draw conclusions from its details, but it is certainly as old as the tenth century in its main outline." One cannot but bow to such an authority, and yet one is tempted to ask whether "the main outline" implies more than the foundations? For the Bill which was so altered that nothing was left of it but the word "whereas" involuntarily comes to our recollection when we try to accept the statement. Certainly a good two-thirds of the numerous columns would seem to be of very much later date, nor have they any appearance of being designed either for this or any one building. The destruction of a large part of Cairo in 1302, and the pious munificence of a Cairene merchant, who collected the debris and formed one mosque out of many, is perhaps the origin of the present Mosque el Amr. One column there is to which we may accord antiquity, and something more, according to the serious asseverations of the guardians. When Amr was building this mosque, he asked his master, the Khalif Omar, for a column from Mecca. The Khalif thereupon addressed himself to one of the columns there, and commanded it to migrate to the Nile; but the column would not stir. He repeated his command more urgently, but still the column remained immovable. A third time he repeated his command angrily, striking the column with his kourbash, but still without effect. At length he shouted,

[1] Stanley Lane Poole, "Art of the Saracens in Egypt."

"I command thee, in the name of God, O column ! arise and betake thyself to Cairo." Upon which the column went, and a vein of the marble is shown as the still visible mark of the whip. Two other columns are there of some interest. Placed near together, salvation is promised to the man who can pass between them. Ismail, it is said, came to visit the mosque. A glance convinced him that his portly form could not stand the test, so, determined that the salvation denied to a Khedive should not be granted to his subjects, he ordered the space to be closed.

After the assassination of the Khalif Ali (A.D. 661), Moawiyeh established the Ommiade dynasty, which lasted eighty years. To its credit we may place the first Nilometer at the island of Roda and the first Arab coinage, inspired by the horror of Abdelmalek ibn Merwan, who finding on the Greek Byzantine coins then in use the words "Father, Son, and Holy Ghost," substituted his own, with the inscription, "There is no God but God." The Abbasides succeeded, reigning mostly from Bagdad. They built a new quarter of Cairo, called El Askar, a Government-house, and a mosque, of which no traces remain ; and perhaps the fact that Haroun el Raschid of the "Arabian Nights" was of this dynasty forms their sole claim to our gratitude.

In 869 A.D., Ahmad Ibn Tûloon, a governor of the Abbasy Khalifs, asserted his independence while still rendering homage to the Khalif at Bagdad as his spiritual lord, retaining his name on the coinage and in the public prayers. He added to Fostat and El Askar the suburb of El Katai ; and the glory of his suburb was the mosque Ibn Tûloon. Let it be noted that the artist was a Christian, and professed to design it as an imitation of the Kaaba at Mecca. Makrisi tells us that the original idea of Tûloon was to build a mosque of 800 columns, which would have had to be taken from Greek or Roman buildings ; but with a toleration in advance of his age, he abstained from the vandalism, renounced his designs, and determined to build a mosque without columns, save two at the Mihreb or recess which points to Mecca. The work is said by the same authority to have cost £60,000, and to have occupied two years in building. The arches repose on brick piers instead of stone columns, and was the first experiment of the kind. "The bold and massive style," says Mr. Stanley Lane Poole, "recalls our own Norman architecture. . . . Three sides have two rows of arches, the fourth, that which lies on the side towards Mecca, has five. All the rows of arches run parallel to the sides of the court, so that, standing in the latter, you look through the arches. The arches are all pointed, and constitute the first example of the universal employment of pointed arches throughout a building three hundred years before the adoption of the pointed

Mosque el Amr.

style in England. They have a very slight tendency to a return at the spring of the arch, but cannot be said to approach the true horseshoe form." The effect of the long colonnades with the delicate friezed arches is unapproachable in any other building, and only partly destroyed by the senseless closing of some with masonry to form stores and receptacles for rubbish. Not long ago the magnificent courtyard was a sort of asylum for the lame, diseased, and half-witted beggars of Cairo; but happily they have been removed; and if nothing has been done to restore its splendour, we are at least allowed to contemplate it in befitting silence. Ludicrous traditions must, of course, attach

Mosque el Túloon.

to every spot in Egypt. Here, say some, Moses conversed with the Almighty; Abraham sacrificed the ram; and Noah descended from the Ark. Of the other wonders of the Túloonide dynasty nothing remains, and the reports of some of them, including the leather bed floating on the lake of quicksilver, we may relegate to the domains of fiction. Túloon's successors were unable to maintain their power, and after forty years the Abbasy Khalifs recovered their authority, to lose it again in thirty years to Mohammed el Ikshid, who, thirty years later, was unable to resist the Fatimy Khalif el Múizz from Tunis. Hitherto Egypt, though to some extent independent, had yet nominally recognised the authority of the Khalifs of Damascus or of Bagdad, towards whom their position was much that of the Egypt of to-day to the Sultan, but now (969 A.D.) for the first time Egypt became the seat of the Khalifate. Gauhar, general of El Muizz, built a palace for his master, which he styled El Kahira (the Victorious), and from this, after the burning of Fostat, developed the city of Cairo. To Gauhar

Mosque el Azhar.

also we owe the Mosque el Azhar (the Most Splendid), but of the original building little is left ; for, injured by the earthquake of 1302, it has been three times restored, nor has the result left any architectural beauty. But El Azhar is to-day worth a visit as the university of Islam. Here, seated in little groups, may be seen hundreds of students imbibing as much useless information as is consistent with systematic idleness. If the learning by rote of passages of the Koran and of the traditions, if the committing to memory of abstruse platitudes, and the repeating of sounds conveying no idea to either speaker or listener, be education, then the Mosque el Azhar is doing a great work.

The third of the Fatimy Khalifs in Egypt was El Hakim, an illuminé who founded the sect of the Druses, and whose followers still believe that he will reappear as the Mahdi or last prophet. He has left behind him the mosque called after his name, built, but much less carefully and artistically, in imitation of the Mosque el Tûloon. Little remains but the walls and two picturesque mabkharehs which dominate Cairo, and one of which was fortified by the French during their occupation of Egypt. In a corner of the large court is now

Street in Cairo.

the Arab museum, full of lovely lamps, wooden mushrebeeyah work, and other remains of Saracenic art, mainly of the Mamluk period.

The Fatemites held their own for two hundred years, until 1171, but the rivalry of jealous Viziers, and the ever readiness of the Egyptians to call in a new conqueror against the old, proved fatal to them. Then came the great Salah ed din Yusuf ibn Ayyub (better known to us as Saladin), as general to the Sultan of Damascus, to restore order. The brilliant and talented adventurer soon succeeded in getting rid of the last of the Fatimy Khalifs and establishing the Ayoubite dynasty, recognising once more the authority of the Khalifs of Bagdad.

The eighty years which elapsed before the authority of his descendants fell before the power of the Mamluks are celebrated not only in the history of Egypt, but in that of the world. If the Fatemites "had changed Egypt from a province to a kingdom, Saladin transformed the kingdom into an empire. The long struggles with the Crusaders, the victory of Tiberias, the conquest of Jerusalem, the well-known treaty with Cœur de Lion, though most familiar to us, form but a part of Saladin's exploits. He made his power felt far beyond the borders of Palestine; his arms triumphed over hosts of valiant princes to the banks of the Tigris; and when he died in 1193 at the early age of fifty-seven, he left to his sons and kinsmen not only the example of the most chivalrous, honourable, and magnanimous of kings, but substantial legacies of rich provinces, extending from Aleppo and Mesopotamia to Arabia and the country of the Blacks."

Little remains in Egypt to recall the great empire of the Ayubis besides the Citadel and the third wall of Cairo; of the mosque and palaces in the former no trace remains but the walls and part of the interior, as well as probably the deep well with its massive masonry, are Saladin's work—as also the interior of the tomb-mosque of Esh Shafiy. One other memorial of a different sort remains. The "most chivalrous, honourable, and magnanimous of kings" was touched by the petition of the Pisans trading to Alexandria, who complained that they were unable to leave the port without suffering grievous exactions at the hands of his officials, and Saladin granted in pity to the "suppliants at his stirrup" their request, that they should be made to pay nothing but their exact dues, and should decide among themselves without interference their own quarrels. From this first act of generosity, as it was then, of tolerant justice, as we should call it now, has arisen the intolerable injustice which, under the name of Capitulations, forbids the Moslem successors of Saladin to tax or to have jurisdiction over the Christian descendants of "the suppliants at his stirrup."

The Mamluks (Mamluk = owned) were white slaves, imported first by the

Ayubi Es Salik for his protection. Reinforced by continual importations, they formed a valuable mercenary militia. Under Beybass they routed the French, and brought about the capture of St. Louis himself; but the son of Es Salik was a helpless drunkard, and the Mamluks seized the power, which they held for nearly three hundred years, till the conquest by the Turks in 1517.

This is the flowering time of Saracenic art. "We are still," says our chief authority on the subject, "far from an explanation how the Tartars chanced to be the noblest promoters of art, of literature, and of public works that Egypt had known since the days of Alexander the Great" (? Ptolemy). Chief among the mosques remaining of this period are that of El Kalaun (1284), of Sultan Hassan (1356), of Kait Bey (1468), and of Ghoriya (1504).

The Mosque (mausoleum) el Kalaun is one of the most perfect in Cairo; the tomb stands in the centre, surrounded by a mushrebeeyah screen, and over it a stone octagonal baldachin with pointed arches, supported by four granite pillars and four piers. The delicate tracery and mosaic work of the tomb and walls have suffered little from the five hundred years. The columns of the Mihrab, a red stone, and an alleged turban and sash of the Great Kalaun, are said to work marvellous cures.

The Mosque of Sultan Hassan stands at the foot of the Citadel hill, and its exterior effect is undoubtedly the finest in Cairo. It looks, in fact, more like a huge fortress than a place of worship, and it was indeed frequently so used. The dome is weak and unworthy of the rest, but the minaret towers with a majestic grandeur over all the city. The splendid portal, approached by seventeen steps, consists of a square arched niche or recess with delicate stalactite; the interior is cruciform, and each of the four transepts consists of a single deep arch. That to the east is particularly remarkable, both for its height and proportions. In the centre of the east wall is the Mihrab, with two marble columns and a pointed arch vaulted like a shell, while beyond are three tiers of arches differing in style, the first pointed, the second round, and the third trefoil, set in a background of red and green marble. Behind the Mihrab, passing through a magnificent bronze plated door, we reach the singularly simple mausoleum of the founder, the great Sultan Hassan, who survived perpetual war, plague, and deposition only to be assassinated at last.

The legend of the erection of this mosque is worth reproducing :—"Sultan Hassan, wishing to see the world and lay aside for a time the anxieties and cares of royalty, committed the charge of his kingdom to his favourite minister, and taking with him a large amount of treasure in money and jewels, visited several foreign countries in the character of a wealthy merchant. Pleased

Tombs of the Khalifs.

with his tour, and becoming interested in the occupation he had assumed as a disguise, he was absent much longer than he originally intended, and in the course of a few years greatly increased his already large stock of wealth.

His protracted absence, however, proved a temptation too strong for the virtue of the Viceroy, who gradually forming for himself a party among the leading men of the country, at length communicated to the common people the intelligence that the Sultan Hassan was no more, and quietly seated himself on the vacant throne.

"Sultan Hassan returned shortly afterwards from his pilgrimage, and, fortunately for himself, still in disguise, learned as he approached his capital the news of his own death and the usurpation of his minister. Finding, on further inquiry, the party of the usurper to be too strong to render an immediate disclosure prudent, he preserved his incognito, and soon became known in Cairo as the wealthiest of her merchants; nor did it excite any surprise when he announced his

Mosque of Sultan Hassan.

pious intention of devoting a portion of his gains to the erection of a spacious mosque. The work proceeded rapidly under the spur of the great merchant's gold, and on its completion he solicited the honour of the Sultan's presence at the ceremony of naming it. Anticipating the gratification of hearing his own name bestowed upon it, the usurper accepted the invitation, and at the appointed hour the building was filled by him and his most attached adherents. The ceremonies had duly proceeded to the time when it became necessary to give the name. The chief Mollah, turning to the supposed merchant, inquired what should be its name. 'Call it,' he replied, 'the mosque of Sultan Hassan.' All started at the mention of this name, and the questioner, as though not believing he could have heard aright, or to afford an opportunity of correcting what might be a mistake, repeated his demand. 'Call it,' again cried he, 'the mosque of me, Sultan Hassan!' and throwing off his disguise, the legitimate Sultan stood revealed before his traitorous servant. He had no time for reflection; simultaneously with the discovery numerous trap-doors leading to extensive vaults, which had been prepared for the purpose, were flung open, and a multitude of armed men issuing from them, terminated at once the reign and life of the usurper. His followers were mingled in the slaughter, and Sultan Hassan was once more in possession of the throne of his fathers."

Loveliest among the tombs of the Khalifs is the mosque-tomb of Kait Bey, with its slender minaret and its perfect dome. The portal resembles that of Sultan Hassan on a smaller scale. The interior doors are surmounted by carved architraves, and above them small stalactited windows between pillars. Tradition relates that two stones, one of red and the other of black granite, were brought from Mecca, and the pious yet see thereon the impression of the Prophet's feet—a sight denied to the unbeliever. The Mosque el Ghoriya may be regarded as the last legacy of the Mamluk dynasties to Egypt, and was not unworthy of their earlier fame. Hardly had it been completed when the old Sultan seems to have recognised that he must engage in a death-struggle against the Osmanli. Fighting in the plain of Dabik against the army of Sultan Selim, he is said to have been seized with a fit of apoplexy, and died or was killed. His head was carried as a trophy to the conqueror. Within the year Selim had entered Cairo, had hanged Tonan, last of the Mamluks, at the Bab el Zuweillah, hard by old Ghoriya's mosque, and converted Egypt into a Turkish Pashalic.

True to their one never-failing characteristic, the native Egyptians assisted the conqueror; and lest we should think that at any one time within their history of seven thousand years they may have shown a generous courage or sense of independence, let us quote what Richard Knolles, writing some hundred years later, tells us of the taking of Cairo:—"But most part of the Egyptians, diligently observing the fortune both of the one and of the other (accounting them both enemies), with divers affection assailed sometimes the Turks and sometimes the Mamluks, seeming still notably to help that party whom they saw for the time to have the better."

Then, as through all time, the Egyptians sided with the for the time strongest of their conquerors, becoming obedient slaves to whoever held the rod, and having no other idea of independence than that of rebelling against one master in favour of another. From the day when the Turk assumed sway in Egypt until the day that he lost it, history and art alike cease. The triumph of the Turk is marked by ruins and by the moral, political, and social degradation of all with

Tomb of Kait Bey.

whom he comes in contact. Other Pharaohs oppressed the Egyptians, but gave to their Egypt at least a name of glory; these alone were the curse of Egypt and destroyed her place in history. Whatever may have been the motive, whatever may have been the ultimate cost, Egypt owes to Bonaparte a debt of gratitude for having even for a moment lessened the influence of the Porte, and to England must remain the disgrace of having in 1801 replaced her under that yoke. Egypt, the cause of contention of the two greatest empires of the world, was handed over to the Turk without one single stipulation for her future welfare. Never had she sunk lower, never had her condition seemed more desperate, than when, exhausted by two invasions, she again became a satrapy of the Porte. But the hour produced the man. There arose in Egypt the greatest genius whom the East has produced within the last four hundred years. Mohamed Ali was not, of course, an Egyptian; the creator of modern Egypt was a native of Cavalla, a small village of Roumelia. A simple volunteer in the army sent by Turkey, he became bimbashi or colonel of an Albanian corps of a thousand men. In four years (1805) he had succeeded in removing or crushing all his possible competitors; two years later he successfully defeated an English army which invaded Egypt under General Fraser. The massacre of the remaining Mamluks in 1811, treacherous and cruel as it may appear to European ideas, was necessary to the accomplishment of the great work to which he had devoted himself. Justice has never yet been done to that work which he accomplished in the next forty years. That work of a single generation was the creation out of chaos of a government which, at the period, compared favourably with that of many European Powers whose civilisation had been the work of centuries. History records no similar feat, and it bears witness not only to the genius of the Roumeliote, but to the adaptability to government of the Egyptian people. His successors, Ibrahim, Abbas, and Said (1849–63), did little to continue his work, but time developed it. Ismail (1863–79), a man of vast ambition and considerable ability, would probably have made an efficient ruler had his head not been turned by the extraordinary prosperity which the American Civil War produced in Egypt. The rise in the value of Egyptian produce seemed to open to him inexhaustible wealth, and he treated as ordinary, circumstances which were entirely exceptional.

The financial collapse followed; the joint political intervention of England and France resulted in the deposition of Ismail in favour of Tewfik (1879), and in Government under the dual control of those two Powers, which secured to the unhappy Egyptians three years of perhaps the most complete prosperity they have ever enjoyed (1879–82). But the system was one which could only last so long as the two Powers and their representatives acted cordially and loyally together. That condition of things existed, so far as the Governments were concerned, until May 1882, when they joined in an identical note to the Egyptian Government, and it failed when, two months later, France refused to fulfil her share of the engagements, and left the English fleet in the lurch at Alexandria. The causes of that action on the part of the French Government have only been very imperfectly understood. Briefly stated, it amounts to this. The rebellion against the Egyptian Government under Anglo-French control was secretly fomented by Franco-Egyptian officials, and at one time supported by a French representative,

Woman Grinding Corn.

while the two Governments were nominally acting in accord. It was this fact which rendered the French Government unwilling to join in the suppression of a revolt for which they were mainly responsible; and when they evaded their engagements, they were secretly allies of the Egyptian rebels, whose success they anticipated.

The victory of Tel-el-Kebir and the easy suppression of the rebellion showed them that they had miscalculated, and even the exaggerated respect of the English Government to French susceptibility has never succeeded in calming the feeling of disappointed resentment.

England, in undertaking alone the execution of joint obligations, unfortunately committed the blunder of making two totally incompatible promises—to secure Egypt a just and stable Government, and to evacuate within what was understood to be a short period. Either was possible, but each was inconsistent with the other. Repeated threats of evacuation have retarded our work, but the five years of English occupation (1882-87) have undoubtedly been of enormous benefit to Egypt. At no time has the Fellah been treated with more uniform justice and consideration, and, making allowance for unfavourable economic conditions, at no period has his material position been better. But the fabric of British reform rests on no solid foundation. It will collapse the day we leave the country, and who shall say what shall take its place? The only

possible courses are three :—First, to abandon it to the Turk, and to repeat
the disgraceful policy of 1801.   Second, to allow another European Power to
assume the position we now hold ourselves.   Third, to accept permanently the
responsibilities of the existing situation.   A fourth course may be suggested, that
of leaving Egypt to the Egyptians ; but the phrase is one without meaning, and
should be rather, abandoning Egypt to the Soudanese.

Cairo Street.

Worker in Mushrebeeyah.

CHAPTER XXI.

Cairo again—Sakkara and the Tomb of Tih—An Egyptian Pepys—Mitrahenny—
Dervishes—Home again.

THE whole party of travellers were again in Cairo, and with conscientious
minuteness the Scribbler led them through the ever-old yet ever-new city,
trying to make the worn and neglected monuments awaken the historical associations which we have endeavoured very briefly to recall in the last chapter.

The Pyramids of Sakkara indeed carried them back again to a more remote
period. On the walls of the Tomb of Tih they read the journal of that worthy
Privy Councillor of the fifth dynasty. The daily life of Pepys himself is hardly
more graphically told than that of this Egyptian of nearly 6000 years ago, who,
of humble birth, rose to the highest offices in the state, married a wife of royal
blood, whom he chivalrously describes as the "palm of amiability to her husband."
We see how his cattle were killed, how his meat was cooked, and his geese
fattened; nay, the exact list of his cattle and poultry. How his fields were
ploughed, his corn grown, reaped, threshed, and gleaned; how his ships were
built; how he fished and hunted, and how he fulfilled his sterner duties as

judge. And lastly, there is his own portrait, with the matter-of-fact remark (perhaps his own, for the tomb would be decorated for him before his death), "a good likeness;" and we may believe it, for it corresponds at least very minutely with the statue of him at Boolak.

The mausoleum of the Apis bulls, with the wondrous sarcophagi fitted exactly into their places, apparently without turning-room for their manipulation, caused our tourists to utter the same ejaculation as did "the fly in amber." There was the chamber closed for 3700 years, in which were still traceable, when opened,

Ramses II.

the finger-marks of the man who had inserted the last stone, the imprints of the naked feet which last trod the sand. So too, in the temple of King Ounas, excavated at the sole expense of the ever-enterprising Cook, were found the tools and burglarious implements of the last robbers who had penetrated it.

At Mitrahenny on their way they saw the colossal statue of Ramses II., the gift of Mohamed Ali to England, long neglected, and now being raised by private enterprise from the ditch where it long lay hid,—never, let us hope, to disgrace the "city of sweet speech scorned."

But with the exception of this excursion, the remainder of their stay in Cairo

was devoted to the city of the Saracens itself—Masr el Kahira, the city of Mars
the Victorious.[1] The wonders of Arab art, however, seemed to weigh but little

in the estimation of most of the party. The Sketcher, indeed, was never tired of the beauties of the Arab Museum,
its never-to-be-forgotten lamps, its brasswork, its traceries, and
its panellings; but the others were little moved. Hides
remarked that old brass was a glut in the market, and
doubted if the whole lot would fetch fifty dollars. The
Patrician, with superior refinement, said that they had better
work than that in Regent Street; while the Turtle looked
disconsolate, seeing no means of evolving therefrom any
question likely to be embarrassing to the Government.

So with a sigh the Scribbler
turned to the more modern as-
pect of Cairo of to-day, and
piloted them through the numerous lanes and back alleys
thronged with *sayces*, cutters of
tobacco, barbers, workers in
mushrebeeyah woodwork, dealers
in scents and articles from Bro-

A Cairo Lane.

ussa and Birmingham, Damascus and Manchester.
The graceful dance of the Mevlewi Dervishes
excited some admiration from the female members
of the party, and envy from the Patrician, who was
subsequently discovered practising the step in his
own room; but the Turtle deemed it frivolous,
and Hides averred that it was nothing to any one
who, like himself, had danced with Mrs. Abraham
Tucker of Washington. The hideous spectacle

Sayce.

of the howling Dervishes seemed vaguely to remind the legislator of recent
scenes in the first legislative assembly of the world, for he was heard to mutter
the word "Tanner," and absently declined to give the expected baksheesh, on
the ground that he was a "member."

[1] An ingenious Frenchman having discovered that the native term of "Masr" was derived from
Mars, I may perhaps be excused for saying that "Masr" is the old Semitic term for all Egypt. The
planet Mars (Arab, Kahir the Victorious) happened to cross the meridian of the new city as its foundations were laid, and Gohar adopted the name of the planet, calling it El Kahira.

BARBANT

G. MONTBARD

Howling Dervish.

Nor did the party neglect the procession of the Mahmal, the orgies of the Mulid el Hossenayn, and that melancholy festival the Mulid el Nebbi. Are not they written in the book of Murray?

And at last they felt that they had religiously performed their pilgrimage and "done" Egypt. The Scribbler was pining to shake from his feet the classic but unwholesome dust of the East. The Sketcher was mournfully regretting that he was not for ever able to bask in its sunshine. Hides had induced the Patrician to accompany him to the States, and was happy in the temporary sole possession of a Lord. The Doves bemoaned their approaching departure with ostentation, but were secretly longing for the delights of a London season, while the Turtle felt that he had exhausted the Eastern Question, and for the future would be able to pose with increased authority as one who had studied Egypt upon the spot.

Tobacco Cutter.

Street Barber.

APOLOGUE.

Two men were discussing the orthography of the word camel. "Sir," said one, who insisted on spelling it "cammle," "I've seen the hanimal, so I ought to know."

EPILOGUE.

Three months after the date of our Prologue, the Sketcher and Scribbler were again at the Grand Hotel de Nouailles, the former wearily glancing over proofs.

"And do you really mean to publish this?" he asked contemptuously.

"Why not?" said the other in desperation.

"But it's so horribly dull," said the Sketcher.

The Scribbler's face brightened.

"Do you really think so? I was afraid your sketches would give it interest."

"There are, of course, *some* facts in it," said the other, somewhat mollified.

"Yes," said the Scribbler pathetically, "but I couldn't help it. I am cursed with the misfortune of knowing a little of the country, and I fear it will be fatal."

"Ah! well, I expect most people will skip them," said the other encouragingly.

"Of course," said the Scribbler, relieved, "and they'll forget them in any case —so I've some chance."

"There's an absence of local colouring too," said the friendly critic.

"I thought," said the Scribbler despondingly, "to correct that by putting a preface at the end—that would be so excessively Egyptian, you know."

"Precisely! and being at the end, it might be read; but do you think the book will have any other attraction?"

"Well, there's always the cover," said the other, rising; "I look to you for that, and that's the material part of most 'gentleman's library.'"

And so the book was published.

PREFACE.

———

Herodotus, it will be remembered, said that everything in Egypt went by contraries. The British Government, in its policy and action in Egypt, has proved that the truism of the fourth century B.C. holds good in the nineteenth A.D. Further excuse is not needed for a final preface to a book on Egypt. But if any were wanting to prove its inconsistency, it would be sufficient to say that the preface has no other object—a sentence the moral of which lies, as Captain Cuttle would say, in its application.